Case of the Missing Look Alikes

A Laura Jensen Mystery

Case of the Missing Look Alikes

A Laura Jensen Mystery

JEAN MARIE WIESEN

RED SKY PRESENTS
NEW YORK

Contents

Dedication

Mom and Dad, Uncle Donald and Aunt Patricia

Acknowledgements

I was always taught never to give up on my dreams, but there were times I almost walked away from this novel. Had it not been for the love and support from my uncle and my cousins, who are more like sisters to me, I might not have completed it. Thank you! And thanks as well to a special group of friends who stood by me and cheered me on, I love all of you dearly.

This book wouldn't have come about without the professional input from some selfless people who put their lives on the line each and every day to keep all of us safe from harm. My good friend Detective (Retired) James Baker, Westport Police Department, CT, taught me all kinds of interesting things about bugs, fingerprinting and the effects of weather on the human body after it's been in the elements for too long. Another dear friend, Corporal Anastasia Le Beau, Westport Police Department, CT, gave me all kinds of fantastic insight and comparisons between local departments that I wouldn't have otherwise been privy to; she's a true gem to her department. Trooper First Class Gregory Le Beau of the Connecticut State Police imparted some special ghost stories that are not available on the internet, as well as helping me understand the special, integral role the CSP plays.

I would also like to thank the instructors at Bridgeport Shooting Range for showing me the particulars of the Glock Nineteen and patiently answering my questions.

I'm incredibly grateful for our open court system that permitted me to observe murder trials in progress, as well as at sentencing, so I could accurately portray what it felt like to be in a courtroom and to experience the emotions of those around me. The Judicial Marshals at the Bridgeport Superior Court courthouse were very giving of their time in answering my questions and I was amazed by the compassion they showed to each of the prisoners they dealt with.

Thank you to my beta readers, the earliest of whom was Steve

Barber, who at first read said he thought I had a story worth telling and nudged me to keep at it. Thanks to Darrell Stewart who perused one of the early versions and discovered pertinent details that needed correction as well. Others picked at it and made necessary technical corrections, especially Laurie, a retired dispatcher -- hats off to you! Marissa Moran tore through it with a fine red pen and rearranged it so it would read much better. And to Anne Skalitza who read a revised draft and encouraged me to query on. Then…I'm almost finished!! I met David Saperstein who I could go on forever about, but I won't, except to say that I'm extremely fortunate to call him my friend. It's through him that I met my publisher Micky Hyman, and now my book(s) have a home and my dream has come true. Thank you to Lisa Keller, my editor, who's more than an editor.

To thine own self be true,
and it must follow, as the night the day,
thou canst not then be false to any man.
Hamlet

Chapter I

The doors of Jensen and O'Malley Investigations had been open for less than a month, and here I was, all alone, tapping a pencil on my desk, waiting for the phone to ring, scanning our lovely, cramped quarters in Soundview, Connecticut. Granted, it wasn't the corporate office that I'd envisioned all those years ago, while growing up in Augustine Bay, Florida, but for now, it suited my partner Mike O'Malley's needs and mine just fine. We hadn't broken the bank giving it a homey feel, but I thought we'd done okay -- paint the walls white to make the place look larger than its two hundred square feet, toss in a couple of desks, a microwave, a coffee pot, hang a few photographs I'd taken on the wall and presto, you have an office.

My desk had a vase filled with fresh flowers and assorted photos of my Grandma Rose, my parents and my dog Kola Bear.

In contrast, Mike's desk was spare and businesslike. There was a stack of memo pads and a pencil holder containing a small assortment of pens, pencils and markers. The only bits of personality were one photo of Mike and his detective buddies in uniform and another of them fishing.

At the moment, my only company was my pup Kola Bear. Mike was late, which was not like him at all. I told myself I was fully capable of being here alone. What could possibly happen that I couldn't deal with?

The phone rang, and I jumped. Then I just stared at it.

Oh great, why does it have to ring without Mike? Wait a gosh darn second, just because he's the one who's a retired police detective and I'm the one who's been freshly minted with a Master's Degree in Criminal Justice from John Jay College, does not mean I don't know what I'm doing. I did work as an intern for a private detective agency all of those summers. It's only a phone, for heaven's sake.

"Good morning, Jensen and O'Malley Investigations, this is Laura, may I help you?"

"Why, yes, this is Mrs. Spencer, may I please speak with Laura Jensen? It's of the utmost importance. Is she there?"

"Yes Mrs. Spencer, this is she. How may I help you?" I reached behind me and plugged in the coffee pot.

"I'm a desperate woman Laura. I've lost something of tremendous value and need you to find it, immediately. Will you do it?"

"I'll do my best Mrs. Spencer..."

"Not good enough Laura. Lots of people use that ridiculous expression and don't put any meaning into it. Either you will, or you won't. It's as simple as that."

"Okay, then, I will. But first, I need to know what it is that you've lost Mrs. Spencer."

"At least you're polite enough, I'll give you that. I've lost my Sherwood Archery pin that I won in a competition years ago. It's silver, so it's likely been stolen. In this day's economy I don't dare accuse anyone, but I want it back. They're an incredible organization that I know you've heard of."

"Yes Mrs. Spencer, I agree, Sherwood Archery is a terrific organization."

I had no idea who they were.

I sipped some coffee and listened to Mrs. Spencer ramble on.

I sighed.

"No Mrs. Spencer, I'm not bored. Yes, I realize I'm a private investigator. Yes, it is my job to find things, but I don't usually take missing jewelry cases. I'm sorry; I don't mean to insult you. I understand how valuable your Archery pin is to you."

I grimaced and reminded myself how vital new clients, any new clients, were to a neophyte agency.

Suppressing a yawn, I glanced at my wristwatch and prayed for the hands to move faster. It was two minutes before one o'clock. Annie called promptly at three o'clock each afternoon so we could make the ever-important decision of where our dog walk would be. What an opportune time for her to call early.

"Yes Mrs. Spencer, I'm still here. What am I doing? I'm trying to think where else you might look. I'm sure you've tried everything, and yes, that's why you called a private investigator. Oh, I didn't know you'd already spoken with my partner Mike. Yes, he is a wonderful man, and…he said missing jewelry is my area of expertise?"

I looked up as Mike tip-toed in and closed the door behind him. My concentration shifted from Mrs. Spencer to observing Mike remove his tattered navy blue scarf. He folded and smoothed it before placing it on the shelf next to the microwave. Maybe, I would buy him a new one for Christmas.

Next, he removed his faded denim jacket, hung it on the coat rack, stepped back and squinted. He leaned forward and brushed away an imaginary piece of dirt. Mike had to be the most meticulous individual I had ever known. Now and then I checked his jacket to see if I could discover anything out of place. Once, I had spied a tiny piece of lint with the aid of my magnifying glass.

"May I please put you on hold for a moment? Thank you. Yes, I promise I'll be right back."

"Mom, there's a sexy sounding woman on the line dying to speak to you."

"I wish you'd quit calling me that. Just because my initials spell it out doesn't mean that's my name."

Mike reached for the phone on his desk while tossing me the morning edition of the Soundview Times. Right above the fold was a color photograph of a woman resembling me, with the words "Known Artist Missing" written in red, bold typeface. I noted that the photo and accompanying article had been taken and written by my best friend Annie Tyler. Annie had simply used a recent photo she had taken at a gallery gala.

"Why are you wearing that devious smile of yours?" Mike asked.

He shook his fist at me the second he recognized Mrs. Spencer's voice. He stepped around his desk, and sunk into his high back swivel-chair.

"Good afternoon, Jensen and O'Malley Investigations," I said, answering the second phone line. "Yeah, yeah, hi Annie. Thank goodness you're early. Nope, just one of those strange client calls I managed to pass off to Mike. A walk in the woods sounds wonderful."

"I've a great idea Laura, while we're walking the pups today, we can be on the lookout for the missing artist. Can you imagine if that was your first big case, how significant that would be?"

"If you're digging for compliments Annie, I haven't read the article yet. I was on the phone when Mike threw me the paper, but I suspect the column is wonderful. It's a bit eerie how the woman looks like me. It would sort of be like trying to find myself in the woods," I laughed. "Where do you think she is, in a remote hunting cabin, drawing or painting?"

"Sometimes, you are positively impossible Laura Jensen! What if she's been kidnapped, and is being held prisoner in that very same remote hunting cabin with very little food and water? What if we can find her before it's too late? It very well could be just the case you and Mike need."

"We probably have better odds at winning the lottery than finding this woman. It doesn't hurt to try, though. It's not as if we've got clients beating our door down. We may as well see if we can make our own case. Heaven knows you're in the mood to solve this too Annie, to advance your journalism career. Let's meet at our usual spot on Bradley Road at four o'clock and begin with Trout Brook," I said.

"Sounds like a plan. There are some cabins up in that area, so that's an excellent place to begin our hunt. Who knows Laura, we might just find her. Bye."

I hung up and watched Mike thump his forehead on his desk. Poor guy. I suppressed a giggle at the exasperated look on his face. I dug around in my middle desk drawer for my alarm clock, set it and placed it next to Mike's head.

He leapt to his feet when it rang.

"I'm sorry Mrs. Spencer, I've got to go. Yes, it's the fire alarm. I'll call you back once the fire is out and we can discuss how to go about finding your Sherwood Archery pin. Right, bye," he said.

"I can't believe you did that to me," Mike tried to glare at me, but with little success.

He settled back into his chair, pushed the sleeves of his dark green fleece shirt over his elbows and smoothed out a few strands of wavy medium brown hair on his forehead. Mike already had a receding hairline and a slight paunch, which belied his thirty-six years. He had bright, deep set, light green eyes.

Being eleven years my senior, Mike regarded himself as my mentor. The ten years he had spent as a Soundview police officer also supplied a vast amount of information and skills I didn't yet possess to our fledgling agency. He had sworn an oath to my parents to watch over me when I'd moved here from Augustine Bay to begin my career in criminal justice, an oath he took quite seriously.

"Excuse me Mom; you're the one who did it to me. Why on earth would you tell Mrs. Spencer that recovering jewelry is my area of expertise? I'm not even sure a Sherwood Archery pin qualifies as jewelry?"

"Listen you; if you keep calling me 'Mom,' people will get the wrong idea about us.

"Besides, she's a lonely old lady who could use some company. When I was a cop, I used to see her sitting by herself in the hallway at Soundview Health Care Center when we'd assist on a medical call. She had a tough recovery from a hip replacement. By the way, when was the last time you worked a shift?"

"Huh? Oh, right. I'm almost finished with my re-certification class, and then you'll see my name on the schedule."

Mike's question made me realize how much I missed volunteering as an emergency medical technician. I had worked hard over the years with the Soundview Emergency Medical Service and liked to squeeze in extra shifts to help keep my skills sharp.

"Okay, I'll keep bugging you.

"Anyway, I kind of felt sorry for Mrs. Spencer. She lives by herself now, over in your

neck of the woods. And well, when we started the agency, I don't know... I gave her the number. You know, in case she needed something. How'd I know she'd come up with this Sherwood thing? Hey, maybe we should check it out, or, maybe you should."

"Uh-huh. Does she have a first name?"

"Yup. Adelaide. Adelaide Spencer. Has a nice ring to it, don't you think? You should drop in and introduce yourself Laura. You might like her. I'm not saying she would replace your Grandma Rose, but it might be nice for both you and Adelaide."

I considered Mike's remarks as I flipped my jet black hair over my shoulder. With the holidays on the horizon, my nostalgia for a Norman Rockwell style family Christmas intensified with the passing of each day.

My fiancé Matt and I had dreamed of working together in a large New York City criminal law firm. I would head the investigation division and Matt would lead the legal department. Our dreams had died September 11th. Matt had been attending a breakfast meeting with a new client at the Windows on the World Restaurant when the al-Qaeda piloted jet had crashed into the Tower. Recovery had been slow for me, and my soul continued to ache. Maybe it would do me some good to visit Adelaide.

"She doesn't have any family?" I asked.

"Nope, she's all alone. I know she'd love to have another visitor besides me. You could bring her fashion magazines and talk about shopping. You know, woman stuff. I bet she'd love it."

"Uh, excuse me. Is this Jensen and O'Malley Investigations?" A young man stood in the doorway. He stepped into the office and cleared his throat, appearing nervous as he took in the tight surroundings. He looked to be thirty something, with closely cropped, gelled, dark brown hair.

He resembled a mannequin straight from one of the windows of The GAP, dressed in a yellow V-neck sweater over a white T-shirt, loose fitting faded jeans and black cowboy boots. He seemed to be in excellent physical shape, long and lean. I wondered if he worked out at Planet Fitness. Since I'd only been a member for a few months, I'd have to keep my eyes peeled for the gentleman who stood in front of me.

"Yup, you're in the right place." Mike stood with a crooked grin on his face. "Please forgive my partner Laura Jensen. Sometimes she's a bit slow in speaking up. I'm Mike O'Malley," he continued, extending his hand to greet my new love. Mike broke the handshake and wiped his hand on his black corduroy slacks.

My mother had recently mentioned to me, that as deeply as I missed Matt, I might very well fall in love with the first man who paid attention to me. I had assured her I was savvy enough to never allow such a foolish thing to happen…but just now I was thinking…you never know…

"Yes, I'm Arnold Hansen. It's a pleasure to meet you Mike, and you too Laura. I'm sorry, I'm a complete wreck." He remained standing and rubbed his hands together. "I don't mean to be offensive…but, have you been doing this investigation thing for a while? What I mean is, I really need help, I…" his gravelly voice trailed off as he fell into the chair in front of my desk, covering his face with his hands.

"Would you like some coffee?" I stood, summoning my manners. "It might help you relax while you tell us how we can help you. Mike was a cop for ten years. He'd still be a detective if a back injury hadn't pushed him into early retirement. And I've been finding whatever needs to be found for most of my life. I have my Master's Degree in Criminal Justice, and I also interned for several summers at a top tier detective agency in New York. I've actually assisted in solving a few kidnapping cases that involved working with the FBI."

I recalled a brilliant FBI agent I'd worked with, Kai Halstead, a young man I'd grown up with, who had taken Matt and I under his wing. We had learned many so-called tricks of the trade when it came to abductions. He was not only a mentor to us, but a dear friend who encouraged us to follow our dreams. He was crushed when Matt died and had requested a transfer shortly afterwards to the Maryland office.

Out of the corner of my eye, I caught Mike nodding his head.

The mannequin was speaking, "Yes, I think so. Yeah, maybe coffee would help. Milk, no sugar. My wife's gone. I can't find her anywhere. Can you put some brandy in the coffee? It would take the edge off."

"Wait Mr. Hansen, did you say your wife's missing?" I set his coffee on my desk in front of him, sans brandy.

"Call me Arnold, please. Some guy named Marshall at the police department claims he's doing everything he can and...."

"I know Detective Marshall real well Arnold. Worked with him the entire ten years I was on the force. Grady's a stand-up guy. He'll do right by you. These things take time, which is real tough on the family, but finding a missing person can be a long process." Mike stirred an extra heaping spoonful of sugar into his coffee.

"How long has...I'm sorry, what's your wife's name? And, when did you last see or speak with her?" Mike asked, easing back into his chair.

I walked around my desk, picked up my notebook and pen and sat down, prepared to take notes. Since I was treading new water, Mike would lead this interview while I learned from the master. I hoped I would be brave enough to ask a question or two.

"Oh, right." Arnold sipped his coffee. "My wife Gwen, she... uh...well. Oh God, I can't believe this is happening. I'm in a freakin' nightmare! I'm sorry, I don't mean to cry." He wiped tears dribbling down his cheeks with the cuff of his sweater.

I scribbled the name 'Gwen' on the page while wondering what kind of woman would try to pick up a guy whose wife had just gone missing. Maybe my mother had a point.

"Arnold, it's okay to be upset. This is the worst thing in the world that could happen. Can you tell me what Detective Marshall told you? And when you last saw Gwen?" Mike inquired.

"Why are you asking me about Marshall? You think I had something to do with this, don't you? That's right; you did say you're friends with him. Why won't anybody help me! I didn't hurt her. I just want her back. I've been in love with Gwen since the first grade. For God's sake, you two have to find her. I'll pay whatever you want. I'm a rich man. Please." Arnold rubbed his eyes again, reached into his back pocket and pulled out his wallet. I watched him thumb through his billfold while he mouthed counting money.

"Here, two thousand ought to be enough to get the ball rolling." He slapped a pile of crisp hundreds on Mike's desk. "Now, can we get back to discussing my wife?" As he sat back Arnold snatched Mike's pride and joy from the desk, the Plexiglas encased home run baseball hit by Derek Jeter during one of the World Series Games against the Florida Marlins.

I glanced at Mike, and noticed him turning various shades of red. He was biting his lower lip so hard, I was afraid he would require medical attention.

"Nice memento." Arnold put the ball back on Mike's desk. "So, is that enough money, or do you want more?"

"Uh, yeah, that's good. Um, thanks." Mike wiped his brow with the heel of his hand.

"Arnold, neither of us accused you of having anything to do with Gwen's disappearance." Mike leaned forward and put his coffee mug on his desk. "These are questions we have to ask. It's part of the investigation. It's sort of like a giant jigsaw puzzle. You know, the answers are, well, the pieces we put together. That way we get the whole picture, then we know what's going on. Does that make sense?"

"Yes, I think so," Arnold responded softly. He rubbed his chin with his thumb and forefinger while staring at the floor.

"Okay, now we're getting somewhere. Start at the beginning and take it slow. Laura and I aren't in any rush. And if we need to, we'll ask questions, only for clarification purposes."

"That's correct," I said, "and I'll be taking notes, which are completely confidential."

Arnold crossed his arms and cocked his head. "Oh, you mean like client confidentiality?"

"Yes, exactly like that," I said with a smile.

"I have that too, in my business. Did I mention I own a private investment firm? I'm always reminding Eliott about that"

"No, and who's Eliott?" I answered as I doodled in the margins of my notebook.

"He's my old college roommate and business partner."

"What's Eliott's last name?"

"Why do you need that?"

"Remember what I said about the puzzle," Mike interjected.

"Of course, I'm having trouble thinking clearly. It's Potts, Eliott Potts. He's a great guy and he's just as upset as I am about Gwen."

"When did you last see Gwen?" I glanced at Mike, who winked at me.

"Well, I...what's today, Saturday or Sunday?" Arnold wiped his eyes. "I keep forgetting, and I don't know when I last saw my wife. Just find her, damn it! I hate all these questions. You're both just like Marshall. Nobody will go and look for her. No, you just want to ask your stupid questions, while she's God knows where!" Arnold screamed and slammed his coffee mug on my desk, splashing hot coffee onto my lap.

"Hey Arnold, you need to calm down." I wiped my jeans and notepad with a paper towel. "Mike and I want to help you, and we're more than happy to be at your service, but, you've got to keep your temper in check. And it's Sunday."

"Uh, Arnold," Mike said as he pushed his chair back and leaned forward and readied himself to hold Arnold back.

"Please tell me you didn't behave like this in front of Marshall. Because if you did, he's going to think you're involved in your wife's disappearance, no matter what you say. You can't act like that here. I don't care how upset you are. Got it?"

"I'm sorry, really...I haven't slept. I'm usually very cool under pressure, well, like business pressure, not this kind. How can anyone be prepared for something this..."

"No one can," I replied. "Mike and I can't even begin to imagine what you're going through. I do know you have to try to eat and get some sleep Arnold. And you need to answer all of our questions no matter how insignificant they may seem. That's why I'm taking notes, so we can sift through them later and pick up some clues. Does that sound logical to you?"

"Uh, yes, it does. Thank you both for being so kind. You're much more understanding than Marshall."

"Thanks Arnold, but you should know that I am going to have to talk with Marshall. Don't be upset now, I have to get his impression. Okay?"

"I think I'm beginning to get this process," Arnold replied. "I feel a little better now, so let's get back to those questions," he continued as he rubbed his hands together. "I can do this. I have to. For Gwen."

Arnold ran his hands through his hair, inhaled deeply and settled back into his chair.

"Okay, ask away, I'm ready."

I briefly looked at Mike. He grinned from ear to ear. I rearranged my notebook and pen, relieved that my first interview would not be derailed.

Mike and I gently led Arnold through the basic groundwork of the questioning; how long Arnold and Gwen had been married, their favorite haunts and the like. I had my own version of shorthand that only I could interpret and made fast work of the necessary note taking. Later, I would enter the information into the computer and our first real case would be off and running. I listened intently as Arnold told his story.

Arnold had met Gwen while studying oil painting at Soundview Artists' Guild. He had enrolled in painting classes in a futile attempt at relaxation from the demands of his and Eliott's start-up investment firm. According to Arnold, he and Eliott were the newest superstars, on track toward earning their third million in only their second year in business. In his mind, considering his business prowess, there would be no viable reason for Gwen to leave of her own volition.

Arnold moved on to talk about the happiness he and Gwen had enjoyed during their first four years of marriage and related their recent discussions of starting a family. It all sounded so perfect, almost too perfect.

"Structure is crucial to your world. Would that be an accurate description, Arnold?" I asked without looking up from my notes.

"Huh? I'm sorry, I was under the impression that Mike was in charge here," Arnold snapped.

"Laura may not have the number of years' experience that I've got, but, we're a team. So, please give her the same respect you're showing me, if you don't mind. Okay?"

22

"I didn't mean anything by it. I just thought...never mind. I'm sorry if I've offended you Laura. To answer your question, yes, my work requires, no, demands extreme structure in order to be successful. Gwen understands the nature of my business and is fully supportive of me.

"I'm an old fashioned guy. I want to be the breadwinner so Gwen can pursue her artistic career. She's incredibly talented and is in the midst of putting several pieces together for a big show in New York this spring."

"In other words, everything is on track?" I asked.

"Well, yes." Arnold fidgeted with his mug.

"According to plan," I continued.

"This is ridiculous!" Arnold roared. "What exactly are you implying, missy? Are you going to allow this Mike?"

"Think for a minute, will you, what would a lawyer be asking if you were in court. Everybody's a suspect until proven otherwise, especially the spouse. Laura, sorry, my partner Laura is asking a good question.

"Keep going Laura, you're doing fine. As I told you before Arnold, show the same respect to Laura that you're showing me."

"Yes, my life with Gwen is on track. Exactly what is wrong with that?" Arnold gave me a cold stare.

"Nothing," I replied, "unless it no longer jives with the life of a painter. Arnold, I'm not implying anything," I answered, in response to his increasing agitation. "I want to thoroughly look at each and every angle, even if it requires repetition. Think about being cross-examined on the witness stand. Mike and I are doing the same thing.

"Would it be accurate to say Gwen's circle of friends was becoming increasingly different from your own?"

"Well, I guess so. She was getting more and more involved in the art world. Matter of fact, she didn't want to accompany me to the club as much as she used to. Don't know if I mentioned it or not, but we're members at the Masterson Golf and Country Club. I'm on the board that oversees the annual charity golf tournament, and that takes a fair amount of time. Gwen originally wanted to join Indian Harbor for the sailing, but they don't have a golf course, so we joined the Masterson instead. Taking clients out on the golf course is more important to my business than her sailing. I hadn't really given it much thought until now, but she was spending more time with her classmates, coffee dates to compare sketches, I suppose. Gwen liked to paint landscapes, so, if she wasn't with her friends or with me, she would go out by herself looking for new inspiration, as she put it.

"Now that I think about it, she spent a considerable amount of time in some fairly isolated places...hey, we might be getting somewhere. Marshall didn't ask these kinds of questions. Thank God I came here. I know you'll find her. Keep going Laura, you're onto something, I can feel it. Come on, ask something else." Arnold practically levitated with excitement.

Mike nodded to me.

My adrenaline began to pump.

"I am curious about one thing Arnold. What kinds of questions did Marshall ask you?"

"Oh God. Not him again. Please."

"It's important. I need to know, especially since you said he didn't ask about Gwen's routine." No way was I going to upset this guy any further, but of course Marshall had to have asked about her routine.

"He just asked about her looks and how she dressed, and..." Arnold's mouth fell open as Mike and I exchanged looks.

"What is it Arnold?" I reached out to touch his wrist.

"I don't know why I didn't connect this earlier, but Gwen kind of looks...jeez, not kind of looks like you, but, almost as if she could be your sister. Not your twin, mind you. But definitely your dark hair, and build. You're both athletic looking, and, well, you do dress differently. Gwen's more Banana Republic."

"And I'm more GAP."

"Exactly. I think you may be a bit taller than Gwen, an inch or two, but otherwise, you could be related."

"And I'm five-foot eight." I jotted down Gwen's physical description. "I certainly look forward to meeting her one day. In the meantime, let's get back to my line of questioning. When Gwen went off by herself, to look for inspiration, as she called it, do you know where she went?"

"I only know the places by name, from what she would tell me. She mentioned several; Brett Woods, Crow Hill and some others I can't recall. It's hard to remember if you've never been there. I'm sure if you mentioned some places in the woods, they might ring a bell. That is, if you go to places like that."

"As it happens, I go to those kinds of places every day. It's a wonderful way for me and my dog to get exercise and the spots you named are on my regular hiking routes." I put an asterisk followed by a question mark in the margin of my notes to discuss this point further with Mike. It struck me as odd that I not only resembled Gwen, but that I also walked in the same areas as she did. This called for closer scrutiny. I firmly believed coincidence had no place in detective work.

"Do the names, Trout Brook, Jump Hill and the Orchard ring any bells?"

"She's amazing," Arnold said as he looked at Mike. "Where on earth did you find her? All three of those, Gwen spoke of frequently. She loved to watch the changes in the light through the trees, especially around sunset. And she was looking forward to walking in the woods right after the first snowfall. In fact, Gwen spent an inordinate amount of time online watching the weather radar in anticipation of snow. She talked about it all the time. She couldn't wait to paint the scenes. Gwen wanted to put them in the show in New York."

"Any places that were more of a favorite?" I asked.

From the corner of my eye, I noticed Mike lean back in his chair with a satisfied look and take a sip of coffee. It gave me a great boost of confidence, knowing he trusted me enough to take over the interview.

"Well, let me see." Arnold rubbed his chin. "Gwen favored Brett Woods and Trout Brook Valley. She always talked about how the view at the Orchard could not be beaten. Now more than ever I wish I had experienced them with her. Gwen would say how at home she felt while there and sometimes would sit for an hour or so completely lost in..." He began to sob once again.

Another oddity, the Orchard was also one of my favorite spots. It amazed me that such a gorgeous place existed in the middle of Fairfield County. I loved to sit on the knoll with Kola Bear and gaze out over the hills to Long Island Sound while the sun descended behind the trees. It often served as quiet time to think of Matt and how life might have been if he were alive. Maybe the Orchard touched my heart so because I felt connected to Matt while there. At times, I would cry so hard, I honestly thought the well would run dry. If I stayed too long in the woods, which I frequently did, I'd hear the owls awaken the nocturnal residents. Occasionally, one would swoop low over the trail in front of me, dipping his enormous wingspan as he began his evening hunt.

Following Matt's death, each time I would meet an eligible bachelor, I couldn't help but compare him to Matt, right down to his nose hairs. In all honesty, even if he had not been in a panic over his missing wife, Arnold did not measure up to Matt.

At any rate, a number of similarities were adding up, making me wonder what else Gwen and I had in common. I needed to do some serious digging into her background; some without Arnold's knowledge.

Arnold, meanwhile, had pulled himself together surprisingly quickly, had pushed his chair back, and was standing up.

I said, "Arnold, there are a few things that aren't entirely clear to me…"

"I'm sorry Laura, and you too Mike. You've both been fantastic; I appreciate everything you've done so far. I know there's a mountain of information I need to go over with you, but at the moment I'm running late." He tapped his Rolex with his middle-finger.

"I have to stop at the cleaners and pick up some shirts and a sports jacket I'm wearing this evening." Arnold paused and blew his nose. "I have a dinner date with an old friend, so, if you will kindly excuse me, I'll be in touch tomorrow. Thank you again for your time," he said as he moved toward the door.

Arnold pointed at the banner that hung on the wall behind Mike's desk. "By the way, Eliott sells those Yankees' banners on eBay." The banner had been signed by the entire team. "Even the ones from the '03 season." He winked before disappearing behind the door.

Before either of us had an opportunity to respond, he was gone.

"Who the hell is that guy? And how'd he know that banner's from eBay?" Mike asked.

"Never mind the banner, will you please run after him, that was my first official interview and I was on a roll."

Mike just shrugged as we heard Arnold's car peeling away.

I considered several scenarios and they all led me to the same ending: Gwen was no longer alive. I pushed that thought aside while I considered the many unanswered questions Arnold had left us with. One thing Arnold had failed to discuss in detail was his dear business partner Eliott, and his whereabouts. I wondered about the relationship between Gwen and Eliott, as in how far back that went. On the other hand, with the short leash Arnold had Gwen on, if there had been the slightest hint of her having an affair with anyone, would he would have been aware of it?

"Is there really two thousand dollars on your desk?" I asked.

"Huh? I don't know. But, it looks like a whole lot of Ben Franklin's here. It will take me an hour to count it all! The bank sure will be surprised when I walk in tomorrow morning with this big a deposit. Another client like him and..." Mike rumpled his hair with his hands.

"Mike, forget about the money for a minute; he had to be kidding about having a date, right? I mean, how could he with his wife missing? Wow, I'm completely confused."

"Me too Laura. I swear he's guilty...his sports jacket? I know it takes all kinds and believe you me, I've seen lots of bizarre stuff in my time, but this guy...this isn't right...the cleaners aren't open on Sunday...hey, and he flipped me the bird, too. Man, that's not nice..."

"What are you talking about? He was strange, yes, but I didn't see him do that Mike, and I'm not all that inclined to think he's guilty, just yet."

"When he tapped his watch Laura, he did it with his middle finger... that's flipping a guy off. Only a guy would know that, I'm telling you... and, why don't you think he's guilty? Women's intuition?"

"You're being paranoid about the watch thing, and yes, it's women's intuition," I said.

"I am not paranoid., and I'm going to get him back for that. You don't do that to an O'Malley, no way."

"Not to change the subject, but, what if I follow him and find out who his date is?"

"Laura, I don't know about that. This guy's not playing with a full deck, guilty or not. And if anything happened to you...well, I don't want to even think about what your Grandma Rose would do to me."

"Come on Mike, this is what I'm born to do and I've had lots of practice."

"This is not like following the cops in Augustine Bay. On the other hand, would you be using your trusty Nikon with that monster lens? The one you can spot a fly with on a farmer's forehead at a hundred yards? Because if that's the case, then at least I know you'll be at a safe distance."

"Yes Mike," I grinned.

"Alright." He looked up at the ceiling and crossed himself. "While you're focusing in on Arnold, literally, I'll Google the guy and see what pops up. I also have to talk to Marshall. This is just plain weird."

"Mike, do you find it odd that Arnold looked directly at the photo and article about Gwen and didn't comment on it?"

"It's an interesting observation, let's save it for later, in case things pan out in his direction."

I jumped to my feet and ran out the door with my pup close behind, leaving Mike shaking his head. A long walk in the crisp fall air might dispel some of the questions which swirled in my brain. I needed to be one hundred percent while following Arnold in order to be effective. What a potentially hair-raising case, exactly what Jensen and O'Malley needed.

My adrenaline remained on high when I pulled into the parking lot off Bradley Road. As usual, Annie had arrived first. I imagined she was contemplating whether or not we'd pick up any leads on our hike that would put us on Gwen's trail.

Chapter 2

I arrived home promptly at five o'clock, and fed Kola. While my coffee brewed, I changed into my dark-colored sleuthing outfit; black turtleneck sweater, black jeans and fleece-lined black boots. My bag of Nikon camera equipment always remained at the ready on the floor next to the coat rack. Mike teased me mercilessly about when I planned to catch up with the digital world. I reminded him that as long as the FE-2 my Grandma Rose had given me for my eighteenth birthday continued to perform, the answer was "never."

I pulled on my navy pea coat, slung the camera bag over my shoulder, grabbed my thermos of fresh-brewed Hazelnut coffee with milk and made my way out to my Honda Pilot. Kola trotted behind since he accompanied me everywhere, regardless of weather or time of day.

Edging out onto Lyon's Plain Road, I noted the time on my dashboard clock. Even though it read five forty-five, it was already dark. I lived exactly ten minutes from where the Hansen's made their home, on Broad Street in Soundview. I silently prayed Arnold had made plans at a local restaurant; I didn't want to be too far away in case I needed Mike's immediate assistance.

I turned left onto Broad Street and flipped the headlight switch to the off position. I did not want to run the risk of Arnold spotting me as I eased my foot off the gas pedal to find the number on the mailbox. The Hansen's was the seventh house in on the left, number 621.

Having driven down the street numerous times, I had always been curious about the place; there had never been any signs of life. It had to be one of the ugliest dwellings in town. The fact that it was surrounded by at least four foot high weeds certainly did not help. It astounded me that a builder would waste so much money on a gray, multi-layered bunker style building with few windows. Was Arnold making a statement of some kind?

The only thing the house had in its favor was that it had been constructed on the shores of a man-made lake. It was not the kind of home I envisioned an artist would reside in. It did, however, appear to fit the extremes I had observed in Arnold's personality during the interview Mike and I had just concluded.

I observed several lights on as I rolled past the house, one being the dim front light; a twenty-five watt bulb at most. A silver Mercedes SUV and a red Lexus sedan were parked next to each other in the driveway. I recalled Arnold had said he drove a Lexus sedan and Gwen owned a Lexus SUV. That would indicate the Mercedes might belong to the mystery dinner guest.

Once I'd completed my turn around, I stopped well before the driveway. I banked on my silver Pilot blending with the landscape on the moonless night. I poured a steaming cup of coffee, and set it on the dash. I pulled my film-loaded camera from the canvas bag, flipped on the switch for the heated seat and set my mind to patience while waiting for Arnold to make an appearance. Methodically, I replayed the interview in my mind while I sipped my coffee. I wondered if Mike and I had missed anything. Or maybe Arnold lied by omission? In either case it felt as if we'd overlooked a key component.

He had become extremely uncomfortable when I'd referred to his life as "too perfect." It could point to him hiding something and with a bit of luck, maybe I'd get a hint of it this evening.

I gripped my coffee cup to eliminate some of the chill from my hands. Usually, I had my glove liners in my pocket for taking photos in cold weather. I set my coffee down, fished around, found them buried deep in my bag, and slipped them on.

Perfect timing. I looked up just as a tall, dark figure emerged from the garage. It was Arnold. He stepped into the driveway and peered up and down the street. I hunched forward and bent my head down as far as possible. My forehead became one with the top of the steering wheel, and my spine arched like a bow. My back was killing me. I held my breath. Even with my forehead pasted against the steering wheel, I might still be seen. Did Arnold expect to be followed? Just what I needed, an educated suspect on my first surveillance.

After what felt like hours, Arnold, satisfied no one was spying on him, turned slightly and motioned with his hand. My forehead remained glued to the steering wheel while I waited patiently to see who would appear. But my patience was not to be rewarded; the individual wore a cap pulled down low, and he or she was enveloped in a long dark coat with the collar turned up.

Arnold held the passenger door of the Lexus sedan open, while his companion eased into the passenger seat. Meanwhile, I remained in my awkward, bent position, wondering after this night was over would I ever sit straight again, or play tennis?

Arnold closed the door and walked around the back of the car, stopped and looked in my direction. His hand shielded his eyes from the light while he stared. I didn't move a muscle and barely took a breath. I wondered if Mike could be correct about this being too dangerous. At the moment, all I could do was pray that Arnold wouldn't come closer to investigate. Another thing I had failed to take into account had been whether or not my pup would bark. I began to understand Mike's point about this not being small town Augustine Bay.

I broke into a cold sweat while the deafening sound of my heartbeat kept perfect cadence with my watch as it ticked away the seconds. My nose itched, but I didn't dare scratch it. My eyes teared from forcing them upward to keep Arnold in my line of vision while I questioned whose bright idea this had been. With each tick of my watch, the more fear crept in to nibble away at my confidence. If Arnold had murdered his wife and caught me spying, would my body ever be recovered from the bottom of the old gravel pit, which was now a lake? Crystal Lake... the name was ironic, given my present predicament. The hopelessness of my situation was becoming increasingly crystal clear.

A low growl emanating from Kola Bear's toes jolted me back to reality. I blinked to clear my vision while I peeked through the steering wheel, just in time to observe Arnold getting into the Lexus on the driver's side. I listened and watched as the engine roared to life and the headlights illuminated the lake.

"Thank God he didn't see us." I slowly unfolded from my cramped posture and stretched my hand toward the back seat. Kola placed his paw in my upturned palm. "What a good boy you are. However, the next time I decide to do something like this, I'm leaving you home. Okay, our friend is leaving, let's follow him and see where he takes us."

Before turning the key in the ignition, I scratched my nose, rubbed my eyes, caught a few extra breaths and did my best to stretch out my back. I waited until Arnold was around the corner before pulling back onto Broad Street, keeping my headlights off.

I remained three car lengths behind Arnold when he turned right onto Route 57. As he completed the turn, I flipped the headlight switch on and stepped down hard on the gas. The second I made the right turn, another car sped past and squeezed in between Arnold and me. Perfect. All three of us made a right turn onto Ford Street. Never having been on this street in the five years I had lived in the area, I had no idea where it would take us. I increased my speed to keep Arnold's car in sight, only to be met by a series of tough to negotiate curves.

No sooner had I cleared the curves then I bounced in my seat and hit my head on the car roof. I heard a thud as Kola bumped his head too.

"Sorry about that, buddy. Can't let a silly speed bump keep us from our appointed rounds. Oops, there's another one." I banged my head a second time. Why do they have to put those damn things in the middle of the road? Ah, to slow idiots like me down. While rubbing my head, I ran a stop sign. This was not going as I'd planned it.

Finally, we stopped at a red light. Arnold made a quick right onto Main Street, while the car behind him edged up to the line, not leaving me much room to maneuver. I drove over the curb to catch the Lexus. I was two car lengths behind as we passed a cemetery. I prayed it wouldn't soon become my forwarding address.

Arnold went through the next two sets of lights, took a fast left turn and a hard right, as if he suspected someone was tailing him. He then disappeared behind a building. I drove past, circled around the block and parked on the corner in time to see him entering the Sono Seaport Seafood Restaurant. He stopped at the door, and scanned up and down the street to see if the coast remained clear. Satisfied that it was, he and his companion entered the restaurant. Even with the streetlights, it remained impossible to identify who accompanied him.

I exhaled and crossed myself in thanks I hadn't been observed.

Having eaten at the Sono Seaport Seafood a number of times; I recalled I could sit at the bar with a decent view of the dining area. On other occasions, watching the sun dip down over the water was relaxing, but this evening it was already dark and anyway, my eyes would have to be on Arnold. I counted to thirty, exited my Pilot and ran across the street with my camera slapping against my side. Gripping the front door handle, I drew in a deep breath, pulled it open, slipped inside and noticed an empty chair at the far right end of the bar, only a few short steps away. I slid into it gratefully.

I raised my hand to attract the bartender's eye, "May I please have a ginger ale?"

"Sure, unless you need something stronger to slow you down some," the bartender winked. He poured my drink, and set it in front of me.

"Thanks, I'm fine with the ginger ale. Maybe, I'll splurge and have a cherry with the next one." I smiled. I pulled my cell phone out of my right coat pocket, adjusted the ring tone to vibrate and placed it on the varnished wooden bar, I noticed there was a text message from Mike. He wanted to know where I was. I quickly replied. Best to be smart since this was my first outing, especially if anything went awry. I sipped my soda both to quench my thirst and steady my nerves. The last thing I wanted to do was draw attention to myself.

I placed my soda back on the bar, turned in my chair and surveyed the dining room. The tables had begun to fill with a combination of couples out for a quiet evening and young moms and dads with noisy children in tow. The combined smells of clam chowder and plates piled with baby back ribs, lobsters and crab cakes filled my nostrils, reminding me that the last thing I'd eaten was the orange I'd shared with Annie when we'd walked Kola and Casey several hours earlier. The job of a private investigator is a difficult one.

While listening to my stomach growl, I spotted Arnold at a corner table, far from the front door. He was standing with his back to me, helping his dinner partner remove his or her coat. It had to be a woman... unless... I leaned forward in my chair, as another waiter passed by, to see whom Arnold was with. When they were seated, the low brimmed hat came off and thick auburn hair cascaded to his date's shoulders – "it" was most definitely a she.

I shook my head in an attempt to clear my confusion. Could Arnold be that much of a bastard? Mike would be shocked by what I'd discovered. On the other hand, I wondered if it could be possible for our first case to be solved so easily. My mind raced while trying to sort the possibilities; maybe I needed the cherry now.

Something didn't add up, why would Arnold have become involved in an affair immediately following the filing of a missing persons' report? And why would he show up on the doorstep of a brand new private investigation firm to report that his wife was missing, and then mention that he was going on a date? If he was guilty, was he trying to pull a fast one on a neophyte agency, not expecting that a retired cop would catch on to his antics? That made no sense whatsoever. If I were on my own in the business, I could accept that, even though it would be an enormous insult. I swallowed some soda and dismissed my line of thinking; I had to be jumping to conclusions,

Re-scrutinizing the pair, I held my camera up and zoomed in to see Arnold slide a small box across the table to the middle of her place setting. Her face glowed with anticipation as Arnold opened the box. She gasped. The candlelight flickered against its glass cover while she held up a gold bracelet with several charms dangling. I re-focused the lens but could not identify the charms nor tell whether she wore a wedding ring.

The sound of my cell phone vibrating on the bar-top crescendoed in my brain, nearly causing me to drop my camera. I spun in my seat to check the screen to see who was trying to reach me. As I picked up the phone, I felt a single tap on my shoulder.

"What..." I turned and found myself staring at a large, shiny silver belt buckle. I raised my head and put the phone to my ear as my eyes traveled upward, "Uh Mike, I have company." My eyes locked with a set of nearly black eyes.

"Hey Laura, who is it? Does he look like a Fed? Because if he does, get out of there, fast!"

"I don't know Mike. I do know there's a gentleman standing over me who looks an awful lot like Reggie White."

"I'm impressed, a Packer fan in New England, and an aficionado; that's interesting. I'm also flattered that you think I resemble the greatest man to have ever set foot on the gridiron," my new, large African-American friend said, glaring down at me. "But no matter, whatever it is you think you're doing, I highly recommend you gather your things and leave. If there's film in that camera, hand it over," he went on, while putting an upturned palm under my nose.

"I heard that, give it to him," Mike yelled into my ear.

"There's film in my camera, sir, but I promise you I haven't taken one photo..."

"Give it to me anyway."

"Laura, give him the film. This is a really bad time to be stubborn. Trust me on this."

"But..."

"Arnold's under investigation Laura. I did the Google thing and his name popped up all over the place. I don't know what he did, but if he's got the Feds on his tail, it isn't good. I'd give Reggie White's look-alike the film if I were you."

"You might be onto something Mike," I said.

"Sir, I was going to give you the film even if my friend hadn't suggested it. Honest…"

"Do not bat those baby blues. They don't like it when you do that!" Mike screamed.

"But first I'd like to see some ID." I placed my upturned palm over his.

"Laura, what are you doing? Please don't tell me you're holding your hand out. This is not the time to play rock, scissors, paper," Mike pleaded.

"Lady, you've got guts, I admire that. However, you're interfering with an ongoing federal investigation, which I've been working for months. If you blow this case, I'll have you tied up in court so long, by the time you're untied you'll have forgotten you were ever a P.I. That being said, here's my ID. Look fast without so much as a twitch, understand?" he commanded. He shoved his credentials, which were enclosed in a double-sided leather case with a plastic window, under my eyes. It read: Agent Reginald Martin, underneath an exact likeness of the individual presently hovering over me. I managed to catch the signature of James B. Comey, whom I knew to be the Director of the FBI, before Reginald snapped the ID case closed and returned it to the inside pocket of his sports jacket.

"Thanks Reggie. It looks real enough, so I guess you're who you say you are. And I guessed right on your name. Did you hear that Mike?"

"Yes dear. Now, hang up, thank the man for not hauling you off, and kindly pay your rapidly aging partner a visit within the next five minutes. You remember how to get to the office, right?"

"Yes Mike. I'll see you in a couple of minutes. Bye." I hit end, and dropped the phone in my pocket.

"Now Laura, I'm going to sit on the stool next to you and I'd like you to keep a smile glued to your face. I'm going to buy you a drink and we're going to act like old friends who are catching up. In between my laughing you're going to relate all you've discovered about Arnold. When I say we're finished, I'll pat you on the shoulder, give you my business card and you'll get up and leave. Is that clear?"

"Please keep in mind Reggie, my partner expects me in our office in five minutes. Oh, and he's a retired Soundview cop. And what if I have questions of my own?" I managed to take a sip of my ginger ale without choking. All I could think of was the silly deodorant commercial which tells you not to let them see you sweat.

"That's great Laura. Bartender, I'd like a scotch and soda, without the scotch…"

"Guessing you're on duty," I said.

"Did you learn to be so observant in P.I. school or were you like that growing up in Augustine Bay? Yes Ms. Jensen, we know everything about you. You left the Big Apple after 9/11. You excelled at John Jay, earning a Master's in Criminal Justice while interning with a few agencies in the City, along with a local guy in Soundview for the last few years." Reggie scratched his chin while I stared at him. He smiled and continued, "Then you met Mike while you were an EMT with the Soundview Squad and he'd injured his back lifting a patient. Retiring from the Police Department came up and he'd followed your criminal justice career path with interest, so I'd say it was a natural fit." Reggie grinned.

"Do you study everyone this closely," I asked.

"Only those who interest me," Reggie answered. "Now, back to current events, I would say, it can be quite a jolt when you unexpectedly hit those darn speed bumps. Please don't drop your jaw so far." Reggie grinned and continued, "There is one thing I'm unable to confirm; what kind of dog is Kola Bear? One of the guys thinks he's mostly Shepherd but I think he has more Husky in him. So, which is it?"

"You win the bet Reggie. He's mostly Husky," I replied.

"You're doing fine Laura. If and when you consider a career switch, I believe you should study acting. As far as you having questions for me, well, let's just say that's not terribly relevant. The FBI has enough problems sharing information with local authorities, much less a P.I., or, for that matter, your ex-cop partner Mike. I'm sure you understand. Now, onto more pressing matters; our mutual friend Arnold Hansen."

"Well, he came to our office earlier today to hire us regarding a personal matter of his."

"Listen, young lady, we know Gwen's missing and we suspect foul play. It's not exactly a monumental leap. I'm more interested in what else he told you relating to his business with Eliott."

"All he said was, it's a new business and that he and Eliott are doing quite well. He was nervous and extremely jumpy when we pressed for additional information concerning his professional life. He insisted it had nothing to do with Gwen's disappearance. I promise Reggie, that's all I know."

"And you figured following him and his sister would lead you to Gwen? Remember what I said about dropping your jaw? Keep that smile on your face. You're a good kid Laura. I thought I'd throw you a bone." Reggie winked and patted my shoulder.

"And that's my signal to leave. I had a wonderful time Reggie, thanks." I quickly gathered my things. Arnold's sister? The information Reggie had so freely given had to be wrong. I needed to get to the office immediately and try to prove what he'd just told me to be true or false. Something did not add up.

"Me too Laura. We need to do this again sometime. I'll give you a call."

As I exited Sono Seaport Seafood, a sharp chill ran down my spine, and it wasn't the weather.

Chapter 3

A few snowflakes floated gently down as I approached the office. I wondered if the temperature would drop low enough for the snow to stick. There was something magical about the first snowfall of the year that tapped the child in me. It definitely brought the puppy out in Kola Bear.

"Well buddy, it looks as if your favorite time of year has arrived." I pulled into my parking space across the street from Mike's and my office. Kola jumped out, and held his muzzle up to the falling snow. I shivered while we ran across the one-way street. Opening the door to the office, I heard a woman's voice.

"Hi Mike, we're back safe and sound." I smiled weakly through my disappointment. I desperately needed to speak with Mike alone. The wonderful aroma of spiced tea tickled my nostrils. Maybe, a cup of tea would settle me until our guest left.

"Ah, please tell me there's lots more of that tea, I'm chilled to the bone."

"Absolutely Laura, I'll be a gentleman and make you a cup. Before I do that, allow me to introduce you to Adelaide."

I extended my hand to shake hers, "Mike has spoken so well of you...please, don't get up. It's a pleasure to meet you." I moved my chair around my desk and placed it next to Adelaide's. I didn't want the formality of my desk to come between this delightful looking woman and me. I held my mug of steaming tea close, wishing we had a wood-burning stove to warm my body.

Adelaide appeared to be in her early seventies and not the least bit frail. Her thick, ear length hair was entirely white. Her close-set brown eyes still had their youthful sparkle. She kept pushing her non-glare rimless glasses back up onto the bridge of her nose. I estimated her height to be approximately five feet, and she was quite fit and trim. The only indication of any physical ailment was the hand-carved cane leaning against her chair. I supposed it had to do with the hip replacement Mike had spoken of earlier.

Taking a sip of tea, I noticed Mike moving his twenty-inch computer monitor ever so slightly. Quickly scanning the information regarding Arnold, I struggled to maintain my composure.

"I am so pleased to meet you too Laura. Have you made any progress locating my Archery pin? I know Mike has told you how important it is to me."

"Actually, I'm handling that personally. Laura is getting her feet wet with some surveillance," Mike answered.

"That explains why you're dressed all in black." Adelaide appraised me up and down. "I hope you know how dangerous it is to wear dark clothing at night. Accidents happen when drivers can't see you." She went on, "On the other hand, I imagine that would be the point; so whomever you're following won't spot you. But what about your white dog?"

My mouth formed the beginning of an answer when it occurred to me; I hadn't considered Kola's color as being problematic.

"That's an interesting question. But, Kola stays in the back seat of my truck. And we're far enough away to not be seen..."

"What a lovely name. Does he have a middle name?"

"Yes, he does Adelaide. His full name is Kola Bear."

"Does Kola Bear have a lot of friends?"

"Well, he has several. His best friend is Casey." I drank some tea. It was not having the desired effect of relaxation. My anxiety level was on the rise. Mike and I had our first big case to solve, yet I was taken with this sweet woman sitting next to me. I could definitely see us spending some quality time together. However, at the moment, I had to figure out a way to get her to leave without coming across as rude. It was proving impossible to focus on Adelaide while the information about Arnold on the monitor held the majority of my attention.

"I'm enjoying talking about your pup and his friends," Adelaide said as she dropped her hand down to pat Kola on the head. "But, we really need to stick with the issue at hand. What's the progress with my pin?" She looked back and forth between Mike and me while petting Kola.

I looked at Mike and nodded my head toward the monitor.

"Well Adelaide, truth is there's not much to report at the moment. Laura and I just landed our first big case and...you know what, I'll pop over in the morning and have a look around. What time's good for you?"

"I suppose that's a good idea. We could share a bran muffin and coffee. As I always say, you can never have enough fiber, so, why don't we make it around eight o'clock. And Laura, I want you to come also.

"Now that we've gotten that established, I do have something else I want to discuss with both of you. It's quite serious, so, I hope I've got your complete attention. In other words Laura, please quit looking at that darn computer screen." Adelaide placed her hand gently on mine.

My inner voice told me she was an expert in getting her way, and at the moment she was showing me she had a handle on when and how to turn on the take charge button. She must have been quite the dynamo in her younger days.

"Okay, you've got my attention," Mike responded, "and Laura's all ears too."

"I'm sorry Adelaide, I am distracted by our new case, and some of what I've recently learned. How can we help you? It sounds as if it doesn't have anything to do with your Archery pin."

"I can't be completely sure, but, I don't think it does. Has Mike told you where I live?"

"He said you're near me, and I'm in the farthest eastern corner of town, right off Lyon's Plain Road."

"What do you know, we're practically neighbors. You must pay me a social call, not in a work capacity. I'd love it. Especially since the holidays are right around the corner, and I'm by myself now that my Henry is gone.

"We'll have to talk about that later though, I've got something much more important to tell you. There have been some strange goings on in my woods recently. I've lived there for fifty years, so I would know better than anyone when something is out of whack. And I'm here to tell you, things are just not right. Even the animals know it, especially the wild ones. Although my little cocker spaniel Chloe is upset, too."

"Um, can you describe more of what you mean by 'out of whack' Adelaide? I'm not sure I'm understanding you." Mike leaned forward. He put his elbows on his desk and rested his chin on his folded hands.

"I hear a lot of noises that I don't normally hear; leaves rustling when they shouldn't be, and I've seen tracks that shouldn't be there either. There are lots of horses that go through those woods every day, but, they don't walk as close to each other as these do. I know horses

41

real well, and these tracks aren't right.

"And then there are some strange people around there, lately. It seems like they're poking around where they shouldn't."

"Without sounding too much like a smart aleck Adelaide, you have to admit there are strange people everywhere these days," I said with a grin.

"I can't argue with that Laura," Adelaide laughed. "However, these folks seem a little bit stranger than average. And I also find things out of place. It's hard to explain, but the woods look disturbed."

"Can you describe these peculiar people and tell me what time of day you see them?" Mike maintained his position of concentration.

"I don't always look at the clock or my watch, but it seems as if it's later in the day. There are usually lots of shadows around, especially when someone who's fond of the color brown is wandering through."

"Brown?" I asked. "Can you elaborate?"

"Well, I can try. I don't know if it's a man or woman, that's another thing that's hard to tell these days. I wish everyone would stop dressing the same. It was so much easier when girls wore girl clothes..." Adelaide trailed off.

"Sorry I keep getting off the subject, I've just got so much on my mind. When you two come over tomorrow morning, I'll show you some of the areas I'm referring to. After our coffee and bran, it would be a good idea to take a walk to get things moving. That's important in the morning, too.

"Okay, back to Brown. Like I said, it's hard to tell the gender of this person. Whoever it is always has a hood up."

"Uh, is 'Brown' ever with anyone?" I asked.

"Nope. Brown is always alone, never talks, always looks straight ahead and keeps a steady pace. He or she wears sunglasses most of the time, even if it's cloudy or dark out."

"Okay, now what about the horses, they have to be with someone, don't they?" I pressed as I looked at Mike, wondering if he planned on jumping into this odd conversation.

"You don't know too much about horses, do you?" Adelaide snorted. "What do you think? It's not like there are wild horses wandering around. I'm sorry Laura; I don't mean to make fun of you. I probably wasn't clear, it's late and sometimes I think I've said things when I've only thought them. Does that ever happen to you dear?"

"Sure it does, my mouth goes a lot faster than my head…"

"I'm not touching that with a ten foot pole," Mike laughed and sat back in his chair. "We can take this up tomorrow morning when we regroup at your house Adelaide. I'd feel a lot better if I knew you were safe and sound at home before too much snow piles up on the roads."

"I suppose you're right, and I know you and Laura have other business to attend to. Speaking of which, you'd both better get to bed early tonight, so you'll be bright-eyed and bushy-tailed in the morning. I want you in top form to solve both of my cases." Adelaide leaned forward, and with the aid of her cane, slowly rose from her chair. She brushed my hand aside as I attempted to assist her.

"Before you leave Adelaide, I don't recall you mentioning what woods you live in the middle of," I asked.

"Oh, thought I had. I live on a no name street, deep in Trout Brook Valley. Mike can give you directions so you won't get lost tomorrow morning."

"I walk there a lot, so I'll recognize the general area. What a great location."

"You, of course, are not the least bit strange looking, and I can definitely tell what gender you are," Adelaide quipped. "I thought I knew everyone who walked through my woods. I'm certainly glad we're finally acquainted."

"Me too Adelaide. I look forward to seeing you in the morning." I opened the door and watched Adelaide make her way down the short hallway.

"Horses taking themselves for a walk." She laughed while she nimbly made her way out to the street.

"She's a pistol, huh?" Mike said.

I didn't answer. My mind was already elsewhere. I sat down and stared at the monitor with Arnold's mug shot plastered like a photo in the middle of the screen. It was surrounded by a lengthy list of alleged crimes, including embezzlement of client funds and insider trading.

"Oh my gosh, I cannot believe how much money he spent on art, Mike. I can't add that fast, but, it looks to be millions!"

"Scroll down and check out how much his buddy Eliott spent on dog toys. And I thought you were bad with Kola. I don't think you could spend that much in a lifetime…well, maybe," Mike grinned.

"How in heaven's name have they gotten away with this? Until now, that is."

"When you think about it, it's not as hard as it sounds. I should clarify that otherwise…well, never mind…"

"Mike, what are you talking about?"

"Sorry Laura, I'm getting like you, thinking on a couple of tracks at the same time. Okay, look at this way. Say you got a lot of money invested with guys like Arnold and Eliott and they send you a statement every month…"

"I'm taking their word for it, aren't I? Wow! And nobody would be the wiser to what they were doing. So, the only way I'd catch on is if I wanted to withdraw some of it?"

"Exactly. I think. I don't have that kind of money outside of my 401k. I'd love to know who reported them. Hold it." Mike turned back to the screen to speed read a bit, and then pointed at an article, "Read this Laura. It highlights what I'm talking about. These guys were definitely spending other people's money. I guess that's why Reggie was following Arnold; and it looks like you did step right into the middle of a federal investigation. When you're finished reading, tell me everything you found out, and don't skip a thing young lady!"

It was a blog, written by an individual claiming to be an independent securities investigator. Much of the information provided would inevitably wind up on the United States Attorney's desk in Manhattan as evidence to indict both Arnold and Eliott. I wondered if the source was one of their clients, and why the Feds were relying on an indie source who signed off on his blog as Anonymous.

According to Anonymous, wiretaps had been set up to record conversations between Arnold and Eliott, catching Arnold bragging about reinvesting their client's funds into a separate hedge fund account in Eliott's name, using inside information from the executive board of a securities firm that Eliott still sat on. Arnold was the silent partner on the hedge fund account, and the other board members were in the dark as to Eliott's extra-curricular activities. Anonymous wrote how Arnold and Eliott phoned each other after every board meeting to use current private stockholder investment information for their own purposes.

"No wonder Reggie was so anxious to get the film from me," I said. "Guess I did step into something big," I added, as I proceeded to relate all I'd seen and heard from the moment I had parked in front of Arnold's house, right up until I left Sono Seaport Seafood. Mike was as stunned as I when I told him the mysterious woman was Arnold's sister. We were both shocked that Reggie would divulge any information about Arnold. I think we'd also both secretly hoped the woman would be a love interest, but it seemed our new case would not prove to be that straightforward.

Chapter 4

I headed over to Adelaide's house right before eight o'clock the next morning. The road to her house was steep, narrow, and windy. Mike's directions were fairly simple -- go straight to the end of Norton and take a right, followed by a left between two oak trees. No problem, I should be able to find that easily enough.

While keeping my eyes open for the oak trees, I was struck by the beauty of the early morning sunlight sparkling on the freshly fallen snow. Roughly three inches of powder had fallen over night. It looked like millions of tiny little diamonds cresting the tips of the statuesque pines.

Mike was parked on the side of the road. Apparently, he didn't think I knew what oak trees looked like. He was leaning against his dark green Jeep Wrangler with his arms crossed, and his navy wool cap pulled down to his eyebrows. Per usual, Mike didn't have a winter coat on, only his faded denim jacket with his tattered blue scarf. His winter gear wouldn't make an appearance unless there was at least three feet of snow on the ground. He was staring down, making some sort of design in the snow with the toe of his boot, indicating he was bored.

"Good morning Mike," I said, pulling up alongside. "The directions you gave me were very accurate, right down to the two oak trees."

"And a good morning to you, too. Here I thought you were going to get them mixed up with the maples that are right down the street." Mike stomped the snow from his boots and climbed into his Jeep, signaling from his window for me to follow him down a somewhat paved road through a forest. All I could think of was the fairy tale Little Red Riding Hood, wondering if I needed to keep my eyes peeled for the Big Bad Wolf. Pretty silly, I thought considering I hike up here all the time and this is another approach to the exact same woods. I'm definitely not a morning person.

After a few minutes, we pulled up to a one story log cabin, smoke curling up from its brick chimney. I felt as if I'd driven on to the set of Bonanza and Michael Landon and Lorne Greene were going to greet me. This place was almost an exact replica of the movie set, including the expansive front porch, with the table and rocker. It actually made me want to go home and watch an episode on TNT. Granted, Adelaide's cabin was on a much smaller scale, but equally as stunning. Not only that, it blended in with the environment; it belonged there. Realizing this was the first time I'd seen the cabin from this proximity, I turned and looked around me to get my bearings.

"What are you looking at?" Mike asked.

"It's fascinating to see this place close up. I'm used to walking by on the trails with Annie and the pups, up over there," I pointed up the hill and swept my hand across the horizon to give Mike an idea of where we hiked. The trails were a fair distance away from Adelaide's fantastic home.

"I have a feeling I'll be visiting her a lot."

"See, I told you. You two have a lot in common, and I mean that in the kindest of ways," Mike replied.

I admired Adelaide's independent spirit for having remained here after losing her husband. The nearest neighbors were close to a mile away, and the closest grocery store was at least five miles away. But then, she'd been here for fifty years and after that many years, where else would she go? If this were my home, I wouldn't leave either.

A few feet from the front door, I bent down to retrieve copies of both the New York Times and Soundview Times from the snow-covered bluestone pathway.

Mike rapped his knuckles twice on the door and while we waited, he brushed the snow off the front step with a broom that leaned against the house next to the door.

"Good morning you two. Come on in after you've wiped your feet off. And thank you Mike for sweeping the snow away," Adelaide greeted us, full of early morning cheer.

The blended aromas of fresh brewed coffee and a wood burning fire wafted through the doorway when she stepped aside to let us in. We left our coats and boots by the front door and followed Adelaide down a short hallway into the den. It was a cozy room, with white painted walls on either side of the floor to ceiling stone fireplace. A large picture window took up most of the other side of the room. It revealed the wooded valley below, a tremendous view that was framed with tieback antique lace curtains. An archway in the far wall led into the kitchen area. Adelaide motioned for me to sit on the couch, facing the warmth of the roaring fire, while she went into the kitchen. She refused help from me or Mike, who sat in a recliner next to me.

Only after Adelaide had set down a tray with three mugs of steaming coffee, a small pitcher of milk, sugar packets and plate of bran muffins, were we permitted to speak.

"It looks and smells wonderful Adelaide, thank you," I said, reaching for the coffee. "Would you like me to fix a cup for you?"

"Thank you, but, if you hadn't noticed, I live in the middle of nowhere. I'm capable of getting my own coffee." Adelaide dragged her cane along, spilling some milk as she poured it into the mug. She inched around the table, whacking the table and the couch with her cane, and settled on the couch across from me.

"Spoon?" I offered.

"Nope. I like to watch the milk swirl with the coffee. It doesn't mix as well, but I like how it looks."

"You have a lovely home Adelaide. I've admired it many times, walking by," I said, feeling greatly relaxed by the warmth of the fire.

"Thank you. Next time you happen by, if you see my papers in the driveway, would you mind bringing them to the door?"

"Of course not, I…"

"Eat your bran muffin while it's still hot Laura. That goes for you too Mike. I have a lot to discuss with you, so we can't take all day drinking coffee. I want to get outside and show you the places I told you about last night. Since the snow is so powdery Mike, I'd like you to bring the broom. You can sweep the snow away so you can see the tracks."

Adelaide turned her head and looked at me with a wide grin on her face. I had a feeling she would never let me off the hook regarding my question about the horses. The best I could muster was a sheepish grin.

Following Adelaide's instructions, Mike and I quickly ate our muffins and drank our coffee. If she wanted to hurry us along, that was fine with me; I had a mountain of work to wade through concerning Arnold. Adelaide's so-called case was nothing more than a diversion, but who could deny the request of such a sweet, not to mention insistent, woman. I hoped Mike wouldn't ask too many in-depth questions, as was his style with new clients. He had to view this as a favor to a friend.

"All right you two, let's get moving, I'm not getting any younger." Adelaide pushed herself forward on the couch and stood with the aid of her cane. "Mike, will you please get my coat. And Laura, will you kindly get my scarf, hat and boots? Everything is on the coat-rack in the hallway; except the boots of course. I have to make a stop at the little girl's room before we leave, and I'd appreciate it if you both would do the same. I don't want to be out in the woods when either of you decides that nature is calling. That's another thing that bothers me about my woods, it's not a bathroom for humans. How would you feel if the wildlife knocked on your door when you're busy and asked to use the toilet?" Adelaide ambled off to the bathroom.

"Don't you dare laugh Laura. God, I love her. She is too much, isn't she?"

"I didn't say a word, she's incredibly sweet and I do want to spend time with her. But, we have so much to do with Arnold's case, we have to go through all..."

"Don't worry, we'll get to it. It's not like we're going to be here that long. Hey, it's not even eight-thirty yet. It'll be fun, you'll see. And just because you walk here all the time, doesn't mean you know these woods as well as Adelaide does. Point being, you might just see something today that you wouldn't otherwise see."

"Mike, please help me with my coat while Laura takes care of business," Adelaide requested as she walked over to him, her coat over her arm.

While Mike was taking his turn, Adelaide put on her scarf and hat and struggled with her boots, refusing my help. With my coat on and my hat pulled down tightly, we walked part way down the driveway and waited for Mike at a trailhead to Trout Brook Valley. I'd let Kola out of the car and he'd trotted ahead of us, taking up a position with his front paws planted squarely on a rock and his hind feet on the ground. He remained still as a statue, not moving a muscle as he sniffed in the direction of the rock precipice on the other side of the trailhead.

"All right, I'm ready for the tour," Mike announced, striding up to us with the broom across his shoulder.

Annie and I had walked many times past what I thought looked like a rockslide. Coming up the trail near Adelaide's house was about a twenty- foot drop down to a ravine on the right. It wasn't unusual for Kola and Casey, Annie's pup, to climb up over the rocks and nose around. Now and then, Casey would come back with a glove or a T-shirt dangling from his mouth.

I shoved my hands deep into my pockets and bounced on my toes to keep warm while eyeing Kola as he slowly made his way to the edge of the precipice. His present behavior wasn't out of the ordinary. Then he lowered his body and began to whine. Whining was not normal.

"Look at that Laura, Kola knows something is wrong," Adelaide commented.

"What are you doing?" Mike asked.

"At the moment, we're watching Kola. I say he's on to something," Adelaide said, pointing toward the rocks.

"Oh, he probably smells some raccoon's house, that's all. So, where do we start?" Mike asked.

"I want to take you down that trail over there," Adelaide said, "the one where Kola's looking, the one where you say he's only looking at a raccoon's house," she continued as she slapped Mike's arm. "What is wrong with you two? Raccoons do live in rock crevices up high, as well as in trees. But they always live close to where there's food available. They don't live in bare rocks. And horses don't take themselves for walks! It's a good thing I didn't lose something out here, neither of you would ever find it." With that, Adelaide proceeded down the trail with Kola in tow. Mike and I both followed, feeling a bit chagrined. To make matters worse, my pup had clearly decided that Adelaide was the pack leader.

While we made our way along the trail, Kola kept looking to the rock ledge and sniffing the air. Each time he would stop, Adelaide reprimanded him. "Kola, I promise we'll check on whatever's got your sniffer going, but we have to do first things first," She reached down and petted him.

"Adelaide, maybe Mike and I should take a thorough look over…"

"Every time we stop, we're simply stalling and I want to show you what I want to show you. You two are so slow, and here I thought the coffee and bran would get you moving along. Now let's go, the day will be over before you know it.

"Kola, why are young people so slow? I thought you and your mom hiked every day. That's right my boy, she should be in better shape."

Mike and I exchanged glances as we picked up our pace. The

ground had the first-freeze crunch to it, so Kola would not disturb any tracks. Adelaide led us along in silence, with Kola trotting at her side, until we arrived on the other side of the stream at a small pond. I threw in a handful of treats for Kola and we watched as he swam after and gobbled each one.

"Do you always do that?" Adelaide inquired.

"Absolutely. Annie and I call it 'fishing.' The pups love it, even when it's freezing."

"Look behind you Laura...at the ground, silly. Do you see the line of snow covered hoofprints?"

I followed the direction Adelaide's cane pointed in, to the deep impressions which could still be seen under the soft layer of snow. There was no mistaking the prints, and as Adelaide had said the previous night; they were almost on top of each other.

"There are a number of barns in the area Adelaide. What makes you suspicious?" I looked at Mike who still had the broom over his shoulder and quietly stared at the set of prints.

"You're not paying attention Laura. When people trail ride, they don't get that close to each other, it's too dangerous. And someone is riding the first horse. How do I know that? Because the impressions are deeper than the prints of the other one, which says the rider is leading a horse. I want to know why."

"Well, maybe the rider is bringing the other horse along for the exercise."

"Let's keep walking and I'll show you why I don't think that's true. Mike, are you awake? Your partner needs your help."

"Huh? Yeah, I was just thinking...never mind, take us to the next spot Adelaide."

Kola made his way out of the pond, shook himself as free of water as possible and fell in behind Adelaide. We made our way up an incline and entered a small stand of pines. Several inches of pine needles underfoot created a soft carpet. Snow had begun to cover the edges of the deep green canopy overhead and gave me the feeling of walking into a greenhouse. The dampness brought out the aroma of the pine, reminding me the holidays were approaching.

Mike started whistling Whistle While You Work and twirling the broom on his shoulder. It amazed me at times how he could enjoy the simplest of things.

"Okay Mike, or should I call you 'Happy?' And you too Laura, come over here." Again Adelaide pointed with her cane toward a small clearing surrounded by mountain laurel trees and scrub brush. "Mike, please sweep the snow away from that one particular spot over to the right. Do you see where I mean?"

"Yup. I'm on it Adelaide." Mike stepped with care around the area Adelaide pointed to.

"Please make it snappy, it's too cold to stand here all day."

"Sorry, but I have to be careful, to preserve any evidence." Mike bent down and knelt on the ground. He shortened his hold on the broom and gently swept the powdery snow away.

I lowered into a squat while Kola lay down next to me. The three of us silently watched Mike's methodical progress. Mike finally sat back and leaned on the broom as he laid it across his knees. His efforts revealed an area down to the dirt with leaves shoved to each side. The breadth of the space looked to be around three feet and the length approximately six feet.

"Now do you understand why I brought the two of you out here? This is not normal. We don't have hikers come through and sweep the woods free of leaves while moving backwards. And look behind you Mike, you'll see more hoofprints and this time, they're equal in depth. What does that mean? I know the answer. I just want to see if the two of you are listening to me."

I raised my hand. "No riders on either horse, or a rider on each horse!"

"I knew that too. Laura's not the only smart one," Mike said.

"That's all well and good class, now I would like an interpretation."

I crawled carefully forward and knelt beside Mike. I then inched ahead, staying between the two areas, and stopped at the top of the section Mike had just swept. Remaining on my knees, I leaned on one hand and moved some snow aside with the edge of my other hand. The heel prints were deeper than those in the section Mike had cleared.

"I'm not sure there's anything to worry about Adelaide, except maybe an out of bounds hunter. You should call the Department of Environmental Energy Protection about that." I tapped Mike on the shoulder to get his attention.

"What? I was thinking and you just interrupted me. Yeah, I tend to agree with Laura. I think. I mean, it could be a hunter, or on the other hand, it could be riders taking turns. Are there any more tracks you've discovered Adelaide?"

"Well, I know the horses go up the hill and out to the street. After that, I've no idea. Riders around here don't ride then decide to walk, unless there's an obstacle in their way. There's something not right. I have seen hunters go out with deer across their horses, even though I don't think they're supposed to, so that could answer why the depth of the hoofprints is different even if it's not by a lot., Did you notice another set of footprints near the hoof marks? Looks to me like hiking boots," Adelaide said.

"In other words, now there's something or someone on the second horse. And the hiking bootprints would verify that. So, the hunter has a helper," Mike said.

"Bravo Mike! I knew you were listening," Adelaide laughed and clapped her hands.

Mike grinned broadly, just like a teacher's pet. I half expected him to hand an apple to her.

"Have you seen hunters in other out of bounds areas of the woods Adelaide?" I asked.

"No. But, I have found bloody arrows now and then. Let me see, the last time I found an arrow was...hmm, not since last winter. And it was way over on the other side of the woods by the Bradley Road entrance, but I know they're allowed over there. So, that brings us back to this being only one of the disturbances I've come across lately."

I felt something on my rump and nearly jumped out of my skin. I looked up at Adelaide, whose eyes were twinkling. She had just smacked me with her cane.

"I'll bite, what else have you found?" Mike asked.

"There's another spot, up on the red trail, where there's a nice, comfortable rock. It makes for a terrific view clear across to the top of the ridge behind you both. Anyway, I like to sit up there; it relaxes me. Until recently, I thought it was my secret place. Now I keep finding newspapers, neatly folded, with a small rock on top of them. Naturally, I bring them home and throw them away. I'll never understand why people feel it's necessary to clutter up the woods with garbage. What I find strange is, the section that lists the obituaries is folded back with that specific page in view."

"What paper is it?" Mike asked.

"It's the Soundview Times. Why? An obituary is an obituary; who cares what paper it's in."

"Well, someone is checking on who's dead in this area, that's why. And it's kind of interesting that whoever it is reading those obituaries can see this spot." Mike looked at me with some concern on his face.

"Adelaide, Mike and I need to get to the office. I'll be walking here this afternoon and I promise, I'll bring my camera and take pictures of both places. I am curious though, have you ever noticed any footprints near your rock?"

"A few, but, they aren't the same as these, if that's what you're implying. And no, I didn't keep the papers. Like I said, I threw them out."

"I was about to ask you that exact question." Mike stretched as he stood and placed the broom back over his shoulder. He put his hand out and helped me to my feet. "Looks as if Laura and I have got some work to do, besides our other case. Like I said Adelaide, could be nothing more than a poacher, but, we'll still look into it. This being your woods, I want you to feel safe."

"Thank you for coming out here and checking. I say there's something wrong and I expect you both to report back to me with what you find. The pictures will be nice to have Laura, but I want answers. The sooner the better. So, let's hurry up. I don't want you wasting valuable time. And Laura, when you've finished your walk this afternoon, please stop by and update me."

I was about to reply when Mike clamped his hand across my mouth. He shook his head, took his hand away from my mouth and pushed me forward. I wanted to run back to my car. Adelaide's 'case' was keeping us from investigating Arnold and finding Gwen. That investigation was more important than finding a hunter; that's what the D.E..E.P. was for. Maybe, when we got back to Adelaide's house, I'd write their phone number down for her.

Adelaide stopped and scratched her head, "I just thought of something, I don't know why I forgot this, but I remember seeing Brown in that area where the horse and bootprints are. He was riding a horse, and leading an unsaddled horse out through the woods in the direction of the road. He had his hood up, and was wearing sunglasses, even though the sun had sunk below the tree line."

I looked at Mike, and stared at the ground, stunned…

55

"If you have something on your mind, speak up young lady." Adelaide leaned on her cane, pursed her lips and waited. "Cat got your tongue? I'm running out of patience, and we can't stand here all day. At least, I can't. Listen, I'm old and I live alone, and as I told you, there have been some oddities going on in these woods that have been upsetting me and Chloe. If it will make you happy, I'll start keeping notes of what I see and when."

"I'm sorry Adelaide," I offered, "I just realized that you might be our only eye witness to a killer. I wish you had thought of this a little bit sooner, that's all. Do you have any idea of when you saw Brown?"

"I remember seeing a picture of a missing woman in the paper. Are you looking for her murderer? Do you think Brown was involved? I don't remember exactly when I saw Brown. It was at least a week ago. I'm sorry Laura, that's the best I can do."

"That's great. It gives us a timeframe that jives a bit with what her husband told us. Thank you for being so helpful Adelaide, especially with all the stress you've been under," I said.

"Now she's trying to make nice with me, isn't she?" Adelaide grinned at Mike.

Mike returned the smile and said, "Anything you might have seen that could lead to the apprehension of this guy, or the location of Gwen, is a good thing."

"Did they teach you diplomacy at the academy, because that must have been the one class you stayed awake for," Adelaide chuckled as she headed up the trail.

It took almost forty five minutes to walk back to the beginning of the trail. I pulled back my glove to check the time; it was almost ten o'clock.

"Adelaide, I don't mean to be rude, I need to leave right away. I want to get on this as soon as possible. There are some things I want to look up on the internet which may shed some light on what you showed us. I promise I'll stop by later, probably around five o'clock…and thanks for the coffee and bran muffin."

"Mike," I continued, "I'm heading down to The Soundview Guild, where Gwen was enrolled in art classes, to see what I can dig up." I waved while getting Kola into the car, checked the rearview mirror, and noticed Mike hand gesturing back and forth with Adelaide. The last thing I saw, while going down her driveway, was her smacking his rump with the cane. I laughed. Better him than me.

I tried clearing my head and re-focusing on Arnold and Gwen as I drove off in the direction of the Merritt Parkway, with renewed hopes of obtaining solid information which would point to Gwen's whereabouts.

Chapter 5

The Soundview Artists' Guild was comprised of several one-story buildings in a wooded setting. It was designed specifically for art classes and included a New York style gallery space for students' art shows.

At ten thirty on a Monday morning, I figured the classrooms would be filled with students studying in the variety of arts the Guild offered. They had classes in everything from photography and sculpture to painting, Gwen's specialty. Entering the office, I wondered if Gwen was an intermediate or advanced painter. The fact she had been preparing for a show in New York indicated she either had talent or connections. Maybe both.

"May I help you?" A sixty-ish looking woman with medium-length brown hair, too much make-up and a bright smile, inquired. She wore a broad-brimmed, expensive-looking black straw hat, a long-sleeve dark blue blouse, a matching below-the-knee skirt and black pumps. The deep red lipstick against her pale face verged on frightening. The bright yellow scarf tied loosely around her neck didn't help.

"Well, I hope so. I'm Laura Jensen of Jensen and O'Malley Investigations," I offered my hand to shake hers, but her hand remained at her side. Now and then I noticed people became uncomfortable in the presence of a private investigator, and she was clearly one of them. Probably some curious Freudian association.

"Uh, my agency has been hired to locate one of your students -- the student's husband is trying to locate his wife. She's been missing for almost twenty-four hours now. Her name is Gwen Hansen and…"

"Oh my God, not Gwen!" The woman leaned against the wall and began to sob. I had not expected such a dramatic reaction, but then again, she was a dramatic looking person. What to do? Consoling was Mike's department. I helped her to a chair behind her desk, and pulled out a handful of tissues from a box sitting next to the phone. Her gold bangle bracelets jangled when she brought the tissues to her nose. The sound of her blowing her nose reminded me of the honking geese that flew over my home each evening.

I walked to the side of her desk to fill a cup of water from the cooler and when I turned around, I noticed her nameplate: Penelope Gatsby.

"Here Penelope, take a drink of water," I said, sitting on the edge of the desk while she swallowed several mouthfuls.

She licked her lips and looked up at me with her eyes narrowed, "How did you know my name?"

"The nameplate on your desk."

"Of course. I can't believe Gwen is missing; she was just here early Saturday morning, working on her latest piece. I'm not usually here on the weekend, but, I was asked to show some out of town prospective students around."

"What time was that Penelope? And, do you recall what kind of mood she was in?" I pulled my notebook and pen from my coat pocket, ready to jot down her answers.

"Oh, I think it was just before nine o'clock. Her mood? Well, it was typical Gwen, cheery and in a hurry to get to work on her painting."

"Do you have any idea how long Gwen was here?"

"I...well...I spent an hour or so with the group. After they left, I went out for a late breakfast by myself at a nearby diner. That took about an hour and a half...are you keeping track of this?"

"Absolutely Penelope. I'm taking notes on everything you're telling me."

"Do you want me to continue? I'm so very upset about this?"

"Why don't you take another drink of water? Then maybe you can take me to Gwen's workspace and show me her paintings. We'll talk while we walk and that may help you relax a bit."

Penelope drank the remaining water and dabbed her eyes to clear away some of her smeared make-up, "I suppose under the circumstances it will be okay if I show you her work. Individuals who aren't members of the Guild are normally not permitted to view pieces in progress without the artists' permission. But if you think it will help, then by all means."

"According to what you've told me so far, would it be accurate to say you didn't get back here until noon?"

Penelope picked up the box of tissues as she stood and tucked it under her arm. We made our way down the hallway, the clicking of her heels on the stone floor, the only sound.

"I believe I did arrive back here by noon, and yes, Gwen was still busy painting. She's always plugged in to her iPod, so I doubt she heard me when I opened the door to check on her. Not wanting to disturb her, I didn't say..." Penelope turned on the waterworks again. She had used most of the tissues while I failed to calm her.

"I should have...I can't talk anymore about this. It's too upsetting. I hope you understand Laura. Please, take as much time as you feel is necessary to look at her paintings and whatever else you need to," Penelope pointed toward the room Gwen used and turned to walk back to her desk. "Please, tell me about anything that you find."

I stood at the door to the studio and listened to the fading echo of Penelope's pumps. I did not have a good feeling about Gwen. As far as I knew, Penelope had been the last person to see her. Arnold had evaded Mike's and my questions as to when he'd last seen Gwen, but maybe he had leveled with Detective Marshall. Well, Mike and I will compare notes later. I pushed the door open.

The pungent odor of oil paints enveloped me as I surveyed the studio space. There was no question regarding Gwen's tidiness. A gray, rickety looking metal locker leaned against the back wall. Several easels were neatly stacked alongside the locker. A cloth-draped open easel with a barstool in front of it was diagonal to the locker. The set-up faced a double set of windows that looked out into the woods, a tranquil setting for an artist.

Next to the covered easel was a cherry-wood, narrow chest of drawers approximately three feet in height. I walked over and opened the top drawer. It had a silverware-type tray inside filled with brushes of varying sizes. The next couple of drawers contained partially used tubes of paint, rags, colored pencils, a palette and paint cleaner. Nothing unusual so far, I thought, as I contemplated removing the cover from the work in progress.

I sat on the barstool and imagined myself as Gwen. I wondered if she had any particular

ritual she followed prior to beginning her work, aside from listening to her iPod. I opened the top drawer of the chest and fiddled with the brushes before choosing one I supposed was for detailed painting. While sitting there with my brush, it occurred to me my fingers had gone over an object that didn't belong in that drawer. Getting off the barstool, I lifted out the tray and placed it on the table, carefully sifting through the various brushes. Someone had used a small piece of masking tape to attach what looked to be a safety deposit box key to the side of the drawer.

Time to call Mike.

"Mike, I believe I've found an important key to our case," I said.

"Where are you?" Mike asked.

"I told you I was going to The Soundview Artists' Guild, silly. Weren't you listening? Oh right, you were getting caned," I laughed.

"Not funny. Adelaide thought you were going to stick around for lunch or something, and I was sticking up for you. That cane of hers is a weapon. So what did you find? I sure hope it's useful. Arnold's been calling every half hour to check on our progress. The guy's flipping out, and now he says he can't reach his partner Eliott."

"Great, first he loses his wife, now his partner? I'm afraid to ask who's next," I said. "I found something that's going to require Grady's help, and it's literally a key. From the looks of it, it's the key to a safety deposit box. It was hidden in Gwen's paintbrush drawer. Before you ask, I didn't remove it, nor did I touch it...well, my fingers might have brushed over it while I was looking for a brush."

"Will you stop already with the puns?" Mike said.

"Only if you promise not to make me wait too long to get Grady down here with his search warrant! Oh, and bring your own car so we can transport some of these paintings back with us."

"Anything else, oh excellent partner of mine?" Mike asked.

"No, I think that covers it. I'm sorry, thank you." I smiled. Now back to the task at hand.

I took a deep breath, but it did not alleviate the guilt I felt about invading Gwen's privacy. An unfinished piece had to be as sacred as a photography project was for me. However, if the painting held any clues to Gwen's whereabouts, then I believed she would grant me permission to look at it.

I stood, held the cloth at the bottom and delicately lifted it up. Allowing the cover to drop behind the easel, I was stunned by what I saw. The scene didn't match the description of the peaceful woman who loved the outdoors. After a moment, I collected myself and backed up to the door, brush still in hand. I pushed the door open behind me without diverting my eyes from what was on the easel. I walked at a brisk pace down the hallway, hoping to find Penelope at her desk and not off on some errand.

We nearly collided when she exited a room in front of me, "Ah Penelope, there you are."

"I'm sorry, I'm not myself today. Did you find anything of consequence?"

"I may have…I mean…would you mind helping me with something? If you're not busy, I would appreciate it."

"I'm on my way to make copies of the art show announcement for next month. The students get so thrilled, so I do my best to get the announcements up early enough for the students to properly prepare. This one will be a mixed medium show, which is extra special. We only have those twice a year."

She paused at my confusion.

"Please forgive me. A mixed medium show is a representation of all the arts taught here."

"Thank you for the explanation, I'd love to attend."

"Of course, let me put these on my desk and I'll be right with you Laura."

I glanced at my watch, anxiously waiting for Penelope to return. It was hard to believe I'd already been at the Guild for almost an hour.

After what seemed like an eternity, she finally appeared. "I apologize Laura, one of the instructors had a question. Now, what would you like me to do?"

"I was looking at Gwen's new painting and…can you please take a look? I could use your input."

Penelope nodded and led the way back to Gwen's studio.

"Uh, is it standard practice for students to have private studios?"

"Heavens no! We don't have that many studios available. It simply is not feasible. For students who are in the upper tax brackets, such as Gwen, they pay a substantial quarterly fee for the space. Believe me; Gwen and Arnold are certainly in the upper echelon. Did you happen to notice the enormous skylight directly over the middle of the room? Well, Arnold had it installed for her.

"So, would you say Arnold was in love with his wife?" I asked.

"I don't believe that would best describe his feelings for her. Mind you, this is only my opinion, but, I think Arnold wanted to remain married to Gwen because she looked stunning on his arm at business functions. Gwen accepted it, as he allowed her complete freedom with her painting career. Arnold's real marriage was to his business."

"Hmm, sounds as if they didn't enjoy each other's company."

"Initially, I'm sure they were in love. Of late it's my opinion that their marriage had grown into one of convenience."

"Without being rude Penelope, what is your position here?"

"Why, I'm the director."

"But your desk is at the front entrance. Don't you have an office?"

"Of course I have an office. I like to spend my mornings out in the open. I want to be readily available to everyone, students and visitors alike. It's one of my personal touches, which creates a family environment. Artists thrive in that particular atmosphere.

"I spend afternoons in my office, returning phone messages and doing paperwork. Now, show me what it is you need my help with."

I held the door open for Penelope. With one foot in the door, she exclaimed, "Oh my word, that poor child." She pulled a tissue from her sleeve and wiped her eyes. "I find it difficult to believe Gwen painted this; it had to have been done by someone who has a turbulent life. I don't understand..." Penelope moved closer to examine the dark, violent, apparently unfinished scene.

I stepped forward too, to interpret what might very well be a message of some kind. It was a horizontal seascape depicting the harshest of storms. The sea was painted such an intense dark gray, it was almost black, and the waves were nearly boiling. Driftwood had crashed on what little beach there was and the sky was equally dark, with lightning bolts shattering the menacing clouds. I leaned a little closer and realized she had not painted any rain falling. Well, it is a work in progress.

Something bothered me about the way Gwen had depicted a black-cloaked figure to the far right of the painting, so far to the right it was almost off the canvas. On the extreme left a life-ring floated on the crest of a crashing wave.

"What do you think Penelope? If Gwen didn't paint this, then who did?"

"I don't know...I can't...oh, poor Gwen, if this is her work, she hid her inner self so well," Penelope gestured toward the painting. "I do need to examine the brush strokes first; that's how you identify a particular artist. Well, if you're familiar with his or her work, that is.

Gwen traces over her strokes…do you see? Come closer Laura and I'll point it out."

As I stepped next to Penelope, my eyes remained glued to the dark figure. It was a provocative image. I wondered if it was meant to be Gwen herself. It was difficult to tell if the figure was entering or leaving the scene. I pulled my magnifying glass from the inside pocket of my coat.

"What are you looking for Laura?"

"I'm curious about who this is supposed to be. It's hard to tell. Maybe, if it's magnified, I'll be able to see more detail." I moved the glass over the figure to obtain the maximum effect of the magnifier. "Hmm."

"What? Laura, what have you found?"

"Was Gwen a sailor?"

"I…you know, I can't quite put my finger on it, but, there is a familiarity there. Give me a moment to think."

While Penelope considered my question, I continued to look at the dark figure and determined that it wore foul weather gear.

"I do believe Gwen sailed with friends. I don't recall her having her own boat. Are you suggesting this is a self-portrait?"

"At the moment, I don't know. I'd love to compare this work with some of her others after I've checked a few more things. I'm guessing the rest of Gwen's paintings are in the locker?"

"Actually Laura, yes they are. Gwen kept them locked up and supplied me with a duplicate key in case of an emergency. I don't imagine this is what she had in mind."

"Most likely not." I moved the glass to my left toward the life ring, determined to uncover anything which could be interpreted as a clue; something not apparent to the naked eye. Come on Gwen, speak to me, I want to help you.

"What? Huh? Penelope, use my magnifier and look at the life ring. I believe I've found a clear message from Gwen."

Penelope removed her dark-rimmed eyeglasses and moved my glass back and forth until the writing on the life ring came into focus. "Why wasn't I aware of this? I failed her miserably Laura…I…"

While Penelope pulled more tissue from her sleeve, I took the glass and zeroed in on Gwen's S.O.S. message painted in the smallest of cream colored letters. The size of the letters, coupled with the color

Gwen had chosen to write them in -- set against the white of the life ring -- would never have been spotted without the aid of a magnifying glass. Gwen was calling for help in the tiniest of voices. Why? What was she frightened of? Was Arnold responsible for her disappearance? What was in the safety deposit box? Maybe Gwen had stumbled onto something to do with Arnold's business, and it was her ace in the hole?

"You can't blame yourself Penelope. It seems as if Gwen was too afraid to confide in anyone. She used her painting to cry for help. I'm wondering what was going on in her life to cause so much fear? Could it have been her marriage?

"May I see her other paintings? And would you be able to give me the names of classmates she was close to?"

Penelope wiped her eyes, blew her nose and sat on the stool in front of the unfinished seascape.

"She met on a regular basis with four women to discuss techniques they were learning and how these methods applied to their current works. Gwen was the only one in the group who had been accepted into the spring show in New York, and…are you implying they had something to do with her disappearance?" Penelope glared at me.

"Penelope, I have to speak with anyone who knew Gwen. I have no idea where the next lead may come from. What if I hadn't taken the time to inspect this canvas? What if you had not given me permission to look through her studio? I've spoken with Arnold and now you. I need every ounce of information I can get my hands on, if Mike and I are going to have any chance of finding Gwen. That reminds me, what, if anything, do you know about her sister-in-law?"

"Judy? Aside from her name, nothing. Gwen mentioned her in passing. I got the impression they're not close.

"I am beside myself. I should have seen the signs, I…"

"Penelope, let's do what we can to help Gwen right now. I need her classmates' names, and please get the key to the locker. Oh, and I'm expecting two other gentlemen who should be arriving very shortly. One is my partner Mike, and the other is a lieutenant with the Soundview Police Department. I found something that I'm unable to discuss with you, but Lieutenant Grady Marshall will go over it with you when he gets here."

Penelope gave me a cold stare, and said, "I've been nothing but open with you, and you're keeping information from me?"

"Penelope, you've been wonderful. I appreciate your help and your insight, it's valuable to the case, and I apologize for not being able to talk about this. Once the Lieutenant arrives, he can explain."

"I'll be back in a moment with the list and I do have to be here while you go through the contents of the locker." Penelope left before I could respond.

I walked over to the window and stared into the woods. A series of deep breaths did not relieve the guilt I felt over pressing Penelope for information. Mike had taught me to be firm with potential witnesses when interviewing them. At the moment, I did not feel he had prepared me for how difficult it would be to lean on individuals consumed by grief. It was impossible to know if Penelope held any pertinent information which could lead us to Gwen unless I pushed her.

My success as a P.I. depended on my thoroughness and following Mike's instructions to the letter until I learned enough to develop my own routine.

"Laura, I'm back."

"Oh…yes, great. Well, let's see what's in the locker."

Penelope grasped the lock and inserted the key. She turned the key numerous times and yanked on the lock until it finally opened.

There were fourteen canvases neatly stacked in groups of two, the backs facing each other. Along the right side, a divider separated the main part of the locker from another section, about a foot wide, with four evenly spaced shelves and a large section at the bottom that contained an umbrella and a pair of hiking boots.

I rummaged through the shelves finding neatly folded aprons, towels, several pairs of socks, deodorant, a toothbrush and toothpaste. Gwen certainly spent a lot of time here.

A silver rain jacket hung next to the umbrella. I reached into the left front pocket. It was empty. Penelope stood with her arms crossed while I continued to search for anything out of the ordinary. I hoped whatever it was would make itself known and I would recognize it when I found it.

I twisted the coat toward me and thrust my hand into the right front pocket, "What do you know…?"

"What did you find? I want to see it first, it might be too personal."

"It's a book Penelope, and we'll open it together. Okay?"

"I suppose that will be all right. You're already hiding one thing from me."

It was a small, black hardcover book with a piece of elastic holding it closed. Penelope removed the elastic and opened it to the first page.

My newfound career is everything to me. My painting has revealed my soul to me. Why can't Arnold allow me this? Why will he not allow me to breathe? What will become of me, if he takes this away? Will I

Penelope thumbed through the remaining pages. They were blank. She silently placed a folded piece of paper in Gwen's notebook, and handed it to me. She began sobbing once more and hurried out the door.

With the journal tucked away in my back pocket, I went through the fourteen completed pieces, which I guessed were for the spring show. These looked more like what I expected to see from Arnold's description as well as Penelope's.

I knelt on the floor to get a better look and was amazed both by the beauty of the paintings and Gwen's talent. Her depiction of the view from the Orchard was exquisite. The fall colors were shown with a brilliance enhanced by the sunlight as it streamed in from behind the observer. I was instantaneously pulled into the scene, even to the point of feeling the ever present wind on my face. Gwen's talent overwhelmed me. She would do well in the New York show. Were her classmates jealous? Was her success too much for Arnold?

While I was still on the floor, Penelope led Mike and Grady into the studio. I immediately handed Mike the journal I'd discovered in Gwen's jacket. "Seems like trouble in Arnold's paradise," he muttered. He handed it to Grady, who read it with raised eyebrows, prior to putting it in a separate evidence bag.

Penelope remained planted in the doorway with her arms crossed. None of us were escaping without her permission. She moved into the room and hovered over Grady while he went through the motions of taking photographs of the taped key prior to removing it. He also took a set of fingerprints, then placed the key in an evidence bag, numbered and dated it, and was ready to leave, until I informed him that we were permitted to take some of the paintings for further perusal.

Chapter 6

It seemed like days before we made our way back to the office with Gwen's paintings, and even longer before we managed to lug them inside.

"How many paintings are there?" Mike asked.

"Fifteen. Let's line them up against the walls. I especially want you to take a close look at the one she was working on. Gwen was in fear of her life Mike. It's in the painting she was working on...and Arnold's involved in her disappearance, I just know it."

"What, is your gut talking to you again? Never mind, mine wants lunch before we start on this. If you're lining these up on the floor, does that mean I have to crawl around?"

"Well, yes, you have to get on the floor. I'll buy lunch today. How's that for a fair exchange?"

"Okay, okay, I'll help. Guess my info on Arnold can wait a minute or two."

"I can't wait to hear what you've found out about Arnold... but first you've gotta see

Gwen's art, Mike, you won't believe it."

I carefully leaned the three canvases I'd carried in against the wall behind my desk, wondering if we had enough room to line all of them up. I moved one of the chairs we used for clients to a corner and placed the seascape on it. This painting demanded our immediate attention. I desperately wanted Mike's prompt input. Gwen's life could depend on it.

"These things are awkward to carry. Where do you want them? Right, on the floor, how could I forget? Will you please order me a pizza with extra cheese and anchovies? And before you complain, I'll leave it in the hall so it doesn't stink up the office."

"I honestly don't understand why you want fish bait on your pizza. No wonder you don't have any success finding a date."

I reached in the drawer and grabbed the menu for Main Pizza while Mike finished setting up the paintings.

"They're going to deliver, right? Wow, this ocean thing is wild."

"It's referred to as a seascape Mike. You really need to get out more."

Mike sat on the floor in front of the seascape, legs crossed, and silently stared at it. While he analyzed that piece, I crawled from one to the other. I experienced a visceral reaction to each one.

The majority of the paintings were landscapes, one using soft colors for birch trees, with leaves floating to the ground.

Another had a doe with her fawn grazing in a meadow, as an eagle soared overhead. They were more a realistic style than an impressionist one. Strangely, Gwen's art style mimicked my photography.

"Mike, do you see any similarities between Gwen's paintings and my photography?"

"Interesting question; I thought I was seeing things because I'm starving. You two sure seem to like a lot of the same stuff."

"Do you think it's a coincidence, or, should I be worried?"

"Nope to both. Don't forget; there's no such thing as a coincidence in P.I. work. However, with me around to watch your back there's nothing to worry about. Always pay attention to your surroundings, Laura, and quit hiking by yourself when Annie's out of town. Do those two things on a regular basis and you'll be fine. Well, I guess Kola will protect you when you're not hiking with Annie.

"There's something eerie about this sea... whatever you want to call it. It doesn't go with the rest of her work. The other stuff makes you feel peaceful when you look at it, like your photos. This one is scary, and makes me seasick. I don't know much about fine art, but anyone can see that she's screaming for help. But from what?"

"Wow. I had a sour feeling about the guy with the way he walked out on us, and it only got worse with the Google info. I don't know how he's involved with his wife's disappearance, but, I'm guessing he's going to jail for something when this is over.

"What's this list of names?"

"Those are the classmates Gwen was closest to, according to

Penelope Gatsby, the woman you met earlier. She's the director of Soundview Artists' Guild."

We were interrupted by several knocks on the door. Before I opened the door, I took some money out of my desk drawer.

Kola barked, until he smelled the pizza and my chicken salad. I had no sooner closed the door when I heard another knock.

"Yes, may I help you?"

"Hi, I'm from Soundview Artists' Guild and Ms. Gatsby wanted me to bring this package to you. She said it's real important, so here," said the young delivery man.

"Okay, thanks very much and please thank Ms. Gatsby for me. Would you like an anchovy pizza before you leave?" I asked.

"Don't you give my lunch away! You bring that over here straight away. Sorry about that."

"Uh, thanks for the offer, but, I don't eat fish bait. Bye."

"Smart young man." I closed the door and turned the package over, looking for a return address. Finding none, I realized it had been sent to Gwen in care of Penelope, and she had not opened it.

"What's that Laura?" Mike had already gulped one slice and was busy with the second one.

"It's something that was mailed to Gwen at the school, but, it doesn't say who it's from. Thank goodness Penelope had the sense to send it over to us..." I ripped the outer wrapping paper off and opened the white gift box.

"Put it down Laura!"

"Why, it's just a burgundy beret. It's enclosed in tissue and there's a card with it: Knock 'em dead in New York, love E. Who's 'E'?"

"Laura, before you touch anything more, set it gently in the middle of my desk. I have to call Grady right away. He'll want to see this. Could be prints on there that might tell us who's responsible for Gwen's disappearance." Mike punched in one number, since he had Grady on speed dial.

"I'm sorry, I wasn't thinking..."

"It's okay Laura...Grady, yeah, it's Mike. I know we just left you a little while ago. Going fishing, huh? Sounds great. You're taking the boys, aren't you? You guys will have a great time. Wish I could go with you and get out of this cold for a while. Are you kidding, Florida's the place to be this time of year.

"Hey Grady, something just came up that could have to do with this Arnold Hansen character. Yup, that's him alright, arrogant as all get out. Well, my fearless partner…ah, she's great, best thing I ever did. I love working with her. She sure is better looking than you, and yeah, she definitely smells better.

"Listen, I could shoot the breeze all day, but I need your help. Why? Because, we got a package here that was sent to Arnold's wife and it may have some good prints on it. Nope, we don't have any real leads either, outside of the safety deposit key you picked up this morning. Of course I'd call you if I had something Grady. Okay, two minutes is great. Thanks buddy."

"Thanks for the compliments Mike, especially the one about me smelling better. I'm sorry I didn't put the package down right away. That is such a rookie mistake. At least I didn't touch the key this morning." I sunk into my chair and stared morosely at my chicken salad.

"Hey Laura, it's okay. It's been a long day, and you're right, you did the correct thing earlier. Far as this beret thing goes, you didn't know." Mike sat on the edge of my desk and gently patted me on the shoulder. "You wouldn't believe the stuff I screwed up on when I first started on patrol with Grady. Do me a favor; don't ask him to tell you any stories when he gets here. Otherwise, he'll be here all day. Jeez, I better get the anchovy pizza out of here; he'll bug me about fishing." Mike got up, picked the pizza box up off the floor and slid it under his desk.

"Uh Mike, Grady's a fisherman, I'm pretty sure he'll smell the anchovies anyhow. And thanks for the pep talk. I always think I should know more than I do."

"I know, it's like that for everyone in this line of work. Besides, you've dug up some great info. Hey, you think I would've partnered with you if I didn't think you had a lot of smarts? You're a quick learner kiddo…"

"Hello. Someone call for a real detective?" Grady poked his head through the doorway.

"Twice in the same day? We're going to have to stop meeting like this; people will start getting suspicious." Then he and Mike spent the next few minutes exchanging back slaps, acting as if they hadn't seen each other in days when in fact it had only been a few hours. I always found it interesting the way longtime male friends greeted each other; mumbled words, smacks on the back and arms, slugging gestures coupled with continuous laughter.

Watching Mike and Grady was made more humorous by the way Grady's lanky six foot three inch frame towered over Mike's five feet ten inches. Even with several shocks of gray mixed into his brown, curly mop, you wouldn't think Grady had already reached his fortieth birthday.

Grady had been blessed with a laid back, magnetic personality, which ingratiated him with potential witnesses or suspects. As a result, in just five short years, his success with solving cases had propelled him through the ranks to lieutenant in the Soundview Police Detective Division.

"Hi Laura," Grady bent down and kissed me on the cheek. "Mike says you're picking up this P.I. thing fast. This morning proved it; you acted like a complete pro. You two sure make a great team."

"Thanks Grady," I beamed, "Slow and steady, right?"

Mike rolled his eyes, "That's right Laura, that's what I keep telling you, but, no, you only listen when Grady tells you. Must be those big brown eyes of his. They work on everybody; it's amazing."

"Okay you two, what have you got for me? I brought my handy dandy detective kit, decoder ring and all. I never leave home without the darn thing."

"Did you bring your magic iodine crystals too? If you've never seen this fingerprint process Laura, it's super to watch. Move closer so you have a front row seat to observe the magician at work. Give her the full show Grady, she got gypped this morning with the safety deposit key."

"Magic, indeed." Grady opened what looked like a fishing tackle box and removed several items. I immediately recognized the purple latex-free gloves. We used the same ones on the ambulance when treating patients. They provided protection for us from blood borne diseases or any fluids we might come in contact with. The straw-like thing I didn't recognize. Lastly, Grady removed a digital camera and a plastic ruler from the bottom of the box and stared at the package on Mike's desk.

"I love this part Laura. You paying attention?" Mike looked like a wide-eyed kid at Christmas, watching his Lionel trains chugging around the table-top tracks. The only thing missing was his engineer cap.

"Okay class, let me explain what I'm doing here." Grady crouched and then knelt on the floor in front of Mike's desk. "This thing that looks like a straw is called a 'pipette' and is filled with iodine crystals.

When I blow through it, the combination of heat and moisture in my breath will turn the crystals into a yellow cloud. When it makes contact with the box and tissue paper, it will become reddish in color, just like iodine."

Grady blew through the pipette, a few inches from both the box and the tissue-wrapped beret, and it was exactly as he had described. That stuff is sure to ruin the beret, I thought. Well, I'll have it properly cleaned before we return it to Gwen.

Now that the box and beret were covered with reddish dust, previously undetectable fingerprints became visible on the box. I watched, fascinated, as Grady set the ruler alongside each fingerprint to indicate size, and photographed them from a ninety degree angle.

"Grady, how does that work? And what kind of camera are you using?" I couldn't take my eyes away from the fingerprints the iodine crystals had revealed. It was magic.

"One question at a time," Grady admonished. "The iodine reacts with body oils, so it reveals any traces of human contact.

"As for the camera, only a photographer would be interested in that," he laughed, and continued to take photos. "It's a Nikon digital and it's a four point two mega pixel model. Now you're supposed to ask me why I'm taking pictures and what I'm going to do with them."

"Grady, why are you taking pictures and what are you going to do with them?"

"Thought you'd never ask Laura. I need a record of the fingerprints because the iodine fades after a short time." Oh, so I wouldn't have to have the beret cleaned after all. "I'll send them off to the State Police lab, along with the beret, the card and the box it came in. They'll be able to identify everyone who touched all of this. Naturally, I'll need your fingerprints and Mike's."

"I didn't touch anything Grady, only my esteemed partner did," Mike said.

"I wouldn't let him get away with that Laura. Anyway, I know both your prints and Mike's are on file with the State, so that leaves whoever delivered the package here as well as whoever delivered it to the school. Do you happen to know this Penelope person?"

"Yes, and she's been completely cooperative with information regarding Gwen, so, I'm sure she won't mind being fingerprinted."

"Great. Sure makes things easier when a witness wants to help. Wait, is that the same woman who was so gruff with us this morning? Aye. In that case, I'll put a priority on this and drive it to the lab. Hopefully, we'll have an answer soon on both the beret and the key. That reminds me, I want to get over to the bank branch as soon as the prints come back and find out what's in the safe deposit box. I'll give you two a call as soon as the print analysis comes back.

"So, you moved Gwen's studio here?" Grady asked, finally having noticed the paintings.

"These are all her pieces that were accepted into a show in New York. It's slated to open in the spring. This is what she was working on when she went missing Grady. Penelope gave us permission to take them, so we could analyze them.

"I'd like to show you what I think is a message directly from Gwen. Mom hasn't found it yet."

"You're still calling him 'Mom?' I love that... All right. Let me finish with the prints first, then I'll take a look at the paintings. I have a feeling I'm going to be here a while," Grady said.

The three of us gathered around Mike's desk while Grady rummaged in his supply box and pulled out a pair of tweezers. He carefully lifted the tissue away from the beret until it was completely exposed.

"Well, that's interesting, there's a pin on the hat. Bet I find a print or two on it."

"Grady, it's not a hat, it's a beret," I commented.

"Jeez Grady, how come you didn't know that, you being a real detective and all? Hey, what kind of pin is that?"

"Thank God you two have me here to help you!" I shook my head. "The pin is silver and it's a rose."

"You can tell it's silver just by looking at it?" Mike frowned and leaned in to take a closer look.

"At least I knew that. Mike, what is wrong with you?" Grady smiled and knelt on the floor, a fresh pipette in hand. He gently blew the crystals onto the beret. Since the color of the beret was a close match, the only evidence of the substance was on the pin. There was enough of a fingerprint on the silver rose for Grady to photograph.

He laid the ruler alongside the pin. It measured two inches in length.

"Interesting choice of pin design. I wonder what the relationship between 'E' and Gwen is...wait a minute, it's Eliott!" I almost knocked the beret off Mike's desk in my excitement.

"Who's Eliott?" Grady asked.

"You know Laura; I think you may have something there. Not that it matters, but, I don't think Arnold said anything about Eliott being married. This sure puts an interesting spin on things…"

"Hey, will one of you please tell me who the heck Eliott is? Arnold wasn't forthcoming and Reggie was vague."

"What exactly did you and Arnold talk about Grady?" I asked in surprise. "How come you don't know that Eliott is Arnold's partner, and… you do know the Feds are investigating him? I was following Arnold, and in the process I met Reggie Martin, or should I say Agent Reginald Martin."

"I don't get it, I spent two hours with the guy and all I've got to show for it is his address, phone number and a picture of Gwen. How did you two manage…wait a sec, you met Reggie? All right, before we go any further, both of you have to tell me everything you know. And I don't want to hear about client confidentiality either. This case just took a serious turn. Sit."

The three of us spent the next half an hour comparing notes, mostly Mike's and mine.

Grady was shocked at how much information we had gathered in the last twenty-four hours. Grady told us that Reggie had been in touch with him and had shared details of the case he'd been building against Arnold that we were not privy to. Mike and I were left to speculate beyond what had been discovered through Google. Grady did tell us Reggie thought he was close to arresting both Arnold and Eliott.

"Wow, I am impressed with what you've been able to put together. Okay, let me get going. I want to get on the road to the lab before the traffic gets bad."

"Hold it, you can't leave yet," I said.

"Why not?" Grady glanced at me over his shoulder. He was in the middle of putting all his things away and bagging the beret and the box it had come in.

"Laura, the guy has to go. He has to get the stuff…"

"Not until he looks at the message in the seascape I found, the one…"

"I stared at that sea thing before I ate and after I ate, and I didn't find any secret message," Mike said.

"I swear, sometimes you two act like an old married couple," Grady cuffed the top of Mike's head and sat on the floor between us to inspect the seascape. "What am I supposed to be looking at?"

"See Laura, I told you, there's nothing there."

"Here, use my magnifier and look at the life ring." I handed it to Grady, who lay on his stomach with his nose an inch from the canvas.

"If I get any more comfortable, I might just take a nap, except there's not much room for my feet. Sorry Laura, but I have to lean them against your desk, hope you don't mind."

"Grady, where do you think you are? This isn't your living room buddy."

"Mike, will you leave him alone so he can concentrate."

"There's nothing there, I'm telling you. Not even a boat," Mike said.

Grady held the glass over the life ring; stopped and sniffed the floor. He grimaced, glanced at Mike and looked back at the painting. "All right, who or what stinks like an old sock? It's not me, I took a shower this morning, and…jeez Mike, why do you order a perfectly good pizza and then mess it up with fish bait?" Grady rolled on his side and kicked the pizza box toward the door.

"All right already, if it will help your detective nose, I'll take it out of here. Can't a guy eat what he wants anymore?" Mike crawled over to the pizza and shoved it out the door. "You happy now?" He resumed his spot between me and Grady.

"Oh yeah, much better. Now can you open a window?" Grady laughed as he zeroed in on the life ring once again. "Huh? S.O.S. Wow, good catch Laura. Our missing lady must really be in trouble. Okay, now I'm off to the lab and I'll make this a top priority." Grady handed the magnifier back to me, stood up and gathered his things. "I'll call you guys later and let you know if anything comes of these prints. In the meantime, if you come across anything else; call me immediately on my cell if I don't answer at my desk. Understood?"

"Yes Sir Lieutenant, Sir." Mike stood at attention and gave Grady a snappy salute. "Will report any and all findings immediately, Sir. Hey Laura, that means you, too."

"Of course Grady, anything I find, I'll let you know right away."

Grady shook his head and laughed as he left our office. I could hear him laughing as he made his way down the hallway.

"Mike, I'm leaving for my walk, okay?"

"Kind of early, aren't you? It's only…wow, how did it get to be two o'clock already? Anyway, Annie hasn't called yet."

"I'm going to get an early start today and Annie can call me on my cell phone. I want to go over to Trout Brook and look around some more before it gets dark."

"Okay, go ahead and leave me all by myself. No problem, I'll be fine. Besides, I've got a bunch of art stuff to look at. Who knows, maybe I'll find something you missed. Could happen you know. Yeah, and then I can eat my lunch in peace without you bugging me."

"Have fun, the magnifying glass is on my desk, and if you need them, the Tums are in my bottom drawer. I'll check in with you after my walk, okay?"

"Sure kiddo, have a great walk. You too Kola." Mike grinned when I slid his pizza across the floor. "Come to Papa."

Chapter 7

All we had learned regarding Gwen and Arnold whirled through my mind with no resolution; only more questions. Kola and I walked in circles while waiting for Annie. I continued trying to process the information. If I connected the dots one way, Arnold was guilty; if another way, he was innocent. Great, it would definitely be a hung jury unless we found something conclusive. Think. Think. There has to be something I've overlooked...

"What? Hi Annie. Sorry, I'm a little bit preoccupied with this new case and...hey Casey." I bent down to pet him while Kola nosed Annie. Then the dogs greeted each other enthusiastically. Even though we walked every single day, they acted as if it had been days since they had seen each other.

Annie Tyler and I had grown up together. We looked so much alike, we were often taken for sisters. We'd gone to summer camp together when we were kids in Augustine Bay, and when it came time to go to college, we remained inseparable and both enrolled in schools in the Northeast. I'd gone for a career in Criminal Justice and she'd tackled Journalism. After Matt's passing, Annie became my lifeline.

"Day two of our missing person's hunt," Annie said, smiling as she watched the dogs touch noses.

"I'm not sure who's more excited about this, you or Mike? Okay, I'm excited, too," I grinned. "Our first major case! He says it could put us on the P. I. map, and it would do wonders for your journalism career. A woman has literally disappeared without a trace; at least none that we've found. Her husband is in all kinds of trouble, so it could be him. On the other hand, it could be his business partner, or..."

"Somebody else," Annie laughed while handing out treats to the pups.

"Well, yes, that too."

"You should be excited, it could be big for the two of you...that is, if you solve it."

"Minor details. I'd like to walk toward the log cabin, where Adelaide lives…"

"Who's Adelaide?"

"A very sweet woman Mike has known for quite a while. He and I were at her house this morning."

"Is she the one who lost her Archery pin?"

"Rock solid memory you've got Annie. Well, aside from the mystery of the missing pin, she wanted to show us different areas of the woods she insists are disturbed. She claims something sinister is happening here. She's lived here roughly fifty years and says nobody knows these woods better than she does."

"So, why do you want to go over there again if you were already there this morning?"

"Because, I had a funny feeling when we walked by the rocky area just before you get to her house. And Kola acted a little strange, too."

"Are you talking about the spot off to the right, where Casey always goes over to sniff?"

"That's the one. I know it's the long way around to the stream, but I really want to take another peek."

"Hear that Casey, we have to take the long way today! I don't know Casey, Aunt Laura's on a mission of some kind. Don't worry; you'll still get the swim I promised you on the way over here. Besides, there could be a juicy exclusive in it for us."

We headed off in the direction of Adelaide's house. Even though it was just as cold as it had been in the morning; the dogs would still want to swim.

As we approached the rock pile, I threw a stick for Casey, who happily ran off to retrieve it with Kola right behind him. The two of them played Tug O' War with the stick for a bit, until Casey had a change of mind and trotted straight over to the rocks. Well, if there's something there, Casey will find it.

Left with holding one end of the stick, Kola turned and observed Casey paw the fluffy snow. Casey bent his head down, sniffed and clamped his mouth down on something.

"Casey, did you find another piece of clothing?" Annie watched while Casey pulled at whatever it was with no success.

"We're going to be here a long time unless one of us goes over there and helps him. He's your dog Annie."

"So? You're the P.I. and an EMT. You're used to disgusting things, I only write about them. I refuse to look at dead anything. You get it out of his mouth."

"How do you know it's something disgusting? It's probably someone's shirt that's stuck under a rock. Honestly, I don't who's more stubborn, you or Casey!" Reluctantly, I made my way over the snow-covered rocks, curious about what it was Casey was tugging at. This was not an area Adelaide had been concerned with during our early morning jaunt -- In other words, nothing to worry about? -- but we had not gone back to check it out, as she'd promised Kola.

"Casey, what do you have there? Come on guy, let me help you." I knelt down next to Casey, who had a portion of dark, sweatshirt material in his mouth. "Here, I'll trade you a cookie for the shirt. How's that? That's a good boy. Thank you." I grabbed the shirt and tried to pull it away. While I pulled as hard as I could, I noticed something poking up from under the snow just a foot or so from where I was kneeling.

"What the heck..." I tumbled backward as the object released itself. "Ouch, that hurt."

"What is it?" Annie yelled. "Casey, come here, you too Kola... both of you."

"I don't...oh my God." I sat up and brushed my hands off. I reached inside my coat pocket, feeling for my cell phone. I couldn't help staring at the arm that had flopped out from beneath the body. Whose ever hand it was, it wore a navy fleece mitten that had bits of dried leaves stuck to it.

The object sticking up, from what was most likely his or her chest, had some kind of cord holding it together. I had made a mistake by handling the package Penelope sent over, and I wasn't about to make another one by touching anything here.

Phone in hand, I scooted myself backwards until I was several feet away.

"Laura, what is it? You look as if you've seen a ghost."

"You have no idea how right you are." I stood up and kept backing up. My heart raced as I touched the screen, hitting speed dial to reach Mike. "Good thing you didn't go over there Annie; Casey found a body! Now I know why Kola was sniffing around there too. My heart was still going a mile a minute as I considered the possibilities. Not wanting to disturb any evidence, I hadn't checked to see if the body was male or female. We were aware that Gwen was missing and Arnold had indicated he'd been unable to reach Eliott. Unless Eliott showed up, it was only a matter of time before Arnold would have to file a missing person's report on him as well. Could the body be one of them?

"Mike, thank God you answered the phone. Why? Well, you're not going to believe this, but Casey found a body. Where? Down the hill from Adelaide's house. No, the other direction. Remember the rocks where Kola was standing? Yes, where you said he was sniffing a raccoon's house? Well, right over there, under it, actually. Yes, Annie is here too…no, we didn't touch anything. Okay, that's not entirely true. Casey pulled at what we thought was a shirt, and yes, it was on someone. Why? Because Casey always does that and usually the clothes he finds aren't being worn by anyone. Yes, this is a first. And hopefully the last. Yes, I touched the shirt too, but I stopped as soon as I saw what we were dealing with. We'll be waiting right here. I promise. You'll call Grady? Good. I…uh-oh, guess who's at the top of the trail? Keep Adelaide away? Oh sure Mike, that should be easy. Right, I'll do my best. Okay, see you soon, bye."

"Annie, Mike said to wait here."

"That shouldn't be a problem. I'm too scared to move. Who's watching us from up there?" Annie pointed up the hill.

"It looks as if you're about to meet Adelaide. I've got strict instructions from Mike to keep her away," I said.

Adelaide stood at the end of the pathway to her house, with her cane dangling from her crossed arms. She wore the same fur-lined parka she'd had on earlier.

I waved to Adelaide, and then helped Annie with holding back Casey and Kola by looping one leash through their collars.

"I thought you allowed the dogs to run free Laura. Why are you putting them on a leash? And who is that with you? You're up to something and I demand to know what it is. You're in my backyard." Adelaide made her way down the trail at a much faster clip than she had that morning.

"Adelaide, stay where you are, we're headed in your direction anyway. And this is Annie. I told you about her this morning, remember?"

"Annie, let's walk as fast as we can, Mike was very clear about Adelaide not seeing the body. As a matter of fact, he doesn't want her knowing what's going on until absolutely necessary."

"Is that Annie? Laura, she looks just like you. And is that Casey?" Adelaide asked.

Annie and I hurried the dogs along, doing our level best to halt Adelaide before she made it to the bottom of the incline.

"I don't think I've ever seen anyone with a cane come that close to a run. Come on Casey, this is not the time to dawdle, Aunt Laura says we have to move. Casey, don't embarrass me, I know you can go faster than Adelaide," Annie said.

"I'm going to run ahead Annie, otherwise Mike will be very upset with me." I moved as fast as I could and held my coat close to my body to give Adelaide the impression I was now in a hurry due to the cold.

"Wait Adelaide, I'll be right there..." I shouted.

"You stay where you are Laura. You're trying to hide something from me."

"Why would I do that?" I asked.

I don't know, but, just because I'm old, doesn't mean I can't smell a con. You've discovered something and I intend to find out what it is. Are you going to wrestle with an old lady? If you are, keep in mind I have my cane and as you know, it makes a great weapon. I've got one of those colored belt things for cane whacking."

Adelaide brandished her cane at me while I blocked her from advancing down the trail. We shadowed each other side to side for several seconds.

"Great mime show. You two been practicing long? Come up with some other moves and you could take it on the road." Mike approached Adelaide from behind. "Don't hit me Adelaide. Remember how much you like me? What the heck is going on here? Oh, I see, it's not mime. You two have challenged each other to a duel! How are you Annie? Oh yeah Casey, my man. Ah jeez Kola. Help Laura, I'm being licked to death." Casey lay on Mike's chest as he fell backwards and didn't seem to have any intention of letting him up. Being part Shepherd and part Husky, similar to Kola, only black and tan to Kola's white, he was a huge boy at ninety pounds and could hold even Mike down for the count.

"They probably smell the anchovies. When you get out from under, will you please talk to Adelaide?" I asked.

"Casey, let the poor guy up, he's got work to do and so does Aunt

Laura…I mean…hi, you must be Adelaide. It's wonderful to meet you, I'm Annie Tyler," Annie bravely offered her hand to shake hands with Adelaide.

Mike managed to push Casey from his chest, brushed himself off, stood and gently placed both hands on Adelaide's shoulders. "You're going to catch a chill if you stay out here much longer. It'll be dark soon…Annie, would you mind walking Adelaide up to the house?

"What do you say Adelaide? You two have now been properly introduced, so it's not like you're bringing a stranger into your house. Matter of fact, I'd love some coffee. Would you mind putting on a pot for all of us?"

"Mr. O'Malley, you don't fool me. I know as sure as I'm standing here, you're trying to get rid of me," Adelaide turned to face Mike and, with her jaw firmly set, glared up at him.

"Now, why would I do that? All right, Laura did find something, but I can't tell you what it is. That being said, there's a whole bunch of people on their way over here, so I do need you to go inside. Only for your safety. Okay?"

"Not until you tell me what is going on. These are my woods; you can't tell me to leave." Adelaide jammed her cane down on Mike's foot. Mike yelped with pain even though he wore heavy hiking boots.

"Now, do I have your attention? How about you Laura? Annie?" Adelaide asked.

Annie and I backed up as she turned to face us. Mike limped up behind Adelaide, wrapped his arms around her and lifted her off the ground, "Laura, grab the cane before she uses it again. Adelaide, you're going to hurt your hip if you don't quit squirming. I'm not putting you down until you're in front of the nice, warm fire Annie's going to start for you. Got it? And I'm sure she'll be happy to help you make coffee or tea or whatever."

"If you don't put me down this instant, the first thing I'm going to do once you do let me go, is call the police. Then, you'll be sorry!"

"Remember I said a bunch of people were coming over here?"

"Yes."

"When they get here, you'll have a whole fleet of detectives and cops to choose from, but be sure to complain to the real big guy. He's the detective in charge.

"Annie, did you happen to walk over to…you know?" Mike asked between breaths. He was huffing and puffing as he carried Adelaide unceremoniously up the hill and carefully deposited her at the top of the path.

"No way Mike. I didn't move one inch off the trail. Stuff like that gives me nightmares. Adelaide, I'll be happy to start a fire for you." Annie ran ahead of Mike, towing the two dogs on the leash. She reached the top of the hill and turned toward Adelaide's house, just as lights bounced up and down on the trunks of the two giant oaks standing guard at the trailhead.

"Laura, you stay here, they're going to want to talk to you. And make sure you point out exactly where you approached. Please tell me you left the same way. Otherwise, they're going to wonder if you learned anything at that Ivy League school of yours. Not to mention, they'll bug me about not teaching you right."

"Don't worry Mike; the guys will be proud of you!"

"Atta girl! You're awful quiet Adelaide," Mike said.

"I'm plotting my revenge."

"Uh-oh, good things the cops are here to protect me from you."

"Alright, I'll go inside and have some tea. It might help me relax. Besides, that Annie person might burn my house down while trying to make a fire." On that note, Adelaide turned and went up her walkway.

I leaned against a tree and drew in a deep breath. While kicking at the snow underfoot, I wondered if it was Gwen that Casey had found. My nervousness grew as darkness descended over the woods and more lights converged in Adelaide's driveway. Please God, don't let it be Gwen. Oh, that sounds awful, I'm sorry, I don't want it to be anybody. I feel terrible for whoever it is, I'm so confused, I don't know how I'm supposed to feel...

"Laura, it's me Grady, are you all right?"

"Hi Grady, I didn't hear you," I pretended to rub my eyes from fatigue. I didn't want him to see my tears.

"Hey, it's okay," Grady held me in a bear hug. "Crying is perfectly natural. I'd be worried if you weren't upset. Finding someone who's been murdered is real tough, especially when you think you could have done something to prevent it...which you couldn't. You do realize that, don't you?"

"Isn't that my job? I feel as if I've just blown our first major case."

"Hey Laura, hold on, we don't even know who it is." He let go of me and stepped back as his team of detectives approached and flashlight beams shone in all directions.

"Hi Grady. Sorry, took a while to get Adelaide settled. I've got Laura's friend Annie babysitting, and she swore she wouldn't let Adelaide or the dogs get away. See you've got your boys here and they look ready to go." Mike zipped his coat and pulled his leather gloves on.

"Yup, we're all set. Laura, would you please take the flashlight and shine it where you found the body?" Grady handed me his flashlight. I cast the light down the trail until I spotted a newly fallen log. I moved the beam to the left and over the rocks. The lack of moonlight added to the surreal atmosphere. The light of the beam created an unnatural shadow over the object sticking up from the deceased's chest.

"Right there, that's it."

"Okay. And you walked in at the log?"

"Yes."

"And you followed the exact same path on your way out?"

"Absolutely."

"Okay Laura, you did all the right things. Stay right here.

"Tim. Get over here with your camera and photograph the soles of Laura's boots. Then we can rule her prints out right away. Tom, you and Jeff tape off the area around the body all the way out to the trail and up over the rocks. Sam, call Fire, we need the ladder truck with a couple of halogens to light this place up.

"Okay," We listened as Grady made a mental checklist. "I've got my insect collection kit and I can hear the crime van generator from here. Pete's bringing down our halogens, I've got my witness. Looks like we've got an official investigation underway. Excellent. We are truly like a well-oiled machine. Have to love that about my crew."

"Can't argue with that buddy. You got the best of the best." Mike affirmed. He and I backed up while the yellow tape was rolled out, wrapped around a tree and rolled out to the next tree, designating the periphery of the crime scene.

Chapter 8

I brushed the snow from a rock and sat down. Tim handed me a yellow plastic ruler. I rested one ankle on my opposite knee. He knelt down two feet away from me and waited patiently while I aligned the ruler with the sole of my boot.

"Is this the right way?" I asked holding the ruler between my left thumb and forefinger.

"Yup, that's perfect…okay, hold still and smile. Wow, nice clean soles. Done with that one. Now, do the exact same thing with your other foot."

"Are you going to photograph the scene, too?"

"Oh yeah, and it's bound to take some time. We take photos before we touch or move anything, and every step of the way while we collect and process evidence. We have to cover every single detail perfectly, so when we catch the guy who did this, the prosecutor can nail his butt to the wall. My worst nightmare would come true if I was in too much of a hurry and skipped photo-ing something major. Can you imagine?"

"I can't. Is there anything I can help with?" I asked.

"Sorry, no civilians allowed in a crime scene. You can watch from behind the tape. Mike'll explain what we're doing."

I stood up and walked toward Mike.

"Hey, I need my ruler," Tim smiled.

"Sorry Tim."

"Trying to grab a souvenir?" Mike quipped.

"Not funny. I can't help but think it may be Gwen over there," I said.

"If it is, nothing we could have done differently to help her. On the other hand, we don't know how long whoever it is has been here. So, we wait while Grady does his fly thing."

"Huh?"

"Yeah, it's pretty gross. He's looking for blow fly eggs or larvae."

"Mike, it's too cold for flies."

"Not during the day. Night, yeah. Long as the temperature's around forty-five degrees, those things will be cruising around for dead anything. When they find something or someone, they lay eggs. Then we check with the weather experts to get the exact ambient temp changes hour by hour over the last few days. That will give us an idea how long the body's been here."

"I thought they figured out time of death by the temperature of the body and lividity?"

"Who dity?"

"The blood pooling Mike. I can't believe you don't know that."

"Course I did, just checking to see if you did." Mike grinned and rubbed his gloved hands together.

"Uh-huh." I pulled my hat down to my eyes.

"It's going to be lots colder before Grady's done, about six hours from now."

"That long?"

"Yup. Takes a long time to check the area. Don't forget, the snow might be covering a clue that could lead us to the killer. They have to go over this entire area in a grid pattern, like a giant checkerboard." Mike waved his hand from the log where I'd entered all the way up to the trail head.

I followed the sweep of his hand, and understood why we would be there so many hours. I re-scanned the taped off section, noting the rocky outcroppings, which would take a good deal of time and effort to search. Grady's detectives would have to crawl over the rocks, poking though crevices, looking for anything out of place.

"Laura, I thought you said you didn't touch the body, just the shirt?" Grady called out his question, so we could hear him. He was crouched near the body, while we remained behind the yellow tape, several yards away.

"I didn't Grady, I…"

"Marshall, don't pick on my partner."

"Jeez O'Malley, I'm not, but, somebody moved her arm. Who?"

"Her?" I glanced at Mike.

"Yeah, 'her.' Back to, who moved her arm? And I don't know who she is yet."

"Casey grabbed the sweatshirt. He likes to pick up clothes he's found and carry them around. That's how we discovered the body. I tried to help him pull the shirt away, until I realized it was on someone. Then, I called Mom right away.

"Sorry if I didn't mention earlier that the arm had been moved."

"It's okay Laura, long as I know the exact sequence…hold it, who's Casey? And why did you let him near the body? You said you were the only one who entered the scene." Grady stood up, hands on hips.

"Casey's a dog," Mike yelled.

"You two stay right where you are. I'm coming over there and this time, I want the entire story; start to finish. And don't leave out a thing, got it!"

Yes Grady," Mike and I replied loudly, in unison.

Mike quipped, "You going to make us stay after school too? I told you Laura was walking the dogs with Annie when I called you, Marsh. Didn't you notice the paw prints leading up to the body?"

"Yes, but, I thought they belonged to…Tim, hold off snapping shots of those other prints, I've just been informed whose they are.

"O'Malley, one of these days…"

Grady made his way over to us, taking care to follow his own prints out. The path he used had already been well searched by several of his detectives. So far, not a speck of evidence had been uncovered.

Grady was a few paces downhill from Mike and I when the ladder truck from Soundview Fire Department arrived. The three of us watched while they parked on a diagonal in Adelaide's driveway. The chucks were put in place behind each wheel before the ladder was extended and turned in our direction. The ladder noise drowned out the hooted conversation two barn owls had been having for the last five minutes.

The halogen lights, which had been attached to the top of the ladder, were switched on. Fire's lights, coupled with the halogen lights Grady's men had set up on the ground, created the illusion of mid-day lighting. I pushed back my coat sleeve; my watch read seven-thirty in the evening.

Grady pulled a notebook and pen from the back pocket of his Levi's and jotted down all that had occurred from the moment Annie and I had arrived at the crime scene.

"Marsh, I told you everything. Why are you riding Laura like this?"

"Listen O'Malley, if you're so adverse to police procedure now that you're a P.I., then leave. Laura's my only witness."

"Can't wait to see you interrogate Casey."

"I'll be sure to have a pocketful of biscuits. Believe it or not, Tim now has to photograph each of the dog's paws to determine if any coyotes have been around. It's all part of the timeline."

"Relax Marsh, will you?" Mike held his hands up.

"I can't, the Chief wants this solved, yesterday. This is the biggest thing to hit Sound- view in decades. And once the media gets hold of this…well, they're going to make my life miserable until we catch whoever killed this woman." Grady hit his forehead with his hand. "I forgot, Annie's here. Hope she hasn't called her station, at least not until I've talked with her."

"Yeah, your handsome mug will be all over the place Marshall. Better brush up on your public speaking while you've still got a few minutes."

"Uh-huh. All right, I'm going back to the body and see how the guys are progressing. I'm surprised the Chief hasn't called me yet."

I watched Grady walk back down the slope. A breeze flitted across the back of my shoulders, shooting tingles down my spine. I spun around, and caught a glimpse of something moving. I stared, astonished; it was a woman, gliding through the trees beyond the halogen light field. Was I seeing things?

"Mike…um…I'm going to see how Annie's doing with Adelaide, and see if she's released any news yet to the public at large."

"You're not going to keep me…Laura, you okay? You're white as a sheet, something scare you?" Mike chuckled.

"I'm fine. I'm tired and worried that it may be Gwen over there, that's all."

"I don't buy it Laura, you don't look right. What's going on? Did you see something that you don't want to tell me about?"

"What makes you think I saw something Mike? There's no one out here, besides us and the detectives and officers."

"Listen to me Laura, if I tell you something, will you be honest with me?" Mike put his hands on my shoulders, and continued. "Before I tell you, you have to promise me you won't say a word to anyone. I mean it, not one word. Except for Annie, since I know you're going to tell her anyway, no matter what I say."

"Okay Mike, you've got my word. No one except Annie."

Mike shuffled his feet, then, guided me by the arm behind a tree, a few feet away from where we'd been standing. He peeked out, his face reddening, toward Grady's position and dropped his voice, "You're going to think I'm nuts when I tell you this, but have you ever heard of the White Lady, or as she's sometimes referred to The Lady in White?"

"Um…no, but you're embarrassed. Why?"

"You saw her, didn't you? I can tell by the look on your face. God Laura, you can't tell the guys about this…quit looking at me like I'm off my rocker. This isn't easy to talk about with anyone."

"I don't know what I saw…it was…a…I felt something brush across my neck and shoulders first. It was kind of like a soft wind that made me feel tingly. Then, I had an urgency -- that's the only way I can describe it -- to turn around…"

"Mike, Laura, where are you two?" Grady said impatiently, "Come on, I need to speak with you. Now!"

"Laura, remember what I said," Mike held a finger up to his lips, and added, "don't breathe a word of this to the guys. We'll talk about it later."

"An identity?" I inhaled, "Gwen?"

"No, "Grady replied.

I exhaled.

"It's odd, though, she fits Gwen's description rather neatly. If it hadn't been for her driver's license poking conspicuously out of her shirt pocket, I would have thought it was Gwen. Name's Toska Non Wrappe. Almost like the opera, but with a 'k', instead of a 'c.' Also, we found a wadded up note in her mouth. It could have been her last words. It reads, "I'm just a hippie."

Based on other things we found, it's a possibility we might have a serial killer on our hands."

"Calling card with the body?" Mike asked.

"Yes, several," Grady responded. "We found an upside down, furled U.S. flag, measures four inches by six inches. The killer has her clutching it in her hands, and it's tied around both hands with some kind of cord. I'd like you to take a look at the cordage. It's not your typical material. At least it's not like anything I've ever seen. I feel like this guy is playing with us. Throwing a look alike at us. Makes me wonder if Gwen isn't around here somewhere. But, why?" Grady rubbed his forehead and looked off in the distance.

"There's this, too. The guy left a note with two lousy words on it, 'Never Forget.' Forget what? It was stuck in the ground, at her left shoulder, with a KA-BAR knife. We dusted it for prints. Nothing. He also left a Beanie Bear in the crook of her right elbow. It's yellow with a red, white and blue ribbon on his neck with the United States Marine Corps insignia on his chest. USMC is stitched in red lettering on its right arm. The cute little guy stands eight and a half inches tall. Sorry, no weight on him as of yet. Poor fella's in a cellophane bag, to protect him from the elements, I'm guessing. I can only show you the note. The bear and the knife are going straight to evidence."

Grady handed the evidence bag to Mike. It contained a note that was written on a white, three by five index card. It was crumpled at the edges where the knife had sliced through between the words, Never and Forget. Mike flipped the bag over to show the back of the card. It was blank.

The three of us looked at each other.

"Obviously, he's not a writer," I concluded.

"Definitely not a man of many words," Mike agreed.

"Just because he's got a knife doesn't make him a woodsman. KA-BAR's can be purchased anywhere these days; Army Navy stores, or online. There's one in town we could check to see if they've had any recent sales. The purchase of the Beanie Bear can't be tracked, since those can be bought online."

"Index cards can be picked up anywhere, the local drugstores have them," I added. "That will be impossible to track down. Everyone has those in their desks.

"I cannot for the life of me figure out why he chose the words he did. What does he not want to forget so badly that he's willing to kill for it?"

"Wait a second Laura, it says, "Never Forget," on the 9/11 decals that a lot of EMS and Fire Trucks display with the Towers in the background," Grady said. "You could be onto something. What if our guy lost a family member or dear friend that day and is holding someone responsible. Soundview is a small town, so it shouldn't take too long to search out victims of that day, and in turn, extend that list to family and friends. If nothing else, it's a starting point."

"Grady," Mike interjected, "there is another thing we forgot to tell you that may or may not have anything to do with this. I completely forgot about it, until just now...we, actually, it was Adelaide, who's another client of ours...Marshall, you can blame me for this one..."

"The two of you forget to tell me anything else, I swear, I'll have you up on charges of obstruction of justice! Now what?"

"Follow along buddy, it's right over here," Mike pointed to the area that Adelaide had shown us earlier. Mike pulled his flashlight out of his jacket pocket as we approached the clearing, and shone the beam where he had swept it with the broom.

Grady knelt down and ran his palm over the heel imprints. "Window of opportunity for solving this murder – because that's what it certainly looks like -- is forty-eight hours. After that, the tracks go cold, literally.

"Laura, O'Malley, we've got ourselves a real hot one."

Chapter 9

The three of us headed back to the area Adelaide had previously shown us. Now, it seemed as if that were days ago. Mike was in the lead, with Grady treading closely on his heels, while I lagged at a safe distance. It seemed a good time for those two to chat and clear the air between them, while I gave the case some thought from my own quiet perspective. No matter how hard I concentrated, I could not shake the feeling that we were being watched by several pairs of eyes. No sooner did that thought cross my consciousness than that now familiar chill send shivers up and down my spine. I quickened my pace and stepped on the top of Grady's boot, causing his heel to pop out.

"Hey Laura, what's with giving me a flat tire…Wow, look at that. So much for a full moon, that's the darkest cloud I've ever seen." He pointed upwards as a long, thin bolt of lightning flashed across the eastern sky.

"Sorry about the flat Grady. I was busy thinking." The lightning gave me shivers, just like the ghost had a few moments ago. Did that ghost have the power to shoot a lightning bolt? Several moments passed, without the thunder that usually follows lightning, convincing me it was not ordinary lightning, and my shivery feeling wasn't just a coincidence.

"Well, here we are," Mike announced. "The heel prints and hoofprints are just like we told you, Marsh, and they appear to be untouched too. I guess the freeze and thaw we've been having, all that weird back and forth weather, hasn't damaged anything. So, you'll be able to take all the mold prints your little heart desires."

"Mike, these silver things, whatever they are, weren't here when Adelaide brought us here. And, neither was my red hair tie. How in the world did they get here? I swear Grady, I have not been near this area since I was here with Mike and Adelaide, so please stop looking at me that way."

"Just when you think you've seen it all. What are eye cleats doing in the middle of the woods?" Grady quizzed no one in particular. He dug into his back pocket for a pair of latex gloves and an evidence bag for the cleats and the hair tie, as well as a Sharpie to mark the bag with the date and the proper numeric.

"What cleats?" I said.

"I was going to say, who cleats? Or, shoe cleats. You know, like for baseball," Mike quipped.

"I'd expect that from you Mike. You've got baseball on the brain year round. These cleats are from a boat. You attach a line to them, say if you need to tie up or to tow something, like a dinghy. Or, if you have to hook up at a dock, or to trailer a boat. It makes no sense that they'd be here. Also, why would Laura's hair tie be here, unless you dropped it when you were here before, Laura. I'm not accusing you of anything, it could have fallen out of your pocket. You do keep them in your jacket and your jeans' pockets?"

"Back to the cleats for a second Grady. What's a dingo? I thought that was an Australian dog. So, why would you tow it behind a boat? Man, you're going to have the ASPCA on your tail...get it, for animal cruelty." Mike chuckled.

"Mike, you had any sleep, lately? Because you're starting to worry me. I realize we're in the middle of the woods and it's a bit bizarre to be talking about boats, however, a dinghy's a boat, not a dog. Get your ears on and listen, okay. A dingo's a dog; separate issue." Grady patted him on the back. "Maybe, we need to rethink this and take a different tack..."

"Ha! I know what that means," Mike interrupted. "You think you can toss these fancy nautical terms out and I won't get them, right? Well, wrong my old friend Loo. I happen to be reading this book and they're talking about tacking..."

"Catching up on Archie Comics? You are half asleep, you just called me 'Loo.'"

"Will you two stop it and stick to what we're doing. Please," I interjected. "Besides, last time I read Archie, they never had anything in there about sailing. I know tacking's for horses But I've no idea what Loo means, well besides a bathroom in England. I've heard you guys use it before, I think..."

Mike and Grady both laughed. Grady spoke up and said, "We're not laughing at your expense Laura. 'Loo' is a cop term for Lieutenant.

Sometimes we'll use an abbreviated term, LT.

I've no idea why Mike came up with it now. I'm not his Lieutenant anymore."

"Okay, okay, back to whatever it is we're talking about, sailing, boating, horses…wait a minute…" Mike spun on his heel as the wind picked up and another bolt of lightning flashed in the sky, but this time it was in the western sky. "That's a bit weird, isn't the reservoir up there, where the lightning is?"

"Yeah. Right underneath, or approximately," I said. "What are you getting at?"

"It's a short ride. The trails are well marked. Granted, the last bit is off limits, but still, it wouldn't be a big deal to get a body across the reservoir in a small boat to the spot where we discovered Ms. Non Wrappe. Of course, it doesn't really explain why the cleats are here, unless someone put them here for us to find. They must have been used to transport the body, by horse, directly from the boat. If memory serves, there's a boat ramp on the other side which would make it very simple for our killer to launch a small boat. All he'd have to do, is back up and in the water you go."

I said, "In theory, a good part of that works, but where are they leaving the horse in the meantime, as in, who's holding it? You can't simply leave it tied to a tree for, say half an hour or more, while you motor or row across the reservoir, in the dark."

One massive bolt of lightning flashed from the west at the exact moment another blazed from the eastern sky. They smashed into each other causing a ripple effect of multiple bolts with a colossal explosive ball on the left. It looked as if they had buckled into enormous, stacked rollercoaster highways above our heads that continued to flash for what felt like forever, when in reality, it was only seconds.

The three of us turned and stared at each other, speechless, backed up a few steps and gaped at the blackened, smoky sky. What was this phenomenon? We remained frozen in our tracks for several moments and then without a word to one another, we headed in unison to the reservoir like moths to a flame. Grady led the way as if it was the natural order of things. Mike followed and I took up the rear.

We paused for a moment so that Grady could call in to his crew. He told Sergeant Thomas that we were working on a hunch, and that we'd be back within the hour. The sergeant agreed to take over until Grady returned. Then we hiked quietly to the reservoir, sticking to the marked trails until they ended, and then used the deer trails up to the dam.

"That was definitely not the norm." Grady was the first to utter a word.

"Wow, that's heavy and profound. I might even write it down for posterity," Mike said.

"Here's a pen and paper." I handed Mike a pen and notepad.

"You've nothing to say Miss I-Never-Miss-A-Comeback? Seriously? After what we just witnessed. Say something! Anything. But, don't just hand me a pen!"

"You said not to," I whispered.

"Not to what?" Grady demanded.

"Nothing Grady. You're going to think I'm nuts if I tell you, so I'm not going to and that's the end of it." Mike was deadly serious.

"If it's about the ghost stories and all, Mike, believe me, I've heard them. We…I mean the guys… don't talk about them too much. Especially, after dark and now being in the woods, because it's scary as hell," Grady said in a low tone. "After what we just saw in the sky, I'm never talking about those stories out loud again. I've never in my entire life seen anything like that. And now, I'm trying to figure out what the hell we're doing here. It wasn't my idea to come here. It's like I was drawn here. This is beyond creepy. I'd much rather be at home with my wife and kids eating dinner, or watching some scary movie rather than being in one. Do you have any idea how far away we are from my guys? Okay, yeah, they could get here by… I don't know, boat, I suppose.

I was gazing at the ground as I listened to Grady, and something caught my eye. "Um, guys, here's another one of my hair ties. I was up here with Adelaide yesterday, and before you say it Grady, I don't carry that many hair ties in my pockets. It doesn't make sense." I bent down to retrieve the red tie and spotted a cleat underneath some brush.

"Grady, there's another cleat over here."

"This keeps up, I'm going to run out of gloves and evidence bags in short order and then we'll have a great reason to leave. I'd love to know who's putting these out for us to find. It's like Hansel and Gretel dropping breadcrumbs. I guess the next question is, will we find any viable prints on them?"

"You mean, does Casper leave prints behind?"

"Not funny O'Malley. I can see me trying to explain this to the

Mayor. Yeah, we've got a friendly ghost helping us out. I'll be tossed out on my ear, looking for another job, or better yet, they'll lock me up in the psych ward and throw away the key. Shut up, you two!

"By the way, let's not mention the lightning show to the guys, unless of course they happen to bring it up. I have this odd feeling we're the only ones who saw it. If we tell them, some of them might want to leave the investigation, and I need all the guys I can get on this -- especially until we've located Gwen."

"Mum's the word," Mike said.

"Without creeping you out any more than you already are, I don't think we're the only ones here, Grady. When we were down below, by the horse hoofprints, I kept getting shivers up and down my spine and feeling like we were being watched."

"Thanks a lot Laura. I've got that warm, fuzzy thing going on right about now. You know, the kind I've got when I'm nice and safe at home, not in the middle of nowhere with unexplained lightning storms that aren't and boat cleats showing up that shouldn't be." Grady locked his hands together behind his head, looked up at the sky and closed his eyes. "Aside from all the hocus pocus, I hate to say it folks, but I have a strong suspicion we may have more than one body out here and we simply haven't found the other one or other ones as of yet. And, furthermore, what if we're looking at several different ways of getting them here?"

"Are you implying we're in a killer's dumping ground, first off? And if so, the horse is his ground transportation when it's convenient or easier, or whatever for him...and when the situation or need arises, he uses a boat?" I asked with some hesitation.

"On the money Laura," Grady answered.

Mike rubbed his chin, "You're saying that we've got an above average freaky guy on our hands. Most killers stick with what they know and that's their game; they don't deviate from it. But this guy may be more flexible, and more devious."

Mike continued. "So, now we have to broaden our search area to look for more bodies. Guess that means we have to check for Gwen, since it's likely she's around here...here being a huge area. We'll have to look for boat owners in the vicinity. A good deal of the small boats around here are unregistered, so that means we're going to have to drive up and down streets looking in people's driveways. We also have to hunt around for horse people, and there are a lot of them in this part of town."

"Don't forget to check and see if anyone in the area's harboring any unaccounted for ghosts," I quipped.

"Ha, ha," Grady almost smiled. "Let's not jump to conclusions about Gwen, at least not yet. Maybe, she's with a friend. Laura, you were going back to the art school to interview some of Gwen's friends weren't you, or is that my over active imagination from these woods?"

"I had been thinking about it. I only had the opportunity to talk to the director, Penelope, when I was there the first time. I wanted to talk to Gwen's fellow students, but they were in class. Arnold mentioned that she had a specific group that she spent a lot of time with."

"Yeah, that was right before he jumped up and said he had a dinner date and had to go to the cleaners to pick up his sports jacket. One eccentric guy, I'm telling you, but he did say Gwen hung out with the same group of women from the school and that they were real close. He said they went places together, met in coffee shops and talked about their painting projects and stuff like that. He sounded rather jealous of them when Mike and I were interviewing him, real angry at their closeness, like he wanted that with her. Now he regrets it, almost like he knows she's dead. But, what makes him think that, when there aren't any signs. There's absolutely no trace of her anywhere. Okay, there's the one thing in her painting, but it's not likely Arnold knew about that.

"You guys remember what I'm talking about, right, the S.O.S. that she painted in tiny letters on that life thingie, right? That was definitely weird. That painting was so dark and stormy, kind of like tonight. Speaking of which, can we get out of here, because I'm getting spooked, again?" I hugged myself in an unsuccessful effort to stop shivering.

As we started walking, Grady shadow-boxed around Mike and then fired off a light right hook mid-chest, his way of changing the mood. Mike clutched his chest and feigned a serious injury as he landed with a thud in a soft bed of pine needles. Grady bent forward with his hand outstretched, grabbed Mike's hand, and helped him to his feet. The buddy back slapping ensued with the usual grins and laughs while we made our way down the trail. We had a long hike ahead of us in the pitch dark and after what we'd experienced; it was good to have a few laughs to break the eeriness.

Grady took up the lead, flicked on his flashlight. Mike followed and I took up the rear. One of these days, I would have to speak up regarding being the caboose.

100

The trail going down from the reservoir was slippery, so I instinctively grabbed a tree to keep my feet steady. I peeked over my shoulder back toward the reservoir that was now partially lit by the moonlight and there she was, a woman with long dark hair wearing a full length white nightgown. I couldn't swear to it, but she appeared to be barefoot and seemed to be hovering several inches above the dam wall that we'd been standing underneath just moments ago. She was smiling and I could have sworn she waved at me. A gentle breeze picked up, rustling through the trees. By all rights, I should have been frightened out of my skull, but then came that familiar tingle up and down my spine. She was Casper! Well, now I'd have to change it to Casperina.

I tapped Mike on the shoulder and turned back, but Casperina was gone. "Never mind. Thought I saw something."

"That's not funny. Great breeze, though. Hurry up, will you."

I thought about the legend of the White Lady while we hiked along, and wondered if that's who we'd encountered. Could it be that she had been causing all these strange happenings? I'd heard stories of her, years ago, so I wasn't too surprised when Mike had briefly brought it up. As the legend goes, back in the early 1800's, a young woman was run over by a horse-drawn carriage while waiting for her boyfriend outside what is now a cemetery. No one is one hundred percent sure if this is true, due to lack of record keeping, but it's generally agreed that this is her spirit, and it's a friendly one. She's been spotted by the cemetery and alongside the Merritt Parkway. It's documented that people have called 9-1-1, stating that a dark haired woman dressed in a white, flowing gown is all alone on the roadside and needs help. The dispatchers have grown accustomed to those calls, and most likely get a good laugh out of them.

We intersected with the main trail and Grady's flashlight began to flicker. He smacked it a few times and it came back on. We picked up our pace and moved as fast as we could. At least we were on a flat trail. However, there were numerous exposed tree roots that could literally trip us up, so we desperately needed our one and only flashlight. For future night hikes, I would most definitely put one in my pocket. Of course, this type of excursion had not been planned, and they never are.

"What's that smell?" I asked.

"Smells like something is burning, kind of like BBQ," Mike replied.

"How can you possibly be thinking about food at a time like this?" I asked.

"Let me think Laura, it's been hours since I've eaten a thing and ribs were the first thing that came to mind. That's how. Maybe, it's venison?"

"Will you two quit it? You're starting to sound like a married couple arguing over what to have for dinner. I don't think what we're smelling is food, per se. If I were a betting man, I'd put money down on the possibility that the lightening hit a person," Grady said.

I responded, "Grady, your men are back at the crime scene. Who could possibly have been hit by lightning?"

"What are we looking for Laura? I mean, really looking for. While considering that, let's head off in the direction of the scent."

"I get the feeling we're not going to find BBQ, venison or even smoked salmon." Mike shook his head.

"I think I've got the answer Grady. It goes back to the potential of our being in the killer's dumping grounds. You not only believe the lightning show hit a person, but may have struck another body, right? That's pretty strange." I put my head in my hands, wondering if that was Gwen's fate.

"You win the roulette wheel bet Laura. Well, we'll find out in a minute if that's true…there, over there, see it? Smoke's making its way up on the other side of that stand of Mountain Laurel, near the rocks. What is it with this guy and rocks?" Grady asked.

"Maybe he worked in a quarry and got laid off. Or, maybe he carved headstones and got tired of it." Mike shrugged.

Grady turned and stared at his longtime friend Mike, shook his head, and continued walking towards the tiny wisp of smoke. I remained several yards away with Mike and waited for some sort of signal from Grady as to what was smoldering. Whatever it was, was leaving a charcoal aroma mixed with an almost perfume scent that I couldn't identify, hanging over us.

"Not like any BBQ I've ever been to. How about you Laura?"

"Me either. I've got a bad feeling about this. Somehow, I don't think this is some campers' leftover pig roast."

"Nope. I'm going to go with your bad feeling. Although, I have to say, a side of bacon sounds really great right about now.'

Mike called out, "So Grady, you going to leave us over here guessing what it is you found? Because, so far, it's between a bad feeling and a pig roast gone awry. We going to draw straws over which one's correct, or are you going to let us in on the truth? Me, I'm going with the bad feeling. No way anyone's leaving bacon in the woods."

"O'Malley, is it possible for you to think about anything else aside from food? Just once, that's all I ask. If it's not anchovy pizza, it's bacon with anything. You'd probably put bacon on your Cheerios."

"You've been peeking in my windows again, haven't you? I told you to stop it, the neighbors are going to start talking more than they already do."

"I don't mean to ruin your appetite, but it appears we've got a serial killer on our hands. Same set of calling cards, minus the wadded up note in her mouth. That must have been something specifically for Ms. Non Wrappe. She must have really pissed him off. Otherwise, with the exception of being hit by lightning, the signs are identical.

"We need a lot more guys, but even if my guys are finished with the first scene, they need a break. A page has to go out for every available guy we've got, uniforms included, before this thing explodes. I think it's time to call the State in too. We need the manpower. Meantime, I have to call the crew on the other scene. I can't believe this Mike...I'm sorry...Laura, it's not Gwen, according to her license," Grady said as he made his way back over to Mike and I. "I took the liberty of taking the ID out of her shirt pocket – it was right there, in the same place as Ms. Non Wrappe's ID."

"Before you go over there and take a look, there's something else I need to tell you straight away," Grady said, as he went down on one knee, "This victim also looks an awful lot like you Laura, as well as Gwen and that Non Wrappe girl. Pretty disturbing, actually how much she resembles you. Thought I'd give you a head's up that looking at her might be a bit like looking in the mirror.

"I'm going to text one of the guys with our location, so someone can come and stay with her until we can get everything photographed, logged in, and all that before moving her down to base camp."

I breathed a sigh of relief that it wasn't Gwen, even though we had another body to contend with. This was the second time I felt that Gwen had dodged a bullet. The more time that lapsed that she remained missing, the smaller was the chance that she was still alive. On the flip side, each time we found a body that wasn't hers, it afforded us more opportunities to locate her before the killer did.

"Gee Grady, thanks for letting me know. I think. Remind me to hang out in the woods with you more often. I can't remember the last time I've had this much fun," I commented.

"Hey, me either buddy. Don't suppose you want to go hunting come fall?" Mike chimed in.

"Did you fail your last psych exam with the department?" Grady shook his head and then went on, "Since no one's asked, the license says that this young lady's name is Wendy Appleton."

"She holding the yellow Marine teddy in her right arm?" I asked.

"Everything Laura. The same flag, and her hands are tied with that string stuff, too. Oh, and the note, too, 'Never Forget,' on the index card. The whole nine yards, it's all the same. I'm guessing the only difference, if our theory holds true, would be how he transported her. Did Wendy go by boat and Non Wrappe by horse? I did find some cleats next to her, which may or may not indicate her mode of arrival.

"So, you two going to take a peek, or should we wait for a team to arrive?"

I was about to make my way over to the recently deceased, when I heard the sound of heavy footfalls approaching from the direction of the reservoir. Aside from Casperina, we were the only three who had been up there.

Mike tossed a twig at Grady's foot. The twig hit my arm instead.

Grady nodded, pointed to his right, indicating he would circle in that direction, while Mike would go the other way. Grady motioned for me to stay put. I wasn't about to move. These woods were becoming rather crowded: ghosts, dead bodies and now who knew what was coming down the path. While I waited, thoughts about mortality tumbled around in my head. I was beginning to buy into the legend of the White Lady. Although I'd heard about it, I'd never given it much credence. If we made it back out of here alive, I would have to Google it. I had always been intrigued about what happened after you left this world. At this rate, it might be sooner rather than later.

"Put your hands up! Don't move, or..."A burly shape stepped out of the woods. "Grady, you're supposed to identify yourself as a Police Officer, first. It's me, Dave Bodach. Get a grip buddy. Having a tough night?" Dave laughed.

"You don't know the half of it. We've got two dead bodies, so far. I think we've got a serial killer on our hands...what the hell are you doing out here this time of night, anyway? Mike, Laura and I were just up at the reservoir and we didn't see you. And, why are you carrying a nine iron?"

"Wait a second, a serial killer? In these woods?" Dave asked. "How bizarre is that! And, you're already up to two bodies." He curbed his enthusiasm abruptly when he saw the looks on our faces. "Okay, okay, I was looking for good hunting spots before the season opens, and practicing my chip shots, killing two birds with one stone. It was still light when I started out."

Dave had been a Soundview paramedic for close to thirty years. Two of his greatest pleasures, outside of spending time with family, were hunting and golf. Apparently, he'd discovered a way to combine the two. He enjoyed the outdoors almost as much as I did, yet he didn't have a weathered look about him. He almost always wore a baseball cap, even now, regardless of the fact that the sun had gone down hours ago. He and Mike resembled each other in that they both had medium builds and were in good physical shape. Where Mike's hair was brown and on the shorter side, Dave's was graying and a bit longer.

Dave's knowledge in the medical field, or, "street medicine," as it was commonly referred to, was legendary and generously shared with any up and coming EMT who was interested in learning from a pro.

"Yeah, we found the second body because it had been hit by lightning. I kept smelling BBQ, but no such luck. Never know what you're going to find out here," Mike added.

"Being a medic, at least I can tell you where the entrance and exit wounds are," Dave offered. "Oh, and since you're going to ask, no I didn't see anyone else. You were going to ask, right?"

"I was getting to it," Grady said. "I suppose knowing the entrance and exit wounds would be of help, although knowing who the hell the killer is would be better."

"Sorry pal, wish I could help you there."

"Wait a minute Dave, maybe you can. Look, so far we think this guy moves around both by boat and horseback. We think he uses the reservoir to transport the bodies..."

"I'm hunting in his dumping grounds?"

"You could very well be hunting in both his dumping grounds as well as his hunting ground."

"You two might know each other. You may have hunted together," I said.

"That gives me the willies." Dave shook his head and followed Grady towards Wendy Appleton's body.

"Okay then, she's definitely dead, as in there's no pulse and she's rather crispy," Dave stated. "And, I'm going to guess it's been roughly two to three hours since she was killed.

But, the ME has to establish the time of death, not me. She still feels a tad warm to me and rigor hasn't set in just yet.

"It's going to be hard to find the entrance and exit wounds, though, since she's burned...I don't get it, I didn't see any lightning, and the ground surrounding her isn't even singed. Are you sure you guys saw a lightning storm?"

"We all saw the same thing Dave. It was the most extraordinary, uncanny thing I've ever witnessed in my life. Whatever word I come up with to try and describe it won't do it justice, but it was as real as all of us standing here, talking to each other," Grady said. "Well, with the exception of Appleton, there, who of course is dead. But it doesn't make sense. Nothing else around her has been burnt, and we're apparently the only ones who saw the crazy lightning.

"Great, just great," Grady fumed. "How the hell am I going to write this up in a report that the Chief will believe. Or, for that matter, how am I supposed to explain this to the woman's next of kin, 'A massive bolt of lightning shot out of the sky, after a serial killer took out your loved one and, possibly destroyed any evidence of finding the murderer.' Somehow, I don't see this testimony holding up in court either. If anyone has anything to add, please do."

I raised my hand. Grady, Mike and Dave looked at me and waited.

"Speak now or forever hold your peace Laura," Grady said.

"I suppose now's as good a time as any. I saw the White Lady when we were at the reservoir. Well, it was when we were leaving, but she's not doing this, well, not all of it. She smiled and waved when we were leaving; she didn't seem angry or evil and, I mean, I think she's the White Lady. Either that or she's Casper, which would have to be changed to Casperina, since she's a..."

"Laura," Grady interrupted, "you're rambling. I get that you're nervous; we all are. Okay, I'm scared and about to wet my pants...and if you ever repeat that, I'll flat out deny it."

"I think I did," Mike said.

"Sorry buddy. No one can blame you if you did. Seriously? You wimp." It was amazing that Grady's sense of humor was still intact after all that had happened tonight. Then he said, quite seriously, "Laura, it probably was the White Lady. These woods are her happy haunting grounds. That's a known fact. Well, one of them. She's got several..."

We were interrupted by a breeze that wafted around our heads, and as it did, all four of us heard, crystal clear, the name Chrisloki. We broke into a mad dash, flashlight or not. Grady maintained the lead with Mike and Dave in the middle and yes, I took up the rear. I tripped several times, once as we crossed a stream, the water soaking my feet. My shoes made gurgling and squishing noises with each step I took the remainder of the way, but I didn't care. All I wanted was to get as far away from these woods that I dearly loved as quickly as possible, go home, turn on every single light in my house and sleep with all of them on until the next morning. From now on, I would be a true believer in the light.

Just before we arrived back at the crime scene, we stopped to catch our collective breath, and to compose ourselves. After a moment, Grady said, "I heard a word. It just came out of the air; sounded like 'Chrisloki.' Did you hear that?"

"Yes, I heard it too. What could it mean?" I asked, perplexed.

"I have no idea," Mike said, 'but I kind of don't want to find out."

Chapter 10

Finally, you're back Loo!" Joanna Hitchens jumped up and down, grinned, clapped and ended with a curtsey. She was a ballroom dancer in her spare time, and I was surprised she didn't grab one of Grady's guys and tango through the crime scene. She was also one of the newest, brightest young female detectives to have been promoted through the ranks in some time. When she locked onto a piece of evidence that was a potential case breaker, she could break the dam with her enthusiasm. Though she stood just five foot, even, I wouldn't want to be any hardened criminal facing her in a darkened alley.

"We were somewhat detained in our search," Grady said.

"What a shame Loo. But I bet you'll be ecstatic with what I've discovered. Come closer and take a look at our victim's neck. I do believe I've found the cause of death. The exact cause, that is. See this puncture wound? Isn't it great?" Her entire face lit up, even her green eyes behind her Woody Allen style glasses. It was incongruous to listen to someone so 'put together' exclaiming about such a morbid discovery. Really, she was a bit of a fashion plate. Her blonde hair was neatly tied back. Everything about her was in place and color coordinated. Not expensively dressed, either. Joanna knew how and where to shop.

She deftly moved aside Ms. Non Wrappe's mousy brown hair, revealing a rather large puncture wound on the right side of her neck, right on top of the external jugular vein.

"That's a sizable wound," I commented.

"Same as the one I spotted on Crispy Appleton," Dave said.

"Wow, that's huge. That could be from one of those monster needles you guys have on the ambulance, right Dave?" Mike asked.

Dave nodded.

"If that's what it is, then what was in it?" Mike held up his hand. "Before you tell me, Grady, I already know what you're going to say: 'That's what the Medical Examiner's going to tell us.'"

Grady raised his eyes upward and exclaimed, "Thank you for permitting my buddy to not have forgotten everything he learned in all his years on the force."

"Grady, you're no fun," Dave grinned and added, "I know you're remediating Mike, but I've got to add my two cents. Please? I know I'm only a lowly medic, but I do have a theory, do you want to hear it?"

"Please!" Grady brushed his hair back.

"Okay," Dave began, "theory is your guy's using potassium chloride, which is pretty sick, because it's going to sting like a bitch for a good bit of time, especially with that size of a needle stick. Not only that, you're talking about at least ten minutes before his victims die, and he's watching this. That's one sick, crazy bastard. I know I called him sick more than once, and that I was joking around at first, but you guys need to get on this and catch this guy before the real hunting season opens up. It will kill the peace and quiet in the woods. Okay, that last part sounds kind of strange, huh?"

"The profiling you did was good," Grady mused. "It adds some more to who this guy is. "He's got access to medical items, or at the very least knows someone in the field who can supply him with what he requires. That's information we're going to need to track down, at some point, who his supplier is.

"In the meantime, I'm sure the area's been well scrutinized and no one's found a monster-sized needle?" Grady glanced around and not one of his men, or Joanna, raised their hands.

"Okay," I said, half to myself. "Then we've got a neat freak killer who cleans up after himself, to a point, but likes to leave freaky clues behind in odd places that don't really make a lot of sense...yet."

"Thank you Laura for sizing up our case in a nice little box, which reminds me. This is an aside, guys. While we were gone on our trek, did a storm pass through?" Grady directed his question to the group at large. "No clouds, nothing? Not even any lightning?" He continued. All he received for his trouble were raised eyebrows and a few head shakes, confirming that we four were the only spectators. "Okay, thank you, and carry on with thoroughly checking and flipping over every rock to be sure nothing's been overlooked. I appreciate everyone's hard work, and I know it's been a long, tough night, believe me. We're closing in on the end, so hang tight. I'll send out for fresh coffee and sandwiches." With that announcement, a loud cheer went up, a few rubbed their eyes and then all went back to scouring the area.

"Mike, can you and Laura take a ride up to Town Hall and get a copy of the registered small boat owners in town, the size we discussed, earlier? That would help me out a lot. In the meantime, I'm going to put a call in to the Medical Examiner and see what's holding him up. He should have been here a while ago. Thought he would have had his work done while we were up at the reservoir."

"Grady, for what's it worth, we're going to have to wait on the Town Hall thing, it's three in the morning. Matter of fact Laura and I could use a few hours of shut eye before we pick this up again in a couple of hours. That is, if you want us to be of any use to you. Your guys need some sleep, also."

"It's what time?" Grady asked.

"It's 3 AM! Hey, I was shocked too. Had to look at my watch a few times, but it's what it is. You ought to knock off for a bit and get some sleep, too."

"That is weird. I don't know much about this ghostly stuff, but whatever happened up there changed the time, somehow." Grady looked puzzled.

"We must have been in some kind of, I don't know, altered universe," I whispered. "Seems like time sped up, a lot. I can't stop looking at my watch, because I keep thinking Casperina changed it, but Mike's says the same time as mine, so it's not that."

"That's crazy talk... altered universe? And who the hell is Casperina? You named the ghost? Are you nuts?" Grady buried his face in his hands. "They're going to throw all of us in the loony bin if any of this gets out. We have to swear an oath."

I grinned, "How about a pinky swear?"

"That is so...girly. No way am I doing that!" Grady said. "Laura, you want to be one of the guys, so man up and swear an oath."

"Fine," I rolled my eyes, "I swear, but I am not doing all that boy, back slapping stuff. It's dumb."

"It is not. It's manly. Would you prefer we chest bump?" Mike chuckled.

"No! We can do that other silly thing, bump fists," I laughed.

As we took turns bumping fists, we agreed to keep the Casperina event between ourselves until we could, ultimately, sort out how it played into the three seemingly related cases -- the deaths of Non Wrappe and

Appleton, and the case of Gwen, who remained missing.

On that note, we said our good mornings, and Mike and I dragged our weary bodies up the hill to our respective cars. On the way, I mentally reviewed the cause of death, praying we'd have the definitive results quickly. Whatever Non Wrappe and Appleton had been injected with, I wondered if it had been a torturous or a fast demise. That would answer many questions about our killer. We already knew he was methodical and a neat freak. We also knew he had more than one means of ingress to and egress from this particular area, separating him from your average serial killer, if indeed that was what we had on our hands. He apparently preferred more than one calling card too, putting him in another category as well. Whoever this guy was, he was striving for the over-achiever grouping.

While closing my car door, a chilling thought hit me; this case had to be tied up tightly, no loose ends whatsoever. Every piece of evidence had to point in one direction and one direction only, so that when this guy was caught, he would be found guilty beyond a shadow of a doubt.

Chapter 11

Phones do ring in dreams. It's happened to me many times and I always answer them. This time, it rang louder and louder, and each time I made an attempt to pick it up, I tripped on a rock, fell, and scraped my knees. With any luck, I'd reach it before I knocked myself out and find out who was calling me in the middle of the night.

"Who is this?" I was lying on my stomach on the floor. The rock was an overturned chair.

"Sorry to wake you up Laura, but you won't believe what's outside…"

"Mike! If you called to give me the weather report, it honestly could have waited until morning."

"It's almost eleven. I let you sleep as long as I could. Okay, back to what I wanted to tell you. There's a bunch of flowers and cards, candles, and teddy bears, and well, all kinds of neat stuff outside our office, and it's all addressed to Gwen. It's all piled up under the eaves so it won't get snowed on. It's amazing Laura, how many friends she has and how many people love her. There are even a few here who are holding candles and praying for her safe return. Several people stopped me when I was coming in and asked if I was the detective who's been out looking for her. I said I was one of many. Laura, you have to get down here. This is incredible!"

"Any guys talk to you?" I stumbled around, grabbed the side of the bed and pulled the chain on my table lamp.

"Interesting question, but, no, the people who questioned me were all women. Will you stop making all those clunking around noises, get dressed and get down here. Don't bother with breakfast; I'll make you something, along with a nice huge pot of coffee. We've got a lot of work to do, including you going back to the Soundview Guild to talk to some of Gwen's friends. Don't forget, Grady's got me running up to Town Hall…oh, and wait until you hear the results from the Medical Examiner."

"If you have them now, you'd better tell me, or you're in serious trouble!"

"You're awake now, aren't you?"

"I'm fine, I'm gonna make some coffee here and breakfast for Kola Bear, and then I'll be over."

"You're making coffee for Kola Bear? That's not good for him."

"Mike!"

"Okay, okay, you twisted my arm. ME says both our victims, Toska Non Wrappe and Wendy Appleton died from a 100 milliliter dosage of potassium chloride that was most likely delivered by a 50 cc syringe, which is why the size of the puncture wound is so large. Bodach's theory was on the money. It's the same as the huge needles you EMTs carry on the ambulance for flushing IV lines, cleaning them before fluids actually go in, right?"

"Right. To be sure no blood has come back in once we've set up the IV administration site. Potassium chloride would take roughly five to ten minutes to stop her heart, and injecting it with that size of a needle, wow, that would cause a serious burn. Our killer is clearly into watching his victims suffer prior to death. Like Dave said, he's one sick, crazy bastard. We've got to find Gwen before he gets his hands on her."

"Well, let's hope she's still out there, right? With each day that we don't find her, it cuts down the chances of us finding her alive, Laura. That's the sad truth of this business."

"I'm not giving up Mike, not until we absolutely have to."

"No one says you have to. Just giving you the facts, is all. There's always some kind of hope until we find a body. That said, get moving and get down here already."

I clicked the phone off, tossed it on the couch, rubbed my eyes and stared up from the floor of my living room at the motionless ceiling fan. Kola rested his head on my stomach. I stroked his ears while sorting through the list of last night's events, trying to make some sense out of what we'd seen and heard. It was a bit like deciding what to bring for a scavenger hunt. First, grab everything and then connect the dots, if you can, to make it all come together. Except, this was real life and scavenger hunts were games. In a serial killer's mind, though, I guess this was a game, and we had no choice but to play our part – to connect the dots to see if we could catch him. His part, to outsmart us and to be one step ahead.

All the key elements were right in front of us, and all we had to do was to organize them in a way that made sense. Sounded simple and logical. I started with our list of elements. We had two dead bodies – every murder scene has at least one of those. Check! We had one missing person. Check! So far, so good.

We then had the perfunctory set of serial killer calling cards. Our killer was definitely a Type A personality. He had four clear calling cards. I rubbed my eyes again, as I mentally went down the list: the yellow Marine teddy bear, the small American flag that was held in the cord, tied hands, and the index card with the words, "Never Forget," written on it. Then, of course, there was the methodology of death. If we included that as a calling card, then we were up to five. And, what about the cleats? And my hair ties? And what of the newspapers Adelaide mentioned finding up on the rocks, off one of the uppermost trails that just happened to overlook the area where we'd discovered Non Wrappe and Appleton's bodies? Hmmm…maybe I needed to spend some time with her discussing what else she felt was out of sorts in her woods.

At present, what I needed to do was to get up off the floor, grab my coffee and head down to the office to size up this crowd that Mike had described.

By the time I rounded the corner of the street our office was on, I was puzzling over the prior night's lightning wars, for lack of a better term, and even though Mike had described the scene, I was not prepared for what I encountered. There had to be close to a hundred people paying tribute to Gwen. Some had their heads bent in prayer, holding candles, while others were playing guitars or flutes and singing songs. There was a variety of colored helium balloons tied to tree branches, and all kinds of flowers in plastic wrap leaning against our building. Flickering votive candles in glass jars lined the stairs going up to the front door. Teddy bears were everywhere. It was an eclectic sight to behold.

A familiar figure lurked on the third floor balcony directly above our office, surveying the hub-bub below. Even though the person was in shadow, there was only one individual I knew of with that tremendous bulk; Agent Reggie Martin.

I reached for my cell phone and pressed the numbers. "Mike, my secret agent man is upstairs scanning the crowd."

115

"Really?" Mike changed the subject, "Would you put your money on Arnold being a praying man, or a strummer?"

"Well, well Mom, how about somewhere in the middle."

"The middle? What does that mean?"

"Take a look at the guy with the Teddy bear, right between the woman playing guitar and the guy playing the flute."

"Whoa. It's Arnold! Good eyes, Laura! Are my eyes deceiving me, or is he holding the same bear we found with the bodies? Is he an idiot, arrogant, or asking to be caught?"

"Or, is Arnold baiting us, Mike?"

"I think we ought to invite your secret agent man in for a cup of coffee and discuss the matter. Also, we'd better dial Grady up straight away and let him know our main suspect is practically at our front door.

"Can't be this easy Laura. This is too weird. Come on in, and try and do it without Arnold seeing you, okay?"

"Got it. I'll park down the street and use the back entrance. I won't even wave to Reggie."

"No need to wave to Reggie. He knew you were on your way five minutes before you did. Trust me on this. He has his ways."

"That's scary. On the other hand, with a serial killer on the loose, it makes me feel safer knowing I've got a government paid bodyguard. Hey, I wonder if I can keep him once this case is all wrapped up."

"He's not a pet."

"What if I ask the Director, nicely?"

"Laura, please get off the phone and come in the office. Now!"

"Only a thought, a passing thought. He might come in handy on…"

"Laura!"

"Coming."

Chapter 12

Mike and I were watching the gathering through matching pairs of binoculars, when Grady slipped in.

"Your client's a suspect?" Grady took Mike's binoculars and panned the growing mass. "This crowd gets any bigger and I'm going to have to get a couple of uniforms down here for crowd control." Then he stopped, focusing in on Arnold.

"I cannot believe how brazen this guy is, same damn bear. You said he acted all bizarre on you in the interview, right?"

"Up and walks out in the middle of a crying jag. Shuts the waterworks down in seconds flat, and he's talking about having to pick up a sports jacket at the cleaners. Then, he flips my World Series baseball at me like there's nothing to it."

"I'm surprised Laura didn't have to do CPR on you."

"Hey, that's my prized possession!"

"I'm agreeing with you," Grady said. "Calm down. So, how are we going to nab him without spooking him?" He thought for a moment, then suggested, "We could use the uniform I'm going to send over."

"I think a cop in uniform will surely spook him. Why don't I go down, walk around, straighten up the flowers and see if I can start up a conversation with him? Without Kola, of course. Let me give it a shot. You can have your uniform stand by around the corner. If things start to go wrong, I'll signal you by putting on my gloves."

"I don't know if that's such a great idea. What if, for the sake of argument, he's the killer, Laura? You're his type, and you're going to saunter right up to him?" Grady asked. "What's to prevent him from snatching you right from under our noses? Not even our agent buddy upstairs would be able to reach you in time. There are probably over a hundred people out there, and to make it even more confusing, Annie and her crew are out there filming all this and conducting interviews.

"I don't like it one bit. At the very least, I want one of my plainclothes guys near you, or one of my female officers in street clothes, someone who can blend in with this growing…whatever and pretend to be an onlooker. You've gotta have someone down there with you watching your back."

"He's right," Mike agreed. "It's too dangerous and too stupid for you to go it alone. You need back up and I can't go. He'd figure that out in a second."

"Alright you two, I got it. Hurry up then, Grady, and call in your plainclothes guy…and you'd better let Reggie in on your plans, or…"

"Someone page me?" Reggie walked in the door, as if on cue.

"I was just going to call you," Grady said.

"So I heard. Saved you the trouble. I prefer face to face meetings anyway, as Laura here can tell you. Did I hear you say that you'd be sending Laura to talk to Arnold? No way! If you think going after a serial killer is the same as, say, going on a fishing expedition, well you're in the wrong boat. Arnold might be your bait to catch the killer -- if he is not in fact the killer -- but the killer might not bite. At any rate, once bait spoils, it either gets tossed out, or it gets used as chum to lure bigger fish, maybe a bigger fish than you bargained for. How do you like my fishing analogies so far? I hope you like them because, when this case is solved, and believe you me it will be, I would love to take you out on my boat and teach you all how to fish, except of course for Grady, who I understand is already quite the fisherman. Before that, though, we've gotta hook this killer shark. Are you all onboard with that? I do love my nautical terms." Reggie grinned.

We were about to be schooled.

"Here's the long and short of it, gang. Arnold has everything to do with his wife's disappearance, and more than likely, her death. That's right, her death. Grady, your guys just haven't found her body, but believe me when I tell you, it's out there. Those woods are vast, and it's a monumental task to cover all that ground. You know that your department can't handle it alone, and even with help from the Troopers, you still need the Bureau's assistance on this. Besides, the Bureau has its own interest in the case. We've got a profile on Arnold and his good buddy Eliott, and they're in pretty deep from a financial standpoint – fraud on a federal level.

We thought that was the gist of the problem, until we found out that both Gwen and Eliott were missing. In another weird twist, we found out that good old Eliott had more than a passing interest in Gwen. But, I suppose you figured that out when you discovered his prints on the beret he sent to her. Good job, by the way, on getting those back as quickly as you did, considering how backed up Forensics is.

"On to another question; has it occurred to you where dear old Eliott might have gone off to?"

"Son of a bitch!" Grady exclaimed. "I've been so busy searching for Gwen…what a damned rookie mistake."

"I wouldn't be too hard on yourself, my man, you've had your hands full the last few days with the murders alone, not to mention some pretty strange goings on in those woods of yours. I'm not so sure I'll be able to sleep for a while after my night in the woods."

"Wait, you saw what we saw? I mean, you were out there?" Grady asked.

"I've been tracking and trailing you three the entire time, and in all my years, I have never seen anything like what I saw the other night. It doesn't jibe with any reality I know. My Grandpop would tell stories about ghosts, and I used to think they were just to entertain us kids, even though he insisted they were true. Until the other night, I never believed a word of it. Now I regret thinking he was a bit of a kook all of those years growing up. I suppose I owe him an apology, and when this is done, I'll go to his grave, kneel down, tell him that I'm indeed sorry and pray that he forgives me. You have no idea how difficult that day will be."

"I'm just glad you saw what we saw," Grady said, "because I keep thinking I'm losing my ever loving mind. Bad enough that a small town like Soundview has a serial killer, but, ghosts? My guys and I have all heard the stories about the White Lady., and you ought to see it on Halloween Eve; it's a regular carnival around here. I have to put extra patrols on the cemetery because of all the tourists who want to take the ghost's picture. Like she's going to show up and stand front and center at the cemetery gates, posing, and showing her better side. I never believed a word of it, but to see her up close and personal like that…. I never in a million years thought I'd actually be out in the woods with the White Lady, not to mention everything else that was going on, especially the lightning and that whispering voice.

"Okay, enough of that." Grady abruptly changed direction. "Can we please get back to discussing normal stuff, like our serial killer friend and what Arnold's connection is, if any? And, what happened to Eliott?"

"I believe Arnold disposed of Eliott, but more about that later." Reggie suddenly paused, as if listening to some inner voice, "Right now, we've got to get Arnold out of this scene ASAP!" As he spoke, Reggie moved toward the window. "I've got one of my female agents on her way over here right now. She's just a couple of blocks away." At our looks of confusion, Reggie tapped his ear and continued, "I'm wearing a headset. We need to get Arnold out of here with as few people as possible noticing, media included. I don't want a riot on our hands, and we'll have just that if people think Arnold has something to do with Gwen's disappearance.

"By the by, thanks for the tip on Gwen's safety deposit box. I did get a search warrant, and voila, Gwen had a copy of Arnold and Eliott's client list in there. I believe it was her trump card for an impending divorce. Not only that, one of the clients was a fella by the name of Bill Appleton."

Mike, Grady and I stared at each other.

"I thought that might get your attention." Reggie winked. He continued, "I'm guessing Mrs. Appleton figured the scam out, and went to either Arnold or Eliott, demanding their money back. Instead, she wound up in the woods."

"Wait a second," Grady asked, "now you're implicating Eliott? I don't get it? I thought we were after Arnold for these killings?"

"Let's just say I'm not completely convinced Arnold is alone in this. It will play itself out. In the meantime, we have to move fast, that's why I've got my agent Jill on her way. She knows what she's doing. She'll have him off the scene before anyone suspects a thing. With a bit of luck, I'll be questioning our dear suspect within the next hour. Grady if you'd like to observe, you're more than welcome.

"Sorry Laura and Mike, you'll have to wait for the outcome. Mike, I'd love to extend professional courtesy to you, but that wouldn't be fair to Laura. If anything pops, Grady will keep you apprised, and in the meantime, there's plenty of detective work to be done. Gwen and Eliott need to be found."

Reggie turned to the window, again scanning the crowd. "Jill's arrived. Looks like I have a couple of minutes while she works her way over to Arnold. Should be just enough time to tell you why I think Arnold killed Elliot, and how I think he pulled it off. Here's the short version. I believe Eliott was getting ready to turn state's evidence against Arnold, and God knows Arnold can't have that. So Arnold calls Eliott to a meeting at his home, his lakeside home. An argument ensues and poor unsuspecting Eliott meets his untimely death. The fact that Arnold lives on a lake makes for dumping a body incredibly convenient, almost ridiculously so, if you ask me. If I were a betting man, which I'm not, I would take a drive over to Arnold's house, go around back and check out his little rowboat, the one with the three horsepower motor on it. It's tied up at his dock, complete with extra lines and a tarp inside it -- perfect for dumping a body into that manmade lake. By the time you've checked out that little boat, I should have a confession out of Arnold for killing Eliott. Then we can get a dive team out there to find the body. At least we'll have him locked up for that one. After that, we'll move on to nailing him for the rest. If he's not the one who killed those women, he surely knows who did. Most likely, he's an accomplice. Maybe, the killer is Arnold's errand boy, or maybe it's the other way around, and the killer's his mentor."

"I've given you plenty to begin your search under probable cause. While Jill and I are driving Arnold over to FBI HQ, I'll call up my favorite judge and have a search warrant drawn up. Someone will drive it over the second the ink's dry."

Again Reggie paused, hand to his ear. "Jill's just a few feet away from Arnold. She's just let me know that she's about to take him into custody." Reggie didn't bother with any good byes. He took the stairs two at a time, leaving the three of us standing there.

"Grady, hurry up and follow him before you get left out of the biggest case of your life, man." Mike shoved Grady, hard, through the doorway.

I ran to the window in time to see Reggie get into the driver's seat of a dark sedan, Grady get in the passenger side and a woman who must have been Reggie's agent Jill, assisting a handcuffed Arnold into the backseat. Within seconds, they were gone, destination unknown.

"Mike, you said Reggie knew things, for example, he was aware of my whereabouts, that sort of thing. But, he was following us in the woods? And, he knows all this about Arnold? It appears as if he's got this case all figured out. I get he's FBI and has eons of experience behind him, but..."

"Your head's spinning. Don't feel badly Laura, mine is, too. This is why we have inter-agency sharing of information, we need each other when it comes to cases like these. First we go to the State, which we did, then the Bureau drops in, which they did. We're lucky to have Reggie. He's incredible. Let's try to follow his line of thinking for a moment.

"Think about it, if your business is dropping down the rabbit hole faster than you can sneeze, you've been caught skimming off the top, and you've got a partner with a conscience who's about to turn you in, which it sounds like Eliott was, what's a guy like Arnold do? He panics. Couple that with thinking he can get away with anything in the middle of Main Street USA, and no one's going to notice; you've got the recipe for disaster on your hands. Murder's definitely stepping it up a notch, but if he's sure he's going away for cooking the books, then he might think, oh what the hell, I've got a nice deep water quarry in my backyard. They'll think Eliott fled the state out of fear of prosecution and maybe I'll go to prison for a shorter stint. End of story.

"Jump to the killer being Arnold's mentor, and now you're in another ballgame altogether. I've no idea where that comes from. Reggie must have some background info that we're not privy to. Maybe, he'll squeeze it out during the confession and Grady will share it with us. Meantime, let's get over to Arnold's and check out that boat of his. And while we're at it, why don't we see if Arnold happens to have any extra cleats lying around, you know, like the ones we found in the woods."

"I always thought it would be great if our first case shot out of the starting gate like a cannon, but I sure didn't anticipate anything close to this Mike," I said.

"Don't you mean; out of the starting gate like a horse? Wow, sure am glad Adelaide didn't hear you say that." Mike laughed.

Chapter 13

A chorus of barks emanated from within my coat pocket. Mike looked from side to side.

"Please keep your eyes on the road. It's my phone."

"Why can't you get a normal ring tone like everyone else? Scares me when a bunch of dogs start barking."

"Oh, and your Andy Griffith theme song is normal?"

"Don't knock it, happens to be a classic."

"I don't recognize the number," I said.

"Answer it to shut the dogs up, will you. It's making me nervous and it's bad enough that we're almost at Arnold's."

"Hello, this is Laura Jensen. Adelaide, what a lovely surprise. Yes, I'm here with Mike and we're on the case that's all over the news. Yes, it has made quite a big splash across town. Yes, they will be talking about it for years, especially if we don't solve it. Yes, exactly how they still discuss Jack the Ripper having gotten away with it. Yes, I suppose the headlines will be screaming about this and nothing else for days. You don't appreciate all the attention from the hordes of reporters that this has brought to your quiet and once peaceful home? It used to be so out of the way and now everyone knows where you live. Yes, I'm repeating every word so Mike can hear."

Mike and I glanced at each other. I shrugged my shoulders and he shook his head.

"What does he have to say? Nothing yet. Why? I haven't had a chance to ask him because he's driving. We're on our way over to do some more investigating and Mike just mouthed to me that we'll be straight over to speak with you as soon as we're done."

Mike threw me a sideways glance.

I shrugged again.

"We'll call when we're on our way. Bye Adelaide."

"This day's never going to end. Arnold's, Town Hall to dig for boat registrations. Jog over to Adelaide's, and you still have to get back to Soundview Guild to interview Gwen's classmates." Mike groaned.

"Right. All in a day's work. There's Arnold's." I pointed.

"The bunker?"

"Told you."

"Not what I pictured. Mr. Slick in a place like this? It doesn't fit the profile, unless you're going for the cold fish look." Mike scratched his head.

"When was the last time you met a fraternity type serial killer?" I asked.

"Remember Ted Bundy, Laura? He was one hundred percent charmer, and all about blending in. But even the smartest of criminals screw up, eventually."

"Well, if Arnold is interested in blending in, he's not doing a very good job of it. This house doesn't jibe with the rest of his upscale image, that's for sure. I guess we should be thankful that not all criminals are as smart as Ted Bundy was." I stated.

We parked in the driveway, quite a different experience from my last visit, when I'd hidden down the street.

We followed an uneven brick walkway to the back of the house. It led us out onto a cedar deck overlooking the man-made lake. A rickety wooden table and chairs and several dead potted plants dotted the forlorn area. All were covered with snow.

A short set of stairs led from the deck down to the dock, where a fiberglass dinghy was tied to a single cleat.

"Guess they forgot to bring in the furniture for the winter," I said as I skirted around the table.

"Not only that, why's the boat in the water? Should be up on the dock, upside down, at least, or in the garage. If she were mine, she'd be nice and warm in there."

"I suppose you'd have a blanket over her?"

"Very funny. Hey, look at that. There's a tarp all scrunched up in the bottom of the boat. We can't touch anything, but we can take plenty of pictures and send them to Grady. He'll love that."

I lay down, on the dock and leaned forward. From this vantage point, I could see inside the boat without disturbing or touching anything.

"How long do you think she is?" I asked.

"Your voice sounds muffled, like it's coming from a well. If you fall in, I am not saving you. Water's too cold. I forgot, you're a body surfer girl from Augustine Bay.

"Anyway, in answer to your question, about eight feet, and that motor there is a three horsepower Evinrude -- just as Reggie said. He does know everything." Mike held his hands up in a gesture of amazement.

"I still would like to double check. I'm great at reading, not so good on measurements. Long enough for a body, wouldn't you say?" I asked.

"Oh yeah. And, the engine doesn't need to be any bigger, either. It's not like you're going all that far. Say, a hundred yards at most, rope around the ankles with a cinder block attached, and he sinks to the bottom. The tarp would keep him covered in case any neighbors wonder what you're up to. After that, you could say it's to keep you warm while you're out in the middle of the lake admiring the moon," Mike said.

"Sure, that's what I always do on a freezing cold, mid-winter night. Especially, if I'm a high-powered exec who loves to relax at home with my gorgeous wife. Oh right, she's missing."

"Mike, I think I found some blood. Over here, right near the bow. Can you get a picture of it?"

"On it Laura. Good eye. Calling Grady right now.

"Hey buddy. Your instincts were on target. We found what could be blood in Arnold's little boat. Okay, Laura found it. Why didn't I find it? Because I wasn't in the mood to get splinters in my belly and...What? Her WHAT is better than mine? Her dexterity? I'll have to look that up later, I think you just insulted me.

"Yes, we'll wait for the dive team because you're about to crack Arnold. Wish I was there to watch. I know, no photos and no video. I guess I'll have to rely on you to tell me all about it. But it's not the same as being there. Next time, can I come? You promise?

"I'm sure, you're having fun playing second fiddle to Reggie. You're talking funny, he must be nearby. Great, send my best to him too.

"That was fast work. I see the lights heading down the street right now.

"Okay, we'll let you know as soon as your guys find anything, or rather, they'll call you. Crack away. Bye."

"Sounds like Grady's enjoying his time with Reggie," I grinned.

"Grady likes to run the show; can't imagine what's going on in that interview room. I put even money on Grady coming out the winner in getting the necessary info out of Arnold."

"He needs to confess to killing Eliott, if he did it. That way, if the dive team finds Eliott's body out in the lake and his DNA in the boat, that's a lock.

"That's a lot of 'ifs,' and it doesn't answer what he was doing with the exact same yellow Marine Corp Beanie Bear that we found with Non Wrappe and Appleton."

"All excellent points Laura. However even if Arnold doesn't confess to Grady and Reggie, a DNA match would still tie him to Eliott's murder. Water's not going to wash that away, and there's plenty to find in the boat. We need to figure out where Eliott was actually killed. Was it the house, outside, or in the boat? Or, was he still alive when he was dumped in the water?

"And what about the bear? Why did he have it? Was there another murder being planned? Is he connected to the killer? If so, how? I know, we've asked these questions already, but we have to keep asking until we have the answers. Don't forget, it's not a lock until the jury says so."

"Mike, what if Eliott's the killer?"

"No way. You asked that before, remember? Even if Mr. FBI thinks it's possible, I'm not buying it."

"No, I don't remember," I said wearily. "One day is merging into the next. Being surrounded by halogen lights for hours didn't help much, and neither did the time warp, or however you'd like to describe that event. At any rate, we have to leave the door open, Mike. There could be multiple killers,"

Our musings were cut short by the arrival of the Soundview Police Department's Dive Team truck.

"My kind of day to jump in a lake and go for a dive. Yes sir. A bit of snow, it's about five degrees today, and part of the lake's frozen," said a young man as he jumped out of the truck. "You couldn't ask for better conditions. We'll just have to do a bit of chipping and away we go... " he stretched and grinned at us.

"Yessiree, can't wait to get in there, poke around and see if it lives up to its name, Crystal Lake. If it does, and there's a body in there, we'll find it right quick. 'Course, if somebody actually saw our suspect shove the body overboard, that would make it easier. But no such luck, so we'll do our search using our side scan sonar.

"How rude, I'm Crosby Lattimer," he said, putting his hand out to shake mine.

"Nice to meet you Crosby, I'm Laura Jensen, Mike's partner. You must be part polar bear to go diving in those icy waters."

"Ah, you're the one he's always bragging on. Great to finally put a face to the accolades. You ought to hear him go on about you.

"As to the cold water, my team and I will all be wearing dry suits that for appearances sake look like wet suits, only they're constructed much differently. Unlike wet suits, which allow water in to help warm us, dry suits don't allow any in at all. They have special seams at the wrists, and we wear specialized hoods, booties and gloves that are lined, so we'll be plenty warm. If you'd like, I can see if we can find one in your size that you can try on?"

"I don't know about that Crosby. I believe you, but I'd rather watch, if you don't mind. Fishing for bodies really isn't my thing."

Mike chuckled, "Good one Laura." Then, to me, sotto-voce, he said, "Don't think that's what he meant. I think it was all about getting you to model a wet suit." And aloud, "We really do have to get you out fishing – for fish, that is." You'd love it. Grady and I are definitely taking you out when this case is over with."

"You fish?" Crosby asked.

"The guys are getting very insistent that I learn, so it's looking as if I'm going to take it up."

"Super, my boat is down near Fisherman's World, the best bait and tackle store anywhere. I know all the guys over there really well and they'll set you up with everything you need; rod and reel, whatever. After we solve this case, of course," Crosby smiled and set about organizing his guys as they donned their dry suits. Next, they loaded the dinghies they'd trailered with the required scuba gear, including extra tanks and ropes for securing the body, in order to bring it onboard one of the dinghies. They had radios to communicate with each other and maps of the lake showing the rocky formations before it had been filled with water.

Mike pored over the maps. "Hate to say it Laura, but if Arnold's our killer, here we go again with bodies in rocky areas. I'm telling you, even if it isn't Arnold; whoever this guy is, he's got a seriously weird attraction to rocks."

"No worries Mike," Crosby interjected, no matter where in the lake this body ended up, we'll find it. We've got the coolest gadget ever made. Like I mentioned before, our side scan sonar will find him."

"Oh yeah? I'm interested; how does it work?" Mike asked.

Mike and I leaned in closely to the dinghy's console so Crosby could give us an on the spot tutorial.

"Why don't you two hop in, it will only take a few minutes to walk you through this. We're only in a few feet of water, but it will give you the general idea. We already know that Crystal Lake's a man-made lake, a filled in quarry, and that the depth is roughly sixty feet. So, we don't have to pull out the big guns for this. Meaning we don't have to tow a piece of sonar equipment behind us with a hundred or more feet of cable, like we would if we were out on Long Island Sound, or out on the ocean. Besides, those things look like torpedoes and scare people. And even with that equipment, we'd still need the assistance of the Coast Guard with onboard computers. So, for our purposes, this baby, which set the Department back around two grand, finds bodies and wrecks --and she can even find fish, too. I call that a great bargain. Oh, and she's got GPS so we don't get lost out on this lake."

Crosby looked up to make sure we were following what he was saying...My kind of guy. We nodded.

He grinned his infectious grin and proceeded, "Her screen is eight inches in diameter with a full color display and she will show us what the bottom looks like, tell us how deep it is and what the water temp is, so we're completely prepared for the conditions before going in for retrieval. See how it shows us a dual image? A split screen, if you will. Well, that's actually identifying and imaging one hundred and twenty five degrees both to the left and to the right at the same time, which gives us a wide viewing area, literally on both sides, hence, side scanning. It's real time too, so whatever's down there, we'll see it. Fortunately for us, this isn't a huge lake, so it shouldn't take too long to survey it and find him...if he's here of course. We still have to use a grid pattern, but it's much easier than it used to be.

"We're going to get started and I'll radio back when we find what we're looking for."

Mike and I climbed out and they were off.

I looked up and saw that a patrol car was parked at the top of the drive to keep the nosey neighbors away. Yellow police tape had already been tied from one lamp post to the other, indicating to the growing crowd to stay out.

While we waited, one of Grady's detectives went methodically over the rowboat, collecting potential evidence, while others scrutinized the premises. At this particular point, there was nothing for us to do aside from stand there and observe.

Mike's phone played the silly Andy Griffith tune. "Hi Grady. Standing here with Laura doing nothing, and you know how much I don't like that. What, you expected him to spill his guts all over Reggie's nice confession table? Oh sure. Bet Reggie's going crazy right about now," Mike laughed. "Crosby's out with the dive boys and his fancy side scan thing that he proudly showed off. Yeah, he said he wants to use it for fishing too. Something about wanting to teach Laura how to fish. Between Reggie and Crosby...oh, now you want to teach her?"

"Laura, there's going to be a fish fight over you. Grady says he's the best teacher...wait a second, he just put me on hold; he's got another call."

The detective who'd been checking the rowboat walked over to us with a very disappointed look on his face. "Thought I'd let you know, boat's clean as a whistle. I already called it in to the Captain. He said I could let you know, seeing as the Lieutenant is busy," he said as he removed his latex gloves. "Sorry, I'm Tom."

"Thanks Tom," I replied. "But, what about the dark spot on the tarp, near the bow?"

"I did a test on it for blood, that's what I thought it was. It's not. Could be anything, juice, who knows."

I sighed and surveyed the scene on the lake. The three dinghies were spread out, each with their assigned search area in varying depths of water, looking for anything out of the ordinary. If Eliott was down there, Crosby was convinced his device would find him. This wasn't fitting as neatly into place as Reggie had thought. Something obviously didn't add up. But what?

"Hey buddy, can you add some music to your hold button. That was a long one. Yeah, some Bob Marley tunes would be great. Bad news on my end...what? You've got bad news for me? Some day this is turning into. Okay, I'll go first. The Captain cleared one of your detectives to say the damn boat's clean. That's nothing compared to what you got? Great. Yeah, Laura and I are both sitting down."

We weren't. I was pacing, wearing the stone walkway smooth.

"No way."

My heart skipped a beat. I stopped pacing and felt an icy chill run down my spine. I knew before Mike spoke the words.

"Gwen's dead."

Chapter 14

There was a stone walkway that required more wearing down. It was calling to me.

I paused on the edge of a snow covered oval shaped stone, pointed skyward and shouted, "At least don't make so much noise with the falling snow, damn it!"

Someone placed a Kleenex in my hand, making me conscious of tears flowing down my cheeks.

I felt a light touch on my shoulder, turned and looked into Mike's eyes. "We failed her."

He pulled me against him, rocked me and stroked my hair. We were silent for a moment, then he said "We did sort of anticipate it. Okay, let me rephrase that. We knew it was a possibility, especially, after what Reggie said. I think he knew more than he was telling us at the time.

"It was a deer hunter friend of Bodach's who found Gwen, in case you're wondering. Same as Dave, he was scouting hunting spots."

"So, Grady's crew is out with Gwen now?" I backed up, rubbed my eyes and blew my nose.

"Yeah. He also said the Medical Examiner picked up Appleton. She's on her way to autopsy. That will take a few days, and more than likely from first inspection, will come back with the same results as Non Wrappe's. Grady sent a fresh crew over to check out Gwen, but he's expecting the same mode of death. The initial reports came in with the identical scene description."

We were interrupted by the crackling of noise and chatter on the police radios.

"Headquarters, this is Marine One."

"This is Headquarters, go ahead Marine One."

"Requesting a Ten-Eighty at our location."

"Ten-Four Marine One."

"Since they're asking for the Medical Examiner, I'm guessing

Marine One's found Eliott," Mike stated. "What a day this has turned into. Listen, there's no reason for us to hang around, unless you want to be sure it's him. I was thinking we could do something useful, like head up to Town Hall as we'd originally planned and check on small boat registrations. Get our minds back into this. What do you say?"

"I say, we nail the bastard, and if that's where we begin, then let's go Mom."

"That's the spirit. Besides, once they ID this body, we'll hear about it, and in the meantime we've got lots of legwork to do."

"Before we do that, what if we check the docks all around the lake. Especially since we've got the dinghies here, it wouldn't take nearly as long as it would if we had to drive around to each house, knock on the door, and explain the situation..."

"What a brilliant idea Laura, and Crosby will be up for it, I'm sure. Cruise up to everyone's dock with a detective onboard to inspect their boat. Hey, a little neighborhood participation in order to catch a killer. 'Course, once we find the boat Arnold might have used, the owner will be begging us to get it off their hands. And, that's how Crosby will get a new toy." Mike turned and was about to sprint down the stone pathway toward the dock.

I stood there, hands on my hips. "Mike, you know I didn't mean talking to everyone with a dock on the lake. If we cruise around, we just might see something interesting."

"Yeah, I know. Bad joke. Come on Laura, hurry up or you'll miss your high class dinghy ride of a lifetime. Being your idea, Crosby will let you come."

"What about the body they're bringing ashore?"

"They still have two other boats in the water, and besides, they have to wait for the ME. That will take a bit. I suspect, with the way this day has been going, the next call I get from Grady is going to be him telling me that Reggie had to cut Arnold loose due to lack of evidence -- which means that your light bulb moment might just save the day. If Arnold's out of Reggie's hands, we can't be here."

Mike and I paced the dock, nearly knocking each other into the freezing water. I found a stick, placed it lengthways on the dock and commanded him to stay on his own side.

Mike discussed the plan with Tom, and the detective remained on the dock with us while we waited for Crosby.

We watched the three dinghies head back in, Crosby's boat in the lead with the cargo onboard.

Tom raised Crosby on his cell to relay our intentions and get his input. He also advised Crosby of the potential time shortage if Reggie had to let Arnold walk. We needed something and we needed it fast. Crosby liked the idea and stepped on the gas, so to speak.

My phone barked. "Hi Annie. Nothing…what do you mean, don't lie to you? Right, I keep forgetting you've got that high tech scanner, and know all about the news as it's happening, No, I'm not forgetting that you're a journalist. Ouch! What? Oh, Mike just slapped me as a not very gentle reminder of what Grady will do to him if I even so much as breathe a word to you. Hey, you know Grady always gives you an exclusive. Okay, except for the one time that you were out of town. What was he supposed do, phone it in?" I couldn't help but laugh.

Annie had the most laid back personality, with one exception -- when it came to competing for a story, she was ruthless. But, that's why she was the best. Her news stories were clear, concise, well written and what the public wanted. She gave them the gritty details without the fluff. I was looking forward to reading how she was going to write our case up.

"Alright smarty, you tell me what you think you know already and I can say yes or no. That's right, that's how the game is played. Yes, I am learning from a pro." I laughed.

Mike winked.

I watched Crosby and his men bring a flat board, also known as a long board, over to the boat, while I listened to Annie tell me what she'd learned. She was, surprisingly, right up to date.

They strapped the covered body onto the board and carried it to the waiting Crime Scene van. It would remain inside until the Medical Examiner arrived, and then be properly packaged for transport. Meaning, zipped into a large bag prior to being placed into the ME's truck.

Meanwhile, Annie was asking, "Well, guess what I learned today Laura?"

"Oh, do tell, but hurry because Mike and I are going to have to join up with the head of the dive team in a minute."

"Ah, hope he's cute."

"Annie!" I could feel myself blush.

"Well, it's been a long time. Okay, on to my interesting lesson of the day: A dead body, when immersed in cold water, does not decompose due to lack of oxygen, therefore making positive identification a snap. It will give the body a bit of a waxy appearance, so you could just ship him off…oh, I won't say it."

"To where?…Oh to a wax museum."

"Definitely. You read my mind," she laughed. "You're just as sick as I am for thinking that. I could see your smile through the phone

"Since we're fairly sure who it is, the opportunity to make a quick ID will make Mike happy. And with any luck, the pups might get an early evening walk in. I'll give you a call when we finish up here," I said.

"Happy hunting."

"Gee, thanks. Here comes Crosby, now."

"Great name," Annie said.

"Will you two quit your yakking and come on, already. We have work to do. Bye Annie,"

Mike said loudly.

"You heard him. Talk to you later."

"Take a photo of Crosby and send it to me. No one will know."

"I'm on a crime scene. Are you crazy? I can't take pictures of anything."

Mike grabbed my phone. "Crosby's the spitting image of James Bond," and hung up.

"Which James Bond?" I asked.

"Does it matter? Someone had to end the conversation. Otherwise it would go on all day."

"Ahoy landlubbers!" Crosby called.

"Saved by the dinghy," Mike said.

"Hi James," I said, as I climbed aboard.

"Huh, name's Crosby. You need some coffee to thaw you out. There's a thermos right over there with your name on it. Warm you right up. Obviously, you've been out in the cold too long."

"Mike says you look like James Bond."

"I get that a lot," Crosby laughed, "but which one?"

Tom looked back and forth as he climbed aboard, and shook his head.

"Alright, let's head on out and begin this process of elimination," Crosby said. "Let's make it as simple as we can and circle the lake, starting with the neighboring dock to the right."

"Problem we're going to have is, if there's not a boat tied up, then we have to knock," Tom pointed out.

"If Arnold used a boat on this lake, then it's one that's either tied up at a neighbor's dock, or it's hidden away behind some bushes on the shore," I said.

"If the latter's the case, we're going to have to walk the entire shoreline, Laura, and that will eat up an enormous amount of time. As is, just tooling around the lake is going to take us a while," Crosby noted.

"That's right. Each boat has to be gone over for any tell-tale signs," Mike said.

Crosby eased up on the throttle as we approached the first dock, then he put it in neutral. We slipped across the icy water and the rubber side gently nudged the dock. Tom stepped up and jumped off, equipment bag over his shoulder, prepared to inspect the boat that was similar to Arnold's.

I thought we'd have to wait a while, but it seemed as if Tom did a U-turn. He was back within what felt like seconds.

"She's spotless," he pronounced. He untied Marine One, and stepped onboard. Crosby throttled in reverse and we were off for the next inspection.

We repeated the process three more times before we got a thumbs-up from Tom. He got a positive for blood that he was able to collect a sample of, and a fingerprint he was able to lift. The most significant find, none of us could have anticipated. It was a length of the same odd cord we'd yet to identify that had been discovered with each of the bodies in Trout Brook. Were Eliott's killer and the killer of the three women one and the same? Or, were they working together? Or, had Eliott gotten too close?

"I'm calling Grady," Mike announced.

"He needs to hear this right away... That's weird, he's not picking up. It's going straight to voice mail. He always picks up when it's me. Always."

"Always?" Tom winked.

"More than I want to know," Crosby laughed.

"Is that all guys ever think about?" I shook my head in mock disgust.

"Yes," the three of them replied in unison.

"On that note, if you'll take me back to Arnold's house, where my car's parked, I'll get all my evidence properly logged and head upstate,"

Tom said.

"Hold on folks!" Crosby pushed the throttle forward, the bow lifted off the surface of the water and we raced toward Arnold's dock. The rush of cold, winter air blowing against my face shocked and thrilled me, and for a brief window, I was enveloped in a moment devoid of serial killers and dead bodies.

Chapter 15

Crosby throttled Marine One down to an idle, reached for his binoculars, peered through and inquired, "Anyone know who the knucklehead is on the dock, waving us off?"

"Here, let me take a look," Mike said. "I can't believe it," he shook his head. "No wonder Grady didn't pick up when I called. It's Arnold! He must have been cussing Reggie out for letting the guy go. Damn. Reggie was so sure of himself."

Mike swung his gaze away from Arnold.

"Hey," he pointed where the Crime Scene van was parked, "there's Grady and Reggie, and Grady looks angry. He shuffles his feet when he's upset.

"Looks like we're not docking at Arnold's. I guess, head in where you launched from, Crosby."

"Righto Nav Man. I'll bring her in, bow first, nice and soft, and you can crawl right over the bow and not get wet at all."

"Thanks Crosby, I don't have a change of clothes with me…okay, more info than you needed," I said.

Crosby laughed.

I felt my cheeks flush.

We eased right onto shore, and Grady gave me a hand in getting off. Reggie reintroduced himself, while Crosby's men readied the boats for trailering and departure back to headquarters. The Medical Examiner had already left the scene with Eliott's body. As with the other bodies, we knew it would be some time before we knew the exact cause of death. We were told that the preliminary theory was blunt force trauma to the back of the head, with drowning as a secondary cause. However, he'd been wrapped up in a blanket, and we hadn't seen him, so we couldn't even speculate. We would have to wait for the final report.

"So, uh, crazy guy's been pacing the dock for a while?" Mike asked.

"Since he came home and threw everyone off his property and

started screaming about how he's going to sue not only the Department and the FBI, but each one of us, individually. Includes you two, so don't feel left out. He's suing for invasion of privacy because you've been going through all his stuff." Grady held up his hands and went on, "Yeah, I know, he hired you for that."

"Paid us too. Now, he's going to sue us for doing our job? He is crazy.

"There's a word for people like him...sociopath," Mike said.

"Psychopath, I think," Reggie offered.

"Can someone be both?" I asked.

"Not usually," Reggie answered, "but Arnold's behavior's not following the norm, from my experience. We arrested him and told him why. He didn't care. The fact that he's stolen from so many people, their life's savings at that, didn't faze him in the least. In his mind, he's convinced himself that he's entitled to that money. Somehow, he deserves it, needs it. That makes him a sociopath. Not much in the way of a moral conscience, or moral obligation, if you will.

"Now, when we broke the news of Eliott's death to him, there was nothing, and I mean nothing. No response whatsoever. That's clearly the behavior of a psychopath. We may as well have told him it was sunny and eighty degrees out, or TV has no commercials."

"I'd do cartwheels if TV gave up commercials," Mike laughed.

"I'd pay to see that," Grady grinned. "Reggie's right, though. Think about it -- Eliott's his college roommate and then starts a business with him. We tell Arnold he's dead, and zip. I've dealt with some hardened criminals before, but this guy is in a different realm. I'm telling you, it's eerie.

"Tell them the rest Reggie, you guys won't believe it."

"It's just as Grady said, Arnold's incapable of feeling guilt, remorse, or for that matter, even love. They're all basic human emotions, and it's my opinion that this throws him into the category of being a psychopath too. In other words, to answer your question Laura, yes, you can be both a sociopath and a psychopath at the same time. I believe our friend exhibits behavior of being both by the mere fact that when we informed him of his wife's death, again, no reaction whatsoever. No twitching, no darting of the eyes, no tapping of the feet or fingers, no licking of the lips. This guy sat there, stone cold still, his eyes in a vacant stare. He blinked normally, and thanked us for informing him."

"Excuse me, what? He thanked you? Did I hear you right?" Mike asked.

"Yes old friend, you did," Grady replied. "I couldn't believe my ears, either. Reggie, I have to tell them the last part, do you mind?"

"Go ahead," Reggie said.

"Thanks, because it blew me away. He said he knew he could count on us, as a group, to treat Gwen's body with the utmost respect. He also said he wanted Laura to escort her out of the woods, which could explain why he's standing on the dock, staring at us."

"Why me? That's not my job," I said. "The ME does that, who's working overtime these days, as well as your detectives."

"I explained that to him. He didn't care, said something about you and Gwen having a kinship because of the woods. I further explained to him that regardless of what he thought or believed, it wasn't about to happen.

"Mind you, he said all of this in a very even toned voice, but with the full expectation that we, or you, would accommodate him. So far the only reactions we've seen out of him are the threats of being sued and not allowing Crosby to use his dock."

"Enough about his psychiatric diagnosis. Why is he standing on the dock instead of being locked up like you were so convinced of?" Mike stared at Reggie.

Reggie took a step toward Mike, returning the stare and responded, "Mike, whatever piece of evidence that will make this case airtight died with Eliott. I didn't count on that, and for your information, I can man up…"

"What the hell is that supposed to mean?" Mike demanded. "And, may I remind you that in fact you already believed Eliott was dead. You're the one who suggested we look in the damned lake!" Mike took a step forward.

"Hey, you two, do I need to play ref here?" Grady demanded, readying himself to get in between Mike and Reggie. He waited a second, and went on, "Tensions are running high, and I get that. We all want our man, and we all concur he's right over there. Lack of sleep also doesn't help. Don't think for one second he's not getting some enjoyment out of watching us spin our wheels. The last thing we need is for him to see is us fighting with each other. Come on, we're stronger than him, so let's shake hands and get the hell out of here. We have a ton of work to do."

We headed to our cars.

"I said, shake hands."

Reggie and Mike both turned back and shook hands.

"Excellent. Now, let's all go back to headquarters, order some food and sort this all out."

Chapter 16

I got in the car with Mike, and for the first few minutes, we rode in silence. I had never seen Mike so angry. In fact, he was the most level-headed guy I had ever known outside of Matt. That was one of the main reasons I'd decided to partner up with him. After the devastating loss of Matt, I wasn't sure if I'd ever realize my lifelong dream, to have my own Private Detective agency. When Mike had come along and taken me under his wing, it was a natural fit.

Nothing had come easy for me, but I'd worked hard to get through college and proven myself with my internships, and it seemed like my dream had come true. Here we were with our first, knock 'em dead, headliner case...sort of.... I guess I should have been careful what I wished for... Okay, so who plans on having their first client turn into their first suspect? Unless you're reading some James Patterson novel, no one does. And now my steadfast partner was going off the proverbial rails due to some macho, imaginary match he had to win with Reggie. This called for diplomacy – which was not my strongest suit.

"So, um, Mike..."

"Don't you start."

"Not starting anything, just wondering if you're okay, and that's all."

"Fine Laura, fine. Just don't like the fancy FBI coming into town, saying they're going to do all this case solving and then coming up empty-handed. Mr. FBI gets to leave town when this is over, and we're the ones who are going to still be here, the ones that the townspeople will look at and wonder, 'What took you so long to get this thing solved?' You know the saying; out of sight, out of mind, well that's the FBI. Meanwhile, we're always here, right in the line of sight. It's not fair! And that stupid line of his... 'man up?' What was that about?"

"I think Grady has a point; we're all tired and mostly, like you said, we all want this solved yesterday. It's a lot of pressure, and to make matters worse, our first client is the prime suspect. That's plain insane!

Obviously, Reggie thought he had Arnold dead to rights, and didn't, so he took it out on you. He didn't answer your question, which I find interesting. Why didn't he, or couldn't he, hold the guy? He sounded so convinced that there was no possible way of Arnold getting out, and yet there he is, enjoying his moment in the sun."

"Hmmmm... There's gotta be some technicality Reggie slipped up on that has him so pissed off, and that's why he got in my face. That's the only thing I can think of. His case wasn't rock solid enough for the prosecutor to get an indictment, or he's telling the truth about the necessary piece of evidence having died with Eliott... Wait a minute... we never searched Eliott's house! See, this is what I love about you Laura, you keep me thinking straight, even when I let a guy like Reggie get to me." Mike patted me on the shoulder and grinned. "I'll bet you what we need and what Reggie needs to pin Arnold to the embezzlement wall is at Eliott's house. I'll run it by Grady. He can get a search warrant right away and take a look see over there, but we need to get on it before Arnold gets there first and destroys whatever it is. Right now, he thinks he's in the driver's seat. What a bunch of idiots, letting him see us at each other's throats, and then giving him the time to get rid of what will tie him to Eliott's death. We'll still have to get him for the rest of the murders, but this turn of events makes it harder. Damn it Laura, I know he's our guy, and as long as he's out there, no one's safe in this town.

"I'm sure Grady's already thought of it, but I'm going to remind him to put a tail on Arnold, just the same." Mike dialed Grady up and, naturally Grady was on top of it. He nodded to me to let me know that Arnold was already under surveillance. He also took the opportunity to tell Grady about the idea he had; that there might be a clue being hidden in Eliott's house, something that could possibly pin Arnold to Eliott's murder, or at the very least, be sufficient to hold Arnold for questioning while we built a case against him on the other murders.

Mike was grinning when he hung up the phone. "Grady told me it was a brilliant idea. But he said he'd only let me present the idea to Reggie if I remain calm. He also told me that Reggie's already at headquarters and asked what's taking us so long."

Great, a mark in the win column for Reggie and we were only pulling into the parking lot. Let the games begin.

On the way into the conference room adjacent to Grady's office, I, in turn, reminded Mike of Grady's admonishment; we all had to play well with each other while keeping our eyes on the prize.

"I figured I couldn't go wrong with pizza, so I ordered large pies that ought to be here in a few minutes, minus anchovies for Mike," Grady announced to the delight of all present at the meeting. "So, let's see what we've got, to date, before they arrive and you guys all get distracted with stuffing your faces."

The regular crew, including the entire detective squad, many of whom were trained in forensics, were all seated at a large oval wooden table. Pads and pens had been distributed so we could take notes. In the front of the room was a large white board with eight by ten color photos of all our victims, including Eliott and Gwen.

"Excuse me Loo," Joanna piped up, "has anyone heard from, or spoken to, Arnold's sister, Judy?"

"Excellent question," Grady said, as he turned around and wrote 'Judy' in the column labelled 'Witnesses' on an adjacent white board that had been set against the wall, "and I'm really glad you asked, because guess what your assignment is?"

The guys all started ribbing her, telling her, as the newest detective, that when you ask, you get assigned.

Joanna Hitchens smiled, "On it Loo."

"See how easy it is to all get along?" Grady grinned. "Chances are, there's a lot Arnold's sister can tell us, that is if she's willing to cooperate. Of course just the fact that we're talking to her at all will more than likely drive our 'friend' a bit crazy. We need something to push him along to show us a card, something up his sleeve, as soon as possible. If he really is our killer, he's not going to lay low that long. Meaning, he's going to make a move, and we need to be on top of him before anything happens to another woman in this town, or any of our neighboring towns. As Reggie's explained, he very well could expand his hunting grounds, just to throw us off our game and to make the chase more interesting to him, add a few more twists and turns. Right now, he seems to favor his particular dumping grounds, they're comfortable to him, his backyard so to speak. He reads his newspapers in there, can't get too much more in the zone than that.

"Okay, everyone, I'd like to introduce you to Reggie Martin, he's our local FBI guy. I know most of you already have had the pleasure of working with him, but some of you might not have. I spent the afternoon with him while he was questioning Arnold regarding another case they've been working. Seems Arnold and our latest victim, Eliott Potts, had a bit of a scam going. Essentially, they liked taking other people's money. Hey, in this tough economy, that's no real surprise, right? Well, I'll turn it over to Reggie and let him fill you in on the details."

"Hi guys and gals. Okay, so here's the long and short of it," Reggie said, as he shifted about and shoved his hands in his pockets. He surveyed the group, and went on, "I've been after these two for a long time and have been trying to pin their asses to the wall, permanently, but I never had Arnold pegged for a killer, at least not until today. I don't know for certain if he killed all the other women, outside of his wife Gwen, but it's looking suspicious, based on the identical nature of the murders. First off, I highly doubt we've got a copy-cat on our hands, since nothing's been released to the press as of yet. The only reason I can think of for his killing the other two is that they got in his way somehow. That's how a guy like Arnold operates; you annoy him, he disposes of you. Literally. A human being is nothing to him, not flesh and blood, not a life that's to be cherished and loved. He uses you for his own personal gain and then tosses you aside. Non Wrappe, Appleton, Eliott, and possibly Gwen, were either in the way, or expendable. So, leaving aside my reason for tailing him originally, we now need to nail his ass for murder.

"I started this investigation on both Arnold and his partner Eliott, who's now deceased, about six months ago when one of their clients contacted our office, claiming he and his wife had attempted to draw a significant portion of their funds out and were told that it wasn't possible, that according to their contract, they'd have to wait. This couple was further informed that if they wanted their funds any earlier than what the contract stipulated, there would be a severe penalty, amounting to a quarter of their total investment. These particular clients were already in trouble with a mortgage that was two months behind, and were desperate to get the money before they lost their home. Even though they'd sworn they'd never touch this investment, they'd both been laid off from their jobs and had been forced to hit their savings. Like everyone else who'd invested with Arnold and Eliott, they'd been receiving monthly statements reflecting profits from their investment portfolio. The time had arrived for them to draw on some of that profit, as opposed to continuing with reinvesting the monies, hence the phone call.

"This guy tried contacting Arnold a few more times, with no luck. He called the number he'd been given and it had been disconnected, and you guessed it, Arnold's not listed in the book and neither is Eliott. So he marched over to Arnold's office, only to find that it had a closed sign on the door. Imagine his surprise! Poof, the money's disappeared, or so say the clients.

But speak with Arnold and he tells a far different tale. He swears that the money is in an offshore account in the Cayman Islands still building interest, but it's a locked account, under a different brokerage investment name that he and Eliott had been using. According to Arnold, they were having problems with their old company name and it would all be fixed in a matter of a few months. Besides that, Arnold told us that the interest their clients are getting in the Cayman's is far better than what they were getting in the US, so they'd be much happier once they saw the final results. He has promised that everyone's money is completely safe and he can show me the paperwork, if I'm willing to work with him. He went on to say that it was unnecessary to have had him arrested, that had I asked him, he would have cooperated and answered all my questions. He added that no, he's not playing some sort of shell game; that's my overactive FBI imagination.

"On another angle, it turns out, our case and your case converge. One of the client's wives approached either Arnold or Eliott, and wound up dead. We discovered her body out in the woods. That would be Wendy Appleton. You're asking yourselves how we know she and her husband are clients. Laura discovered a key, hidden in Gwen's paint brush drawer in her private art studio at the Soundview Artists' Guild. The key was for a safety deposit box that contained a complete client list, and yes, Arnold is in the dark that we have this in our possession. I intend to keep it that way for a while.

"So, that's exactly where we were when I had to let him go, because believe it or not, he actually produced the paperwork that showed the entire client list and investment portfolios, including the portfolio of the initial guy who contacted me. I'm convinced this guy's Houdini with paperwork. We still don't know if the money has actually 'vanished.' Maybe Eliott knew what really happened, and that's why he's dead.

"In closing, if you can pin Arnold, based on what I've told you, please do, because you would make my career. I want this guy, badly. Especially, if he's killed these women on top of embezzlement and insider trading."

Nobody noticed that the pizza had arrived while Reggie was speaking, not even Mike. No one moved for a full two minutes after Reggie sat down, and no one uttered a word.

Chapter 17

When Tom walked into the room, I recognized him as the detective who'd been with us in the rowboat. He whispered to Grady, who covered his face with one hand and shook his head. Grady patted Tom on the shoulder and Tom then took a seat. Grady began, "Okay, everyone dig in and start eating; pizza's getting cold. I do have an announcement, though. Tom has some info that doesn't help us all that much; the DNA match on what he found in the boat came back as a positive for Eliott, but not for Arnold. It told us one thing that we already knew, that the boat was used to carry Eliott to where the Dive team retrieved him. It also told us that the string-like substance we found on the boat was the same as what was used to tie Gwen, Appleton and Non Wrappe's hands, so it definitely links all the murders. But the forensics still do not link us to the killer. All signs point to Arnold, but this guy is most assuredly slick and is not going down easily. That translates to, all hands on deck until we catch him. And we will do that!

"Joanna, go talk to Arnold's sister. Bring her in right away. And I don't want her comfortable. Got it?"

"Yes sir Loo."

"Reggie, if you know any judges that you can scramble a search warrant out of immediately for Eliott's house, we would be eternally grateful."

"Have a favorite on speed dial Grady. Consider it done," Reggie stood up, grabbed a slice and walked out of the room.

"Soon as he comes back with a go ahead, I want a full team to head over and turn that place upside down, and I mean upside down. Go get your gear ready, and take the pizza with you," Grady ordered.

The room cleared out.

"Mike, Laura, I've got a plan for you two, and you may not like it, but please listen up. I'm going on gut instinct, here."

"I'm here for you buddy."

"Me, too," I added.

"I know I can count on both of you, but this is going to sound silly, so please bear with me," Grady paused. "I need you to keep an eye on Adelaide. She's his next target."

"Hold on a second, you want us to babysit Adelaide?" Mike asked.

"No, I want you to protect her," Grady said. "She's a target, O'Malley."

I slowly nodded as the realization dawned, "She's seen and knows too much, Mike," I said.

"At least one of you gets it." Grady smacked Mike on the back. "Think, will you? Who came to you about seeing weird goings on in her woods? Who saw Brown leading a horse out to the road from the very spot where we discovered the bootprints?"

"You let your guys walk away with my pizza! I'm food deprived, not to mention sleep deprived. I keep forgetting that even though Adelaide's on the older side of life, she's sharp as a tack and knows those woods better than any one of us."

"Mike, she probably knows if a leaf's been moved. And Arnold has got to be aware of that. It never occurred to me that she could be in danger," I said, shoving my hands in my jeans pockets.

"That's why I want the two of you at her side, constantly, whether she likes it or not, and you know she's going to hate it. She's going to hate every second of it, but it's for her very survival. Laura, maybe you can stay there at night? You've got a permit to carry a weapon and we all know what a crack shot you are."

"I'll be happy to Grady, that is if she'll let me. I don't know if I can convince her that her life's in danger. Outside of me, she's the most independent woman I know."

Both Grady and Mike laughed.

"That's a compliment Laura," Grady grinned.

I smiled.

"Who's going to break it to her?" Mike asked.

"You, of course," Grady said. "And, you'll be sleeping in that barn of hers, because if you think I'm going to allow anything to happen to either Laura or Adelaide, you're out of your mind. I also know that there's no way on God's green earth that she'll go for both of you staying there. But, she doesn't have to know you're setting up guard in the barn. Just pack up your stuff first thing in the morning, or hide it."

"Oh, sure, like she won't notice that I'm sleeping there, and she can pick up when a leaf is out of place in the woods? Did you seriously think this through Grady? I might as well sleep in my car...oh, no you don't! I'll freeze my ass off! What kind of friend are you?"

"Mike, it's for the good of the community. We're catching a killer, remember? I'll make sure you get a commendation from the Governor for this."

"How's a commendation going to keep me from getting pneumonia?"

"You're creative; you'll come up with something. Car, or barn and either way, be very careful not to get caught, or you'll catch the wrath of Adelaide's cane," Grady winked.

"Gee, thanks old buddy. We sentinels will do what we must in order to see that the citizenry remains safe," Mike said with a sigh.

"Wow, I see you've been reading the dictionary I bought you. I'm very impressed. Now, both of you, skedaddle, you've got a lot of convincing to do. I'd hate to be in your shoes," Grady laughed.

"Skedaddle? Seriously. Sounds like you've been hanging around Adelaide," I said. "That reminds me, I hope she doesn't mind if I bring my dog Kola Bear. It might be a good thing, since he's got a deep bark that would scare any potential intruder off."

"Arnold's not your typical intruder Laura. Don't underestimate him. If I were you, I'd consider leaving Kola at home for this one so no harm comes to him. Psychos don't have any regard for animals. I don't mean to be harsh, but I'd rather lay it out for you then have something happen to Kola and have kept my mouth shut. I know how much you love your pup."

"Grady, much as I appreciate what you just said, Adelaide's radar will be up in a heartbeat, if I leave Kola at home. And she'd be even more worried about him than about her own situation. I get the feeling that she puts animals first, and she would want all of us to be together, or all of us to be in our respective homes."

"Laura's right," Mike agreed. "If Kola's in the same room with Laura, he should be fine. He'll bark like Laura said, and that will alert her and give her time to call you, or whoever's on duty, or both. Worst case scenario is, she has no time to call anyone, shoots, then calls. If that happens, all our problems are over. I kind of like that last one the best, her being the crack shot she is. Of course," he added, "she wouldn't shoot to kill, only to immobilize."

"Immobilize is right Grady. He's going to stand trial and go to prison for what we hope will be the rest of his life. There's no way I would kill him even if the opportunity presented itself. That's the easy way out. I want him to suffer behind prison walls." At first, it was surprising to hear myself expressing such harsh words, but I realized that Gwen's death had impacted me in some way.

"You and Reggie say that psychopaths and sociopaths have no feelings and emotions? That may be true, but somewhere along the line, while he's sweating it out in a jail cell, year after year, day after day, I'd like to believe that a brain cell lights up, even if it's for one minute out of a month, that screams in agony. And that's good enough for me. That's a reason to not shoot to kill."

"They say there's nothing like your first case to shape you into who you become for your career; I'd say you're well on your way Laura, but never let your guard down. You've got great instincts! Now the two of you, get going. Be safe, and thank you." Grady's phone buzzed, and before he answered, he said, "I've got my hands full with Annie asking for updates every hour,"

"After that speech, I half expect a blessing of some sort. Good luck with Annie," Mike said.

"Stay warm, my friend," Grady said.

"Annie's doing her job, just like we are, and she means well," I said.

Mike and I left Grady's office and bumped into Reggie, running down the hallway, waving the search warrant and grinning like a wild man.

"Out of my way, I have to get this to Grady and get over to Eliott's house before Arnold gets there," Reggie yelled.

"It's a well-oiled machine Laura. Thank God he's on our side. He's a human steamroller."

"Yeah, watch out, the steamroller's back," I said, flattening myself against the wall to avoid being squashed by Reggie, who must have thrown the warrant on Grady's desk, turned around and was once again aiming for us.

"Will you two get out of my way and get to work!" Reggie demanded.

Mike ducked and barely avoided being struck by Reggie's elbow. "Did he do that on purpose?"

"No I don't think so. He's just taking it personally that he had to let Arnold go, and he wants to fix it. You just momentarily got in his way."

"Yeah, he's a bull in a china shop, point well taken. I'm staying out of his way and doing my thing. Let's hope Reggie finds what he needs over at Eliott's and let's hope you and I have a quiet, peaceful evening at Adelaide's. Why do I get the feeling we're in for one hell of a night?"

"With any luck, the White Lady will join us," I smiled.

"Jensen, you're not funny. Not even a little bit. Go get your dog."

JEAN MARIE WIESEN

Chapter 18

I ran home to let Kola out, feed him, throw some clothes in my overnight bag, and prepare to head over to Adelaide's house. Mike and I had concocted a solid enough plan that, if followed to the letter, ought to outwit her. She was a crafty one, and I could tell, in the short period of time that I'd known her, that pulling the proverbial wool over her eyes was not going to be a simple task.

The car was packed with all the essentials for a few nights stay at Adelaide's, including Kola, his food and a couple of his favorite toys. I was ready to go, when my phone rang. It was Penelope Gatsby from The Guild informing me that there would be a memorial for Gwen this coming Sunday, two days from now. She was inquiring whether or not I'd like to attend, since she anticipated an extensive guest list. I told her that I would do my best and greatly appreciated her contacting me. She cried and thanked me for my efforts.

I hung up and cried, too.

I stopped my car at the two oak trees and waited for Mike, as we'd agreed. He pulled up behind me within a couple of minutes.

"Hey, you know your trees?"

"Very funny O'Malley. Let's see how good you are at following me with your lights off. Then, let's see how good you are at finding the barn in the dark."

"All I have to do is follow your tail lights, and the barn's the big building on the right, so I should be fine, unless you decide to run into something," he grinned.

"You honestly don't think Adelaide will be able to tell the difference between one car coming into her driveway and two cars coming?" I asked.

"We'll turn them off at the same time and she'll be none the wiser. Remember, I'll flick my flashlight on and you shut down your engine, okay?" Mike said.

"Okay, got it, but you'd better be right about this. She catches us and it's on you."

"Right, I'm the brains of the outfit."

"Didn't say that; you're the one trying to deceive an old lady."

"Ouch, say it that way, and it sounds terrible." Mike grimaced.

Just then, an owl sounded off.

Mike jumped. "What was that?"

"A barred owl telling you how terrible you are," I laughed. "Now, get in your Jeep and let's get this mission underway, you big chicken."

"You sure that's all that was?"

"I thought you were this big outdoors guy? Boy, are you in for a surprise. A few nights in Adelaide's barn and you'll never be the same: coyotes, bears…"

"Bears?"

"Someone said they saw a black bear in this area a couple of weeks ago, but I'm sure he's moved on by now. Oh, and raccoons nibble on toes, so be sure to tuck yourself in to your sleeping bag and zip it all the way up."

"You're hysterical Laura. I'll sleep in the hayloft, lift the ladder up and no critter will get me."

"Perfect, then when you have to run to my aid, you'll forget to drop the ladder in place, fall and break something. Excellent planning ahead. The other option is convince Adelaide that you have to stay in the house with us and then you won't have to sneak around in the barn. You know she's going to catch you eventually. By the way, what was the reason you gave her for my staying with her?"

"I more or less told her the truth, that all of us, including Reggie, suspect Arnold, and how dangerous we believe him to be. Turns out, she's excited to have you stay with her, she's got a movie all set up and dinner cooking, so let's get going. Me, I get nothing other than what I've loaded on my iPad and whatever I can heat up on a Sterno stove, which is a can of beans."

"Beans for dinner? Good thing you're sleeping with the wild animals. On that note, let's go."

We started our engines in unison and made our way down Adelaide's driveway with me in the lead, as we'd planned, and Mike following closely behind with his headlights off. It seemed luck was on our side. It was a new moon, so very little natural light would be cast on Mike's movements. The exterior of Adelaide's house was pretty dark as well. She didn't believe in sensor lights around the house or barn; she felt they disrupted the night creatures hunting patterns. The only lighting she allowed was low level lanterns, one on either side of the front door and one at the main door of the barn. If she needed to go to the barn to tend to any of her animals during the night, she used a flashlight to find her way along the path. She kept a baby monitor inside the barn and one in her kitchen so she would be alerted to any emergencies among the goats, lambs or donkeys. And, of course her Cocker Spaniel Chloe would bark if anyone approached the house unannounced. In short, Adelaide felt safe enough in her secluded environment. Mike and I intended to keep her that way.

I pulled right up to the front porch, inching a bit forward so I would have Mike's signal in my line of vision prior to shutting off the engine. He had parked his Jeep just uphill from the barn, so when he turned his ignition off, he would roll forward far enough to be out of sight, in case Adelaide came out to the barn in the middle of the night for some unforeseen disturbance with the animals.

I focused for the signal, and there it was.

A short flicker of light.

I breathed a sigh of relief.

"What do you know Kola, phase one went without a hitch. The rest should be a snap, and you get to hang out with a little girl for the evening."

I retrieved my bag and other necessities from my Pilot, and plunked them at the front door.

"You're late," Adelaide announced, opening the door. "Beef stew's warming on the stove, fire is lit, and Chloe's bored to tears waiting for Kola. Casablanca is cued up in my DVR player. Almost forgot, my shotgun is loaded and leaning next to the coat rack, so be careful when you hang up your coat, wouldn't want it to go off prematurely."

"Shotgun?"

"Ever since my husband died, I have to do something to protect myself. It was his and he taught me how to shoot it; it's a lovely Winchester twelve gauge. Chloe can do just so much to protect me, especially with all the nuts walking in my woods these days. So I'm glad I hung on to it. I'm also glad that you're here, even though I don't believe this Arnold fellow is after me. There's nothing that I've seen that can implicate him in anything, at least I don't think so. Granted, the guy's a bit on the odd side, reading newspapers while sitting on the same rock and then leaving them there, as if he's watching for someone or something.

"Okay, enough of speculating about what I did or didn't see. Let's have a wonderful evening, it's been a long time since I've entertained anyone in my home and I'm looking forward to it. First, let's eat."

"It smells fantastic Adelaide," I said, hanging up my coat, keeping a sharp eye on the shotgun. I kicked off my boots, set my bag down, headed for the kitchen and Adelaide showed me where to store Kola's food. While I helped her in the kitchen, Kola and Chloe had found an old towel, and they busied themselves with a game of Tug O' War in front of the roaring fire. The flames flickered across the enormous picture window overlooking Trout Brook Valley, and the fire warmed the entire room. I felt so at home here, as did my pup.

I decided to take a moment to text both Annie and Mike to let them know that all was well. We'd dubbed Adelaide's house Eagle's Nest, which seemed appropriate considering there were actual nests nearby. Once the texts were sent, I felt I could relax. I didn't want Annie to worry, but I did want her to know exactly where I was, just in case anything went wrong. I had total faith in Mike, but what if something happened to him? We were isolated out here, a good mile from the nearest neighbor, and it would take a bit of time for reinforcements to arrive. I knew I could count on Annie to move heaven and earth to get help to us if the chips were really down. Knowing her, she'd have the State Trooper helicopter circling overhead and every town police department with their canines out within minutes, if necessary. She had that much moxie, and the authorities listened when she barked.

"Alright, come on over here and help me with this tray. I'd like to eat in front of the fire. The table's already set, and I'll carry in the tea," Adelaide said, dragging her cane along but not spilling one drop of tea.

"I don't believe in that fancy bread that everyone gets, I like my good old fashioned chunky bread that I can dip right into my stew. It soaks up the broth just fine, and doesn't leave all the flaky crumbs in there making a mess of the stew that's been slow cooking all day. Hope you like it," Adelaide raised her tea cup to clink with mine. "To Chloe and Kola and our friendship."

"To our pups and our new friendship," I said.

I dug into the stew without any hesitation, dipping the bread in and biting off a piece, to Adelaide's satisfaction. It was the first time I'd ever noted a glint in her eye, a hint of contentment.

"The stew is delicious, and you're correct about the bread, chunky is better. This reminds me of the stew my mom used to make on winter evenings when we were kids. It brings back sweet memories, thank you."

"We're not going to travel too far down memory lane, are we? I don't want to have too much of a moment. A brief one now and then is okay, but lingering isn't good for the soul. Bet you've never heard that saying before. My husband used to say that. He had a whole list of them, never wrote them down, and my memory isn't what it used to be, but that one stands out."

"What was his name?"

"Thought you'd never ask. It was Henry. And, before you ask, no we never did have children, only dogs, or pups, as you refer to them. He figured that they never talk back to you," she chuckled. "I agreed with him, but the only problem with that is, there's no one to take care of you when you get old."

"Mike says your parents died in a car accident and you don't see much of your brothers. That's too bad."

"My brothers fought after my parents died, over money, and I didn't want to have anything to do with it, so I moved away to begin my education in criminal justice with my boyfriend Matt. He was killed on 9/11."

"This is turning into a cheery conversation, almost as if we were discussing the killings in my woods."

"Funny you should bring that up, I happen to have a couple of questions on that very subject, beginning with Brown. When did you first notice Brown, and how often did you see him, or her? Also, did you ever see Brown near the rock where you found the newspapers?"

"Interesting line of questioning Laura, because I've never connected the two until now," Adelaide said, spooning the last of the stew soup into her mouth. She sipped some tea, set the cup down and poured some more into both our cups before proceeding. "I always saw this person with his or her hood up, so I was never able to tell if it was a he or a she, but this person was tall, and as I told you, earlier, dressed entirely in brown, right down to the boots."

"How tall do you think Brown was? Say six foot, or less, or more?"

"It's tough to say, I never was close enough to tell, I only watched from my driveway. Do you think that costume was intentional, so I wouldn't be able to identify Brown later on?"

"Could be." I sipped some tea, glanced at the pups curled up in front of the fireplace, and reached over and grabbed a poker to stir the fire. "Was Brown standing near any of the trees that you could point out, so that we can use it as a measuring stick, of sorts?"

Adelaide pointed her finger at me and said, "That's using your noggin, you know I can identify every one of my trees." An enormous smile creased her face as she sat back in her chair and stared into the fire.

I cleared the dishes, put them in the dishwasher, made some more tea, and then we settled in to watch Casablanca.

Chapter 19

I was pulled from a deep sleep by a chorus of a variety of animal noises, some of which were emanating from the baby monitor in the kitchen. In addition, Kola had his paw on my stomach and was growling.

"Glad to see you're awake Sleeping Beauty," Adelaide said.

I looked up to see her standing next to my bed, dressed in a nightgown, flannel pants, heavy boots, a woolen hat pulled down to her eyebrows, her winter parka unzipped, her cane hanging from one arm and her Winchester cradled in the other. "How do I look?"

"You're worried about how you look?"

"If I'm going to die, I want to look as nice as possible. I realize it's the middle of the night, and there's not much a person can do when they're awakened so abruptly, but again, do I look okay?"

"The outfit could use some work, but it's passable under the circumstances," I rubbed my eyes and reached for my Glock Nineteen nine millimeter that I'd stowed in the most obvious and uncomfortable of places; underneath my pillow. "Sounds like everyone in your barn is going crazy, and Kola never growls unless there's something going on, so I'm guessing we've got a visitor."

"I've got two flashlights, one for you so you can check around the house, while I go up to the barn."

"Opposite Adelaide; I'll go to the barn while you check around the house. Only I'd prefer you do it from inside and take the phone with you when you make the rounds.

"No arguing either, because you'll lose." I dressed quickly, grabbed my cell phone and the flashlight, and ran to the front door, "Lock it behind me. Be sure the windows are locked, too. I'm leaving Kola with you. He'll attack anyone who tries to break in. If all else fails, call 9-1-1 right away. Is that clear?"

Adelaide's eyes narrowed. "Clear. You come back Laura, do you understand me?" Her hand rested on Kola's head.

"You have my word."

I heard the latch slip into place as I inched my way off the porch, again grateful for the mostly moonless night. I held the Glock close to my body, pointed downward, and began a slow trot up the incline to the barn. I'd remembered to silence my cell phone. Last thing I needed was for it to ring and have a bunch of dogs barking, giving away my position to whoever might be out there, aside from Mike.

Making my way along, the thought crossed my mind that this was the exact scene that played out in every horror movie I'd ever seen: The dumb girl leaving the safety of the room, or in this case, the house, walking into the obvious trap laid by the killer as the audience screams, "No! Stay where you are! Are you an idiot?"

I wondered how my scene would end.

Mike and I had worked out a code if this situation arose and one of us needed to check on the other. Well, here we were, and I hoped my notoriously miserable whistle wouldn't fail me when I needed it the most. I'd begged him to come up with something different, but he'd insisted on a whistle, said that's what everyone used. We'd agreed on three short bursts. He claimed it would sound akin to an owl and our killer wouldn't know the difference.

I stopped a short distance from the barn to get my breathing under control and to listen for any sounds out of the ordinary, and mostly for Mike. I took a deep breath in through my nose and was letting it out through my mouth, but I never finished the exhale. Suddenly, I felt a sharp pain and heard a sickening thud. It felt as if someone had swung a bat across the back of both my calves. The air I'd let out was instantaneously sucked back in as I landed, first on my knees, then face down with my Glock under my stomach. I lay there, forcing myself not to scream out in pain, trying to determine whether or not I had the energy to turn over and shoot whoever it was, when I felt a hand, first in between my shoulder blades, pressing me down, then another clammy hand against my neck.

"I'm the one you call Brown, my attacker said in a muffled, but decidedly male voice, "and I'm telling you now, you're gonna lose, so back off before I kill you too. Consider this a gift."

From my peripheral vision, I could see a brown, hooded sweatshirt with the drawstring pulled tightly around the face so I couldn't distinguish the features. This guy was smart. He smelled of garlic, but so did lots of people, so that wasn't exactly an identifying factor.

"Stay down and don't move…and. stop looking for me. Listen to what I'm saying or your friends will start dying, one at a time, and I'm not gonna tell you who's first. You and your partner better find another case to work. I like killing and no one's gonna stop me – especially not amateurs like you.

"I'm gonna let go of you now. Stay put, or you're dead, got it?"

I nodded.

"Smart girl."

He did indeed let go, and I braced for the death blow I was sure would come. When it didn't, I rolled quickly onto my side. If I was gonna go, it wouldn't be without a fight. My Glock came up with my finger lightly on the trigger. I aimed at what I was sure would be my assailant, only there was nobody in sight. I sat on one hip, continuing to aim, traversing the hillside from the barn down to the house, and back again. He had disappeared into the woods in a matter of seconds, which it seemed to me was totally impossible. It was at least seventy five yards from where I was to the tree line. Granted, he'd been smart to camouflage himself by wearing the color brown, and it was a very dark night, but still, it was awfully fast to cover all that ground. I slipped my Glock into my waistband and then shone my flashlight around to be sure, but he was definitely gone. I put a call in to Grady and hurriedly told him what happened. I told him I was going to check on Mike, to hurry up and get over here, and to send.an ambulance just in case. He said I didn't need to tell him any of that – he was already in his car and heading my way.

I looked toward the house and noticed the porch lights had been switched on. Immediately, I phoned Adelaide to let her know that I was okay and was on my way to the barn to check on the animals. She said she'd put some water on for me to make some tea, and to hurry back, that Kola was whining. I told her to expect some company, but not to worry; a kindly officer would be knocking on her door shortly, and I asked her to please show him in.

I started over to the barn and almost tripped on a log a few feet away. That must have been what he'd hit me with, the bastard! No wonder I'd gone right down. It probably came from the stack of logs on Adelaide's porch. That meant he'd been on her porch, and we hadn't heard him, which worried me.

I hesitated before entering the barn. My heart was in my throat as I contemplated what I might encounter. That's when I realized how much pain I was in. My gun remained in my waistband as I dialed Mike. While I waited for an answer, my legs buckled under me, and I went down on my knees. I was in the process of trying to stand back up, when I heard Mike's voice respond groggily.

"Yeah? Huh? Where am I? My head hurts. I must've got whacked in the head. Laura, is that you? Are you okay?"

"Mike! You're alive! Don't move! I'm outside the barn and help's on the way. I'll be there in a minute, okay?"

"You say so. My head really hurts. You have any aspirin?"

"You know the rules, if you've been hit on the head, no aspirin, nothing at all until you've been checked out, especially if you lost consciousness. Just hang on!" Mike's speech was a bit slurred, causing me some concern.

"I hate rules."

"It's so good to hear your voice."

"What's taking you so long Laura?" As we talked, I was finally able to stand back up and get my balance.

"Be right there Mike. I tripped, that's all. No big deal. I don't suppose you happened to see who hit you?"

"Nope. I was sound asleep. Then the animals started making a bunch of noise. Next thing I know, you called."

I pushed the heavy barn door open with some difficulty and limped inside.

"Hey, you're walking funny, what happened?"

"Brown's our man Mike. He's the killer, and he sort of ran into me after he belted you." I switched on my flashlight. "Boy, did he get you. No wonder you've got a headache. You're black and blue all over your forehead. Black eye, too. If I didn't know better, I'd say he hit you with the same log he hit me with. Only, I'm guessing he didn't take the time to have a conversation with you?"

Mike tried to sit up, grimaced, and lay back down, "You spoke with him?"

"After he whacked me across the legs…"

"Why were you even outside?" Mike grunted.

"Because, there were all sorts of noises coming from the barn, and Adelaide woke me up, armed to the teeth, so I was headed up here to check on you. Okay, maybe not the best idea, in hindsight. Anyway, he ID'ed himself. He actually said he was 'Brown' so now we know Brown is the killer... Hey, how did he know we call him that? Anyway, we still don't have an accurate description, but he did speak to me, and even though he tried to disguise his voice, I'm pretty sure it's Arnold. He's the right build, too. He threatened that if we keep coming after him, he's going to kill us off, one after the other. Nice guy, right.

"I called Grady. He's on his way and so are his guys. Mike, whoever this guy is, he's fast. I couldn't get a shot off before he got to the tree line. And he's also crafty. This guy knew you and I were here. How's that possible?"

"Last part's easy; he's following us, or he's set up camp around here and as we thought, we're in his hunting grounds. In other words, these aren't only Adelaide's woods, they're his woods too. It's our business now to change that."

"He wasn't wearing gloves. He had his slimy hand on the back of my neck and my back, so maybe they can get some DNA from my jacket. Since Arnold's been arrested, they've got something to match it to."

"You're thinking like a detective Laura. I'd smile, but it hurts too much. It's kind of scary that he identified himself as Brown to you. That means he's listening in on our conversations, somehow."

"We'll have to tell Grady to have our offices swept for listening devices when he gets here," I said.

"What did you want to tell me?" Grady said, walking into the barn with the ambulance crew right behind him. "Oh, wow, you two look awful! I've got one of the officers going down to stay with Adelaide. I know how much she loves having us here," Grady laughed. "Your forehead's a DNA mine site Mike. Why don't we just bag your entire head and take it to the lab."

"Very funny. Get me the refusal form and a glass of water with a bottle of aspirin, and I'll be on my way, or back to sleep, or whatever," Mike groaned.

"Not a chance hard head. You're going to get a scan first, to see if you've got any brains in there and secondly, to see if they're damaged, which we already know the answer to, but we're supposed to check just the same. Officially, that is. It's the liability thing. They make us do it, so be a good boy."

"Grady, you're a pain in the ass."

"Thanks, love you too. Once I'm finished with you O'Malley, I need to speak to you, Laura, that is, after you've been checked out. Don't worry, the log's being put into evidence, but we have to get your complete statement." Grady hesitated for a minute, shuffled his feet, walked over and grabbed Mike's hand and mine, "I don't know what I'd do if anything happened to either of you."

Grady walked out of the barn, the ambulance crew loaded Mike onto the stretcher, I leaned down and gave Mike a quick hug, and off he went to the hospital. I'd also been checked by the medic and deemed to be okay, no X-Rays necessary, but he left me some ice packs for the bruising and swelling that was setting in.

My jacket was bagged and tagged for evidence, and my neck was swabbed for DNA residue.

Next was my interview with Grady, and that could be done seated in the house with a nice cup of tea. We'd decided that keeping this information from Adelaide any longer wasn't going to help anyone down the road.

One thing was definite; we were on Brown's trail and we had rattled him enough for him to show himself, a mistake that would lead us to him in the end. Criminals seem to think they can outsmart the law, but eventually their egos trip them up. They covet the limelight; no fun to remain in the shadows forever. I recalled one of my Criminal Justice Professors telling me something along those lines. Brown was proving that theory to be on the money, I thought to myself as I walked, with some discomfort, and some assistance from Grady, back to the house.

Chapter 20

Y ou're a sight for sore eyes," Adelaide said, standing in the doorway. She put the shotgun back down next to the coat rack, looked up at Grady and said, "Thank you for bringing my young lady back to me." A few tears rolled down her cheeks and onto my neck as she hugged me. "Don't you ever frighten me like that again, is that clear?"

"Perfectly."

Kola bounded over, and would have knocked me over if Grady hadn't been standing right behind me. He put his paws on my shoulders and looked me in the eyes, tail wagging.

"I think he's trying to tell you something," Grady said.

"Yup, and it's that the next time he wants to come with me so he can take a clean bite out of Brown."

"You saw Brown? On my property?" Adelaide asked. "Is that what all the noise in the barn was about?"

"Okay, one question at a time," Grady said. "Yes, yes, and yes, and there's more. First, Laura really needs to sit down, preferably with some pillows underneath her legs and some ice packs, if you've got them. A cup of tea would be fantastic, too. Once we get her settled, I'll tell you everything."

"You will?" I looked at him.

"Might as well. She'll figure it out anyway."

Adelaide nodded, as if to say "Yes, I will!" She disappeared into the kitchen while Grady helped me over to the couch, and she was back in a moment with the ice packs. With a bit of maneuvering, I was able to get into a comfortable position with the ice and pillows, and Adelaide soon reappeared with a fragrant cup of tea. Once I'd swallowed a couple of sips, I began to feel a bit better, and related to both of them, in full detail, what had occurred from the moment I'd left Adelaide's house that night.

Adelaide was startled to discover that Mike had taken up residence in her barn. She was visibly shaken when we told her that he'd been attacked by Brown. It took us some time to reassure her that he would recover with his brains fully intact.

"Makes me want to track him down myself and serve up justice the old fashioned way." Adelaide shook her cane for emphasis. "Drink your tea Laura, we've work to do."

"Adelaide, you're not going anywhere," Grady said. "Let me rephrase that," he said, catching the sideways glance from her.

"You'd better, sonny boy."

I grinned at Grady and waited to see how he was going to dig his way out of this one.

Grady cleared his throat, smoothed his hair, re-tied his shoe laces, and took a sip of tea.

"I'm not getting any younger waiting for this fancy explanation of yours, Mr. Lieutenant, of why I need to stay put in my own home." Adelaide tapped her cane on the floor.

"Please, call me Grady. No need for the formality of…"

"Fine Grady. Move along with your explaining, then."

"Okay. There's no need to actually stay in your house, per se, but could you at the very least not go out on the trails by yourself until we've apprehended the killer?"

Adelaide patted Kola while considering Grady's request. She looked back and forth between the two of us, and said, "I've a demand of sorts of my own."

"All right, seeing as this has been a very tough situation for you, I'll negotiate. It's not every day that someone has a killer roaming around in their backyard."

"No, it isn't, and I'm glad you recognize that. These woods have been so gentle to me for all these years, a special place for me and my Henry, who's no longer here. Right now, the most important things in my life are Chloe and the wildlife, and of course, Mike and Laura. So, here's my demand. I want you to allow both of them to stay with me until this is over with. Will you do that Grady?"

"Oh, that's all you want? Sure, I don't see a problem with that at all. I know Mike'll be happy to stay here. He and Laura were both pretty worried about you, which is why they came up with their plan to stay here, or in Mike's case in your barn, in the first place. Right Laura?"

"Absolutely Adelaide. So Mike will move out of the barn and stay in your other bedroom…with your permission, of course," I said.

166

"He might not like Casablanca, though," Adelaide said.

"We'll make him watch it. Besides, as long as he has pizza, he doesn't care what he watches. But I have a demand of my own. Don't let him order it with anchovies."

"Agreed, no anchovies. My house is not going to stink like fish, and it's too cold to open all the windows. If he wants anchovies, he can eat them in the barn and sleep there, too," Adelaide grinned.

"Okay, then it's settled," Grady said. "For the rest of tonight I'm going to have a couple of officers outside patrolling the grounds, and one inside while you ladies get some sack time. It's only four in the morning, so you've got a couple of hours to catch some beauty sleep. Meanwhile, we'll go into the woods and see if Brown left any other evidence-- aside from the log -- or some kind of a trail we can follow. I like Mike's theory that he has a camp around here somewhere. It's got to be close by for him to be so aware of what's going on."

"I know it's not your favorite area Grady, but it would make sense for him to have an encampment up by the reservoir. If he's been hiding out in the woods for any length of time, he's gotta have a hidden stash of food and supplies somewhere, and that's a likely spot," I said. "The reservoir is far enough off the beaten path, but close to where he needs to go, either by boat or horseback, without raising too much suspicion if he's seen by hikers. And don't forget that Adelaide saw him leading the horse. If he's on foot, he can move rather fast, as I witnessed earlier, and it's apparent that he knows these woods like the back of his hand

"I think you're right about that Laura. If Arnold and Brown are one and the same, then he's learned to blend into both worlds equally well, that of the woodsman and the world of finance. Who in their right mind would suspect a financial type of hideous crimes like these? What a great cover."

"Brilliantly plotted out," I agreed. "You're procrastinating."

"Am not."

"Are too."

Grady sighed. "I really hate the reservoir area."

"Chicken," Adelaide said.

"Come on, you too?" Grady hung his head.

"The White Lady is very nice. You just need to know how to talk to her," Adelaide smiled, stood up, and headed to her bedroom.

"She's kidding, right? Talk to the White Lady? I know that was a joke, it had to be."

I chuckled, stood up myself, although more slowly than Adelaide, and went off to the guest room with Kola in tow. Even though it hurt me to laugh, the look on Grady's face was priceless. "Have fun Grady."

"Neither of you are very funny. Hope you know that. That episode took five years off my life and you're joking about me going back up there. If I remember correctly Laura, you were running down that hill as fast as the rest of us."

"I wasn't running from her, Grady. She actually waved at me. She's the friendly one. I told you that when we were up there. It's the other one you have to watch out for, Chrisloki. He's the scary one. The White Lady will protect you and your team, really."

"You seriously believe that?"

"I do Grady, and you would too if you'd seen the way she looked at me. I'll bet she's been looking out for us all along. The more I think about it... okay, this is going to sound completely insane, but I'm beginning to think that Chrisloki is somehow tied to Brown and the White Lady is on our side. That's why some of the clues popped up in odd places.

Grady was looking at me with interest, so I continued, "Do you have any other explanation for how the cleats and my hair ties wound up in those particular bushes, especially when none of us put them there? It was as if they were placed there for us to find. I've no idea why my hair ties were there. That implicates me, which makes no sense, unless they were clues from the White Lady."

"So you think she wanted you to be the one to find them, or for you to think they fell out of your pocket? Maybe...

"But, anyway, I'm not supposed to be afraid of her, you say? Only him? And, she's protecting us? Fine, and that's supposed to make sense?

"Say good night Laura."

"Good night Grady."

"Good night Laura."

"Will you two quit your chattering," Adelaide said from behind her closed door.

"Good night Adelaide," we said in unison.

"Good night, you two. And, for your information, this is NOT an episode out of The Walton's."

Chapter 21

In what felt like five minutes, but must have been several hours, my phone rang. It was Mike, begging for a ride back to Adelaide's.

"You sure all your brains are where they're supposed to be?" I laughed.

"Very funny, esteemed partner of mine. Are you sure your legs are still attached? Just wait until you try and stand up. Yeah, I'm guessing you're not even out of bed yet. In other words, you haven't tried out those sore legs of yours. What a pair we are, huh?"

"But enough about our bumps and bruises... There's a lot of buzz here at the hospital about an incoming storm, and it sounds as if we're in for a rough time of it. They're doing all kinds of prep work here, so we need to be sure we've got plenty of supplies at Adelaide's house, just in case. Check with Adelaide and see what she might need in the way of food and batteries, and we'll get everything after you pick me up, okay?"

"Oh, just great, a killer out in the woods and now a storm on the way. Does the storm have a name?" I asked.

"Sure enough; Sandy."

"Interesting; could be a woman's name or a man's. Storms named after women usually wreak more havoc. Although now that I think about it, Andrew did an enormous amount of damage, so I'm not so sure my theory holds true. When's it expected to make landfall?"

"They say by Monday. That gives us a few days to prepare, or best scenario, catch this bastard and then hunker down somewhere to celebrate." Mike sighed.

"I'll let Adelaide know about the storm. Grady's out looking for Brown's encampment. I'll call him and let him know too, although I'm sure he's aware of the weather, right?"

"Maybe Chrisloki's interfered with his transmission," Mike chuckled.

"I'm not even going to ask what kind of drugs they gave you Mom. See you in about an hour."

"Nothing stonger than aspirin, I swear!"

"Then, it's patently obvious you're pizza deprived. One hour, be dressed."

"Yes Ma'am."

I rolled over into a sitting position and dangled my feet, gritting my teeth while positioning my hands on the edge of the bed. Mike was correct, my legs were quite sore. I don't know what else I'd anticipated. I had been smacked with a log, after all. Adelaide had given me some topical cream that she swore by, to help with the bruising and pain. I reached for the glass of water and the bottle of aspirin she'd placed on my bedside table. I opened the bottle, slid three tablets on my palm, popped them into my mouth and swallowed them down with the water. Luckily my legs were covered by my pajama pants. No way was I going to look at them; that would make it hurt more. Suck it up and get up, I thought, as I rose and stiffly shuffled to the bathroom.

Kola followed me, wagging his tail.

"Yeah boy, I'm going to make it."

"Oh Adelaide, are you up? I asked, making my way into the kitchen, "I've got news. Some good, some not so good. Which would you prefer, first?"

"Good morning, Lazy Bones. Coffee is on. About time you got up. The day will be half over if you don't get moving, and your poor pup will be starving if you don't feed him.

"If you're going to tell me about Storm Sandy, I already know. It's all over the news. I might live out in the woods, but I do have TV with news channels. That, and Officer Kindly let me in on the information as well. He made up a list of necessities that he said I should send you out for when you go pick up Mike.

"Here's your coffee and bran muffin." Adelaide placed them on the kitchen table, which was set with a vase full of yellow daisies.

"Thanks Adelaide. Mike phoned me and we made plans to shop after I pick him up. I guess Grady chose the right guy to watch out for you," I said, as I looked over the list Adelaide handed me.

"Kola, come on and I'll let you out. Officer Kindly will keep an eye on you while I make your breakfast. If you're good, he might even throw a ball to you," I said.

"How are your legs Laura?" Adelaide asked, when she saw me shuffling along.

"They're a bit stiff, but if I walk a little and put some more cream on them, they'll be okay. Both Mike and I are very lucky, all things considered. We don't need a storm to hamper the investigation, but I'm sure Brown's thrilled by the news, if he even knows about it. I guess he does; he seems to be aware of everything that's going on. With a storm of this magnitude on its way, Grady's going to need every bit of manpower at his disposal to hunt Brown down, both during the storm and immediately afterwards. Grady will also have to keep an eye on Brown's primary targets, namely us. Brown will know that Grady and his force are spread thin, and try to take full advantage of it, I'm sure. In short, Grady's got a very brief window of time to find this guy, or we're going to have to move you to a more easily protected place, Adelaide. We'll have no choice. This is your life we're talking about."

"I'm not leaving Laura, and that's final. This is my home and I've got a barn full of animals to take care of. Grady has a few days to catch Brown, so let's give them to him and see what he comes up with. He also has you and Mike. I have faith in all of you."

Chapter 22

Sandy was forecasted to arrive in our area on Tuesday, and today was Wednesday. That gave us six full days to find our killer. No problem, I tried to convince myself, as I drove down Adelaide's driveway, knowing full well that we'd never been confronted with anything like this, neither the storm that was relentlessly advancing, nor a serial killer who was bent on taking our lives. Were we going to triumph at the last moment, or were we going to be screwed by both Mother Nature and a psychopathic sociopath?

Pulling into Soundview Medical Center, I pondered whether or not Mike held the key to our situation.

"Howdy partner," Mike said. "They wouldn't let me walk out on my own, some dumb thing about rules. You know how much I can't stand rules, especially when I have to be wheeled out in this chair like some old guy," he continued. He frowned a bit when the attendant tried to help him get in the passenger side of my car. "I can do this part, myself, thank you very much. I'm not helpless."

"Mike, the guy's just doing his job. Don't be so gruff."

"Yeah, okay. I just want to get out of here, and get going on our errands. Sorry pal." He patted the attendant on the back. The man nodded, shook his head, and wheeled the chair away for the next person.

Kola greeted Mike as if he'd been gone for a year. "Now, that's what I needed, a puppy hug. I'm feeling tons better already.

"Let's get this chariot in gear Laura, we've got so much to do before this storm hits and so little time, it's unbelievable. I need to be one hundred percent, and so do you, if we're going to catch this guy. When the storm hits, we lose most of Grady's guys, plus we might have to help out with the storm's aftermath. They're saying it's some kind of super storm, whatever that is. All I know is it's got to be manna from heaven for our killer. Talk about the perfect cover for him to get to Adelaide. No matter what, we can't leave her unprotected! If I didn't know better,

I'd think it was special ordered from that Chrisloki guy, or whatever he is. Do you think the White Lady can help us out with this…oh man I got hit harder on the head than I thought I did. I can't believe I just asked you that?"

"Me either. Please don't run that scenario by Adelaide. She will probably suggest having the White Lady over for tea and a bran muffin to talk it over."

Mike and I glanced at each other, and we burst into near hysterics.

"Now, I feel badly for making fun of Adelaide behind her back," I said, when our guffaws had finally subsided to the occasional giggle

"Me, too. What if some of that stuff's true?"

"Well, I've seen the White Lady with my own eyes, but ghosts organizing a storm? I refuse to buy it Mike. That's coincidence, pure and simple."

"Adelaide would disagree, and so would a lot of other people like her. They'd tell you that there are no such things as coincidences. What do you say to that, my friend?"

"Is this a philosophical discussion, or is it your head injury talking?"

"A bit of both, I guess. That and I've had close calls a few times, so it's made me think and wonder about death sometimes, and what comes after. I told you I've run into the White Lady in the past, so she's something that I do believe in. Let me rephrase that; not like Santa Claus, okay. I mean, who knows where we go when we die; it's not like anyone's come back and told us. Not exactly in a way that many of us have paid attention to. Maybe, that's what the White Lady's doing, trying to open our eyes to the possibility that the other so-called realm is right next to us."

"I never knew you were so much of a deep thinker Mike."

"I'm usually not. It takes something serious to bring it out of me, and this was one of those rare instances. It probably won't ever, knock on wood, come up again."

"If I follow your train of thought," I mused, "and I think I do, then I concur. And I want to add, I've deduced that the White Lady is the good one and Chrisloki is the bad one. My theory is that our killer's being influenced by Chrisloki, so the light show we witnessed was a Tug 'O' War between the two."

"I'll go along with that."

"Okay, I'm glad you do, because Grady is pretty skeptical. Anyway, to take it a step further, you remember that the killing of Non Wrappe and Appleton occurred during the light show, right?"

"You might be onto something Laura. I mean as far as who Brown's being influenced by, and in what way. You do realize that if that's the case, if Brown's our killer, he'll use insanity as a defense and say he's hearing voices, right?"

"Yeah, I do, Mike. That puts him into a mental hospital, with the possibility of one day being released, which is obviously what we don't want. You know as well as I do, that Brown's smart enough to bring it up. And, besides, if we say anything about the White Lady or Chrisloki, we'll be right there on the same ward as Brown. So Mom, how do we get around that?

"That's where our FBI friend Reggie comes in," Mike answered. "He has to make his case a complete slam dunk, so this guy goes away, permanently. You know, I'm thrilled that you ran into Reggie that night – although I'm sure you didn't just run into him. I'm sure he'd been watching you – well us – from the moment Arnold walked into our office.

"But I'm rambling. I do hope he digs up something oh so special at Eliott's place that will sink Arnold, who I'm convinced, is Brown. Arnold/Brown might be able to plead insanity to the killing, but he won't be able to say he's nuts for ripping off all those people and burying the money offshore. He might be crazy, but he's also a crook. No jury will absolve him of that, even if they conclude that he's nuts. Juries can come up with some interesting decisions these days."

"We'll come up with plenty of solid evidence Mike, you'll see. Between all of us, there's no way this guy will be able to slide past a jury. Granted, they may have to sift through a mountain of evidence, but this guy Arnold, Brown, whoever he is, will be brought to justice. Reggie's been after Arnold for a long time; that's why he's so intent, so singularly focused. He wants Arnold in the worst way. I doubt any super storm will slow Reggie down on his mission. When he gets done with Eliott's house, he'll move on to Arnold's. Arnold's house might be a bunker, but Reggie'll tear it to pieces, and find what he needs, even if it's on a tiny flash drive. It wouldn't surprise me if he takes a jackhammer to the place. Mike stared at me as I ranted on. "Should we drive by?" I concluded.

"Nope, we've got a shopping list a mile long and a very short amount of time. Once we've accomplished that, we have to locate Grady and see how he's doing, as in, has he invited the White Lady over for dinner? Or, maybe Grady's luck has turned and he's discovered the psycho's camp. I'm hoping for the latter, myself. How about you?"

"I think some of the meds the doc gave me might help you."

"Funny guy O'Malley."

"Back to what we know, or don't. Whatever's influencing Brown -- let's keep referring to him as that for now – it's clear that the guy's a killer, and it does seem that those weird storms are somehow connected to the killings – maybe he's using the storms as a cover. When we found Appleton, she was definitely a bit on the crispy side – unlucky lightning strike, you might say. We could go so far as to say that Brown is at one with nature because he's out in the woods…"

"Seriously? So, now he's a tree hugger? Do you realize you've just categorized environmentalists as potential serial killers?"

"Did not."

"Did too."

"Have to be so politically correct these days," Mike sighed. "What am I supposed to call him?"

"An adaptable killer."

"Can we please stop for pizza while I mull that one over?"

"We can, but it has to be snappy."

"You're beginning to sound a lot like Adelaide."

"If that's a compliment, I accept. On the list, you'll notice I added more ammo, that's for me. I'm low. Adelaide needs more shotgun shells, too. We also need to hit the pet supply store, so eat your pizza while we drive and we can discuss our adaptable killer some more on the way."

"Righto, Adelaide junior. By the way, when you were pinned down by Brown, I don't suppose there's any way you could draw a comparison between him and Arnold, is there? I'm sure Grady asked you that already, but I wanted to ask you myself."

"Funny, he didn't really ask it in quite that way," I said, pulling into a pizza place near the hospital. "I'm going inside to order for you, and yes, it will have your gross bait on it. I do insist on the windows staying down while you eat the disgusting stuff. But, before I go order, I will tell you, I think they were about the same height, Mike, and probably about the same weight. Arnold's never been on top of me, nor has Brown, so I'm just guessing, but they did seem similar in build."

I felt an odd chill when I spoke those words. I went in and ordered Mike's pizza and a chicken wrap for me. While inside, I couldn't shake the feeling that I was being watched. Standing at the coffee and soda machines, I kept turning to see if anyone was staring at me. No one was, but I was sure it wasn't my imagination. I could feel it in my gut. I paid for our food, grabbed our bags, walked out the door, and that's when I saw him, in the reflection of a glass repair truck; it was Brown. In the panes of glass stacked on the side of the truck, I could see him, clear as day. He appeared to be standing right behind me, dressed head to toe in brown, including brown rimmed sunglasses. The hood of his sweatshirt was drawn tightly around his face, the same as the night before, to hide his features. I held my cell phone up and snapped a photo of him, turned and he was gone.

Bastard.

I checked the phone. The photo was there. I ran to the car, got in and locked the doors.

"I have to pee."

"Why didn't you go when you were in the restaurant?" Mike asked. "Here's your food."

"What happened, you're white as a sheet? The ghost, again?"

"No, it was Brown! He followed us. I took his picture with my phone, but he's gone. We have to get it to Grady. Mike, he made me so nervous, I have to pee."

"You're not making any sense...wait, give me your phone.

"Grady, hi, Brown's on our tail and Laura got a photo of him with her phone. Yes, I'm texting it to you right now. I don't think he knows she took it. It's a reflection of him in a pane of glass on a work truck she was standing next to. Yeah, it was fast thinking on her part. So could you send a uniform over here to see if he's still in the area? What? Your guy is on his way already? Great.... Oh, by the way, I can see there's a security camera mounted outside this joint, so you'll be able to check out the surveillance tapes. With any luck, he might show up on them and just maybe, he has a car and we can get the plate numbers. Yeah, that would be a nice bonus, wouldn't it? Yes, we'll stay put and wait for your officer. I agree, we're his current target and as long as we're here, he probably won't go too far.

"Okay buddy. You're looking at the photo? Nice and clear, huh? Man, it would be great if we could haul this guy in before that storm hits.

I heard it's supposed to be real bad. Yeah?

"Hey, you find anything in the woods? No kidding? A lean-to? Camouflaged with what? Pine branches. It had empty soup cans in it, and a couple of empty cans of Sterno? No wonder he was out and about. He needs more stuff. Hold on, Laura just made a hand gesture. I think she wants me off the phone. Yeah, it was not a nice hand gesture. I know she graduated top of her class at John Jay, and, yes, she should be more professional. Yes, I'll remind her, but she's been under a lot of stress in the past couple of days. She just made another hand gesture. Better say good bye. Okay, talk later."

"You have to tell him every little detail?"

"Not really. I was emphasizing how upset you are and was trying to keep the discussion to a minimum.

"You telling him I'm flipping him off is a good way to do that?"

"If I'd just come face to…okay, face to glass with my attacker, I'd be a little freaked out too. Do you still have to pee?"

"Yes! that's why I wanted you to get off the phone!"

"Oh, why didn't you say so?"

"I did!"

"No, you didn't"

"Yes, I…oh never mind."

"Can you wait for Grady's guy to get here?"

"Not really."

"OK, well, go. I'll watch your back while you go in, or I can go with you."

I glared at him.

"Or, I can stay in the car and eat my pizza. Better yet, I'll stand outside and eat. How's that?"

"Suits me fine. That way you can keep an eye out for Brown. I'll be right back. Please call Adelaide and let her know we're running a little behind, but don't tell her why."

Half way to the restaurant, I turned back towards my partner, "Mike, thanks."

Then, "Duck!" I screamed the loudest my lungs could muster, while drawing my Glock to aim towards the glint that shone off the same sheet of glass I'd seen Brown's reflection in. I tracked the glint to a rooftop, across the alley, as a shot rang out. Simultaneously, I dove behind a newspaper stand, the only sort of cover that was within my range. The glint I'd caught was from a rifle! My heart felt as if it was going to beat straight through my chest cavity wall as I held my position, waiting for another shot to surely hit. So, Brown had a gun!

"Mike? You okay? Mike, talk to me." I held my breath.

"Yeah, I'm good. Laura, you okay? You see where the shot came from?"

"Rooftop, across the alley Mike."

"Dammit, this guy is really pissing me off. Nobody shoots my lunch. I didn't even get one lousy bite."

The only thing that had been killed was Mike's pizza. It had exploded all over the panes of glass on the truck. It looked like some kind of expressionist art piece, chunks of anchovy stuck to glass along with tomato sauce and extra cheese.

"I'll call it in, even though I'm sure someone else already has," Mike said.

"Hey Dispatch, this is O'Malley. Right, I figured you'd had a bunch of calls. Okay, yeah I hear the sirens. Far as I know, it's one shooter, and I think it's our guy. Yeah, I sent a photo of him to Grady a bit ago. It's the best w've got. Thanks, you guys are the best."

"Cavalry's on its way Laura. Hang tight until they get here. I'm guessing, unfortunately, this guy is gonna be long gone by then and, we're gonna be without lunch, also unfortunately. In the meantime, don't move, okay."

"I'm staying put."

I looked inside the restaurant. Good thing it wasn't the height of the lunch hour, otherwise it would have been crowded. As it was, there were a handful of people hiding underneath the tables and behind the counter.

Grady pulled up in his unmarked vehicle, slid out and stayed behind his open door, rifle aimed at the rooftop. The tactical team pulled in alongside him, ready for action. These guys were the best of the best and trained consistently for this kind of thing. Luckily, they were rarely if ever, deployed, but at least when the occasion arose, you knew they'd take care of business.

Their first task was to keep the public safe, and the second was determining whether or not the shooter was still in the area. This was not going to be accomplished in a few minutes, so my trip to the bathroom was going to be put on hold. Should have gone when I was in there the first time.

I knew Tactical had to get Mike and me out. We were considered part of the public and we were in the line of fire. As such, we were their top priority.

Chapter 23

My phone began to bark. Just great. If I didn't answer, Annie would fly down here, convinced I was dead. If I did answer it, Mike would yell at me. I was in a no win situation.

"Annie, I'm alive," I whispered, "but if I talk to you, I'm going to be screamed at. The tactical team is here, and they're going to get us out, you have my word on that."

"Get off the phone!" Mike made a motion with his hand across his neck. He pointed to the rooftop.

I nodded. "I'll call you later, and don't come near this place. OK, I know, stupid to even tell you that, because of course you're already on your way. But don't!" I ended the call, silenced the phone, slid it into my pocket, and remained in my kneeling position behind the newspaper bin, wondering how many papers it would take to stop a bullet. Definitely not the best bulwark for protection.

I glanced at Mike, who pointed to a portion of the tactical team. They were heading directly to me, a group of four, one right behind the other. Their shields were facing out toward the alley, touching each other so that no bullet could possibly pass through. They had a nifty shuffle step, and they kept perfect time as they made their way over to my position. It was clear that I was to be taken to a safe area first. Women and children first, the unwritten rule as old as mankind. Far as I could tell, there was ample room behind the shields for both Mike and me, but I sensed there was no room for argument here.

I still couldn't shake the sensation that this was all for naught, that, as Mike had guessed, Brown was long gone. This was a glorified drill for the team. Granted there had been live fire involved, so they'd be doing a complete search of the scene, including where he'd fired from, to see if they could locate any expended shells, footprints, fingerprints, or anything he might have left behind. I could almost bet they wouldn't find anything. This guy was too good for that. He'd simply have stuffed everything into his pockets or into a trash bag, to be disposed of later on. He was more than likely completing his own shopping list and prepping for the storm, while we were holed up in the parking lot, theoretically still pinned down by him, the lone shooter. By the time Annie and her news crew arrived, Brown would likely be sipping coffee and smiling as he listened to her theorize about his whereabouts. I muttered to myself in frustration, while I tip-toed beside the shuffling team of four back to the so called, "safe perimeter." I waited anxiously while they performed the same scenario for Mike, and then watched as they safely extricated the patrons of the pizza place.

I still had to pee.

"Gotta go?" Mike winked.

"That obvious? That's it, I'm going across the street to the deli and beg to use their bathroom. While I'm there, I'm getting a cup of coffee and a sandwich. It doesn't look like I'll be able to get to that chicken wrap I left in the car anytime soon."

"What, you don't want to stick around and be interviewed by Annie?" Mike grinned.

"Hey, where do you two think you're going?" Sam Winston, the head of Tactical, asked. "You can't leave the scene until you've been cleared. You know that, especially you O'Malley. I can't have my people wandering in and out of an active crime scene and right now, you're my people, so stay put. Please."

"Sorry Captain, I know that but Laura's got to go. You know, girl stuff. So she was going to go across the street to the deli and I was going with her, to watch her back."

"Next time, speak up and say so O'Malley. Hold on a second. Pete, I want you to go with these two across the street and make sure they come back in one piece. We still don't know the location of this guy, so keep an eye out."

Witnessing Captain Sam Winston out in the field with his Tactical Team, in full gear for a real life engagement, was something I'd never dreamt I'd see, much less be in the center of. When Mike had been on the force, I'd been invited to some of their drills and was impressed with their precision, skill and dedication to detail, as they repeated exercises under the Captain's commands until perfection was attained. The Captain's men had complete respect for him, since he'd come from the rank and file himself and worked his way up. He was bold and decisive, yet relaxed at the same time, qualities that put others at ease. He spent off hours with his family, and he also spent plenty of time in the gym, which emphasized his already broad shoulders, giving him an imposing stance at six foot two.

"I've never seen the Captain so wound up," I said, as we ran across the street.

"When's the last time Tactical has been out for real Laura. Think about it. Facing down a shooter is scary business, even for a tough guy like Captain Winston. You're used to seeing this cool, calm and collected guy walking around the department, not out in the field, protecting you, me and the public at large. Different ballgame, as they say. I'm glad these guys are so vigilant. We got into this line of work to take down the bad guys, with help from my buddies when necessary. So far, so good. Next time, though, we need to do background checks on our prospective clients prior to taking them on, okay?"

"Agreed. Especially, when they plunk down a pile of cash on our desk. That should have made us suspicious from the get go. Speaking of going, I'm going to go, and while I do, would you kindly order me a chicken wrap and some coffee? Get something for Pete for his trouble too."

On my way out of the restroom, while picking up a couple of bags of chips, I spotted Annie on the TV behind the deli counter, giving her description of the morning's events, and speculating where the shooter might be. She was finishing up her rundown, and about to interview a young woman with a youngster holding her hand, when Mike turned to hand me my coffee, "Your new chicken wrap is almost finished."

"Thanks."

"Annie's doing a great job, as usual. And, as usual, the Captain's staying a mile away from her," Mike said.

"He won't talk to her until he knows exactly what's going on. I know it infuriates her, believe me. I'm surprised one of the people from inside the pizza place managed to...oh, wait a minute, look at that, Annie's not going to be happy."

The Captain had walked over and stopped the interview in mid-sentence. He had Annie and her interviewees move across the street, and had his men roll out yellow crime scene tape. The cameraman had kept his tape rolling long enough to see Annie's face go through several sets of contortions. Fortunately, the audio feed had been cut, otherwise the viewing audience would have gotten an earful, and it wouldn't have been rated PG.

Seconds later, Annie stomped into the deli, walked straight up to Mike and said, "I cannot believe your Captain's impudence! Is he not aware of the freedom of the press?"

Mike took a sip of coffee, and looked at me. I shrugged my shoulders and stirred my coffee.

"What exactly do you mean by impudence? Mike asked.

"Are you being a smart aleck? Because, if you are, you're no better than he is."

"No, I just want to know what context you're using impudence in, that's all."

"Now you're being smug, and that doesn't suit you, not one little bit. Matter of fact, you are being impudent," Annie poked her finger into Mike's chest.

Pete, our accompanying officer, was looking on with apparent amusement at Annie and Mike's exchange.

I chimed in, "Stop, the both of you. Mike, have a little compassion for Annie. She's trying to do her job. And Annie, the Captain is just following procedure, okay. You can't give interviews in the middle of an active crime scene; you know that. How long have you been a reporter?

"You should really apologize to Mike for calling him names. Brown killed his pizza, and you know how fond he is of his anchovies. He's suffered an enormous loss and then you come along and yell at him when you're actually illogically mad at the Captain."

Annie sighed, "I'm sorry, Mike. You two have been under a lot of pressure with this case. I honestly didn't mean anything by what I said. I'll be happy to buy you a couple of slices."

"Thanks Annie, you're a good egg, and I know you didn't mean it." Mike held out his hand to Annie, and she shook it. "We're all a little shaken. I haven't had a bullet whiz by my head in years. It could have ricocheted and really hurt someone. Come to think of it, we've no idea where it ended up, do we?

"Oh well, I'm sure they'll find it when they go over the scene, which reminds me Laura, we need to get back there. I'm surprised he hasn't radioed Pete about us already."

"O'Malley?" Pete said.

"Yeah?"

"I just heard him mumbling something about you."

"Hey, look, isn't that Crosby?" I asked, as he pushed open the door of the deli and walked in. "The last time I saw him, he was wearing a wetsuit."

"Sure is," Mike answered. "Guess you didn't know he's part of the tactical team, now did you," he grinned. "You thought he was only a dive boy. No time for small talk Laura. Grab your sandwich and get your feet moving."

"I'm moving."

"New incentive to avoid the crime scene," Annie said. "I'm staying put. We can film from right here. Laura can always call me with anything I might need to know." At my appraising look, Annie smiled sheepishly, "Okay, okay, I'm coming."

The three of us made our way back across the street under the watchful eye of Pete, the Captain and a few of the tactical team's snipers, who were visually scanning the area, rifles pointed outward in various directions. I was still convinced Brown was long gone, having made fools of us yet again. He was somewhere safe by now, gloating over having thwarted Soundview's finest. With the storm closing in, the window to capture him was also narrowing. The teams would be deployed for storm management, a fact he had to be as aware of as we were.

Chapter 24

Grady approached us the second our feet hit the parking lot, "Seems our guy's fled the scene, and my crew and Tactical found no trace of him whatsoever. If not for your photo and the gunshot, it's as if he were never here. We went over this place with everything at our disposal, including a toothbrush, and we came up empty-handed. The shell casing went with him. If he had a chewing gum wrapper, it's gone. We checked the surveillance tapes from the pizza joint and the deli, and please do not ask me how, but they're both a blur. Somehow, the people and traffic both before and after him can all be seen just fine. Either he's got the best jamming equipment, or Laura's going to tell me some ghosts are working overtime."

"I'm going with the former," I said.

"Maybe, he sprayed the cameras with something," Mike said.

"Both of them? He wouldn't have had the time. Actually, the deli's tape wasn't really focused on the pizza joint parking lot, so some of the fuzziness had to be due to the distance. The deli's camera did catch a car speeding off, but we can't positively ID him as the driver."

"Was it a red Lexus sedan or a red Lexus SUV? Even though there are loads of those around, there's a possibility you can match it to Arnold. The SUV was registered to Gwen and the sedan would be under Arnold's name," I said.

"How can we even confirm it was Arnold's car without a plate number?" Captain Winston asked. He'd given the order for the tactical team to begin wrapping things up, and walked over as Grady was updating us. "It's like you said, Laura, there are loads of those vehicles around. Granted, we've got the photo you took with your cell phone, but we don't have one with him leaving or entering the scene, either in a car or on foot. That means we can't positively ID this guy. At least, when the DNA sample from the log Brown smacked you with comes back from the lab, we'll know if Brown and Arnold are one and the same, like you all seem to believe. But we still won't be able to prove that Brown, or Arnold for that matter, was here.

"There are too many puzzle pieces that don't quite fit. In other words guys, you need to bring me some real solid evidence before I can go after Arnold. As much as it's aggravating me not to net the arrogant SOB right now, I want something rock solid, you can't blow a hole through it, and it won't leak any water at all, to bring to the prosecutor, so that this guy never, ever sees the light of day. Got it? All we have right now are theories. Theories are great, but juries can't weigh evidence they don't have. If they can't see it, touch it, and or feel it, he'll walk. As you know, we've got a long way to go before our guy even faces a jury. First we have to come up with enough evidence to convince the prosecutor we've got a case. Understood?

We all nodded. The captain leaned in towards us as he spoke again. "Most importantly, I do not want any more dead bodies showing up, nor do I want any more shots fired in public places. Is that clear?"

"Yes Sir," Grady said, "And my men will take care of all the scene clean-up," Grady added.

Mike and I nodded again.

Getting reamed out made me feel part of the team. It made me feel proud and accepted.

The Captain turned and strode off, folded himself into the lead vehicle, and headed back to headquarters. His team followed, leaving us to ourselves in the now empty parking lot.

"We've got our work cut out for us," Grady said, toeing the pebbles. "I don't like being outsmarted and made out to be a fool in front of my Captain."

"You're no one's fool Grady, and he knows that. Don't forget, he's got the Chief to answer to and the Chief's got the Mayor to answer to. And, the Mayor has the Governor to answer to, and so forth," Mike said.

"Nice to know you haven't forgotten the chain of command Mike."

"Hey, I'm trying to help out buddy. Listen, it's not going to do any good standing around feeling sorry for ourselves while Brown, or whatever the hell his name is, is laughing at us. He's probably mapping out who his next victim is, hate to say it, but think about it, he hasn't killed anyone, in what, at least a couple of days? For a serial killer, that's a long time. The Captain's only too well aware of that.

"Reminds me, has anyone taken the time to call Adelaide?"

The three of us dialed in unison.

Grady reached her first.

"Great to hear your voice Adelaide. What do you mean, who is this? Why, it's Grady, as in Lieutenant Grady Marshall of the Soundview Police Department. Yes, it was rude of me to not have said immediately who it was; I thought you would have recognized my voice by now... even so, you're right, I should have stated my name and reason for calling. Why am I calling? To check on your welfare. You're not on welfare. Of course you aren't, Henry left you quite comfortable. Okay, sort of comfortable. Okay, it's actually none of my business and why am I asking? I'm not. You started this. No, I'm not accusing you of anything nefarious...is Laura or Mike with me? Yes, why? Because, you'd prefer speaking with either one of them over me. With pleasure. Yes, it's been great, and yes, we should not do this again."

Grady handed the phone to me, smacked his head and walked away. Mike followed him while I took a breath, debating whether I should adopt a cheery tone, or a middle of the road one. I opted for Adelaide taking the lead and simply opening with, "Hi Adelaide, how are you?"

"After that conversation, I'm not too sure. A lot of crazy talk accusing me of not being capable of taking care of myself, prying into my privacy and what Henry left me, or didn't. Why would he do such a thing when I'm so worried about all of you, with all that's on the news? Why is it no one's bothered to call me to let me know that you're safe?"

"I think that's what Grady was trying to do, to let you know that all of us are safe and sound, and most importantly, to keep your doors locked until Mike and I get back. As you know, we had a run-in with Brown..."

"A little more than a run-in; you could have been killed! You were both shot at. I saw the news. Annie was there, too."

"That's true, but it looks much worse on TV than it really was. We're shaken up, but not at all hurt. I'm telling the truth Adelaide."

"Okay, I believe you Laura."

I could hear the trembling in her voice.

"Is Officer Kindly still there with you?" I asked.

"Yes he is. He's sitting right inside the front doorway, near the coat rack. He just waved to me. I made him come inside, it's too cold out there and I want him where I can see him. The only time he goes out is to patrol the perimeter and he takes Kola with him so he can do his business. There's another Officer at the top of the driveway and one at the barn, too."

"Sounds good, as if everything's covered. Mike and I will be back in a little over an hour, once we've finished up our shopping. I promise we're not getting diverted for anything else. We'll finish our list and then head straight back."

"Promise?"

"You've my word. Give my boy a pat for me," I smiled.

"Done."

I felt a tug on my coat, turned and looked into the face of the same youngster who'd been holding his mother's hand while they were being interviewed by Annie. He handed me his cell phone, showing a photo of a license plate on a red Lexus Sedan. It read: TOPS. He took the phone back from me and slid his finger across to show the next photo in the gallery array.

And there was Brown at the wheel of that red sedan.

Chapter 25

I looked around and noted Mike and Grady talking as they walked into the pizza joint. I directed the mother and child and they walked in front of me without a word. We followed them inside and stepped up to the counter next to the two of them. "Mike, this young man, Alex, would like to buy you a slice of pizza. He saw what happened to your other one and feels terrible about it," I said.

Alex fished around in the pocket of his navy pea coat, came up with a fistful of change, and handed it to Mike, "Came out of my piggy bank, Officer. I've been saving it for a really long time and I think you should have it because your lunch got shot."

"That's very kind of you, young man, but I can't take your money. You should put it toward something very special that you've wanted for a long time.

"And I should let you know that I'm not an officer. I retired and now I'm a private detective, but my buddy here, Grady Marshall, is a lieutenant."

Alex's eyes got very wide with that information. He grinned and put his hand out to shake hands with Grady, who good naturedly complied.

I chimed in, "Grady, I'd like you to meet Alex. Our new friend here has some very interesting photos on his cell phone, but I believe that we might want to go somewhere a bit more discreet before you take a look at them. He showed them to me just now, while we were standing out in the parking lot -- probably not the best time or place, but he was anxious to share them. And, let's just say, I know that the Captain will be equally anxious to see them. Matter of fact, you might want to give Alex and his mom a ride to headquarters where all the policemen work. He could meet the Captain there, right Grady?"

"Yeah, I think that's a fine idea. And almost on cue, here comes Annie. How does she do that? A story pops up and she's right there," Grady put his hand on the boy's shoulder and guided him to the door. He winked at Annie as he passed her on the way out.

"Grady's not telling me something. He caught a break, didn't he? It has to do with that little boy. And I even interviewed that kid in the first place! What was it that he didn't he tell me? He was on TV! A chance at fame and he passed it up? He just stood there, quiet as a mouse. That's it, I'm never having kids." Annie stormed out.

Mike laughed, "I can't help it, but that was funny. A nine year old kid ruined her interview. I guess she's gotta work on her interview skills with the younger set."

"She'll get over it. What she doesn't know yet is how brave that kid is. Mike, let's get out of here and I'll tell you what's going on. Once this is over with, Annie can interview Alex to her heart's content. I'll clue her in when it's safe to do so."

Mike gave me a quizzical look. I leaned over and whispered into his ear. He ran to the car like a kid himself, jumped in, and was all ears, waiting for me to get in to spill the beans on the kid's photos. This was the evidence we'd been waiting for, and who could have guessed we'd find it on some kid's cell phone. All we had to do now was go about our business, picking up our storm supplies, and wait for confirmation from Grady that Brown and Arnold were indeed one and the same person. Once that was accomplished, an arrest warrant could be obtained by a judge. That would be the easy part. Next would be locating him. We had him cornered to within, say, a thousand or so acres of land. It'd be tough enough to find him, even without the super storm bearing down on us.

"Mike, I don't think I've ever seen you move so fast, except for food."

"This is big Laura, and the kid had the info on his cell phone the entire time, even with the Captain here. 'Course, what if Brown, or let's just call him Arnold, had driven around the corner and decided to watch the proceedings on TV, you know, and while Annie's interviewing the kid, the kid talks, and then Arnold comes back and snatches him? Damn, do you think that kid might have thought the whole thing through? You think he didn't say anything to Annie in order to protect himself and his mom?"

"Who knows with kids these days, with all the TV shows they watch. Alex does come across as a very bright child, though. Maybe he spotted Arnold again while Annie was doing her interview. Or maybe he thought it best to keep it to himself until he could get the information safely to someone he trusted, someone who would get it to the detective in charge."

"You have that honest face, so he gave it to you." Mike smiled, gripped the wheel and added, "We've got Arnold now and boy does it feel good."

"Let's not forget, we still have to physically find him and bring him in. And he's got the upper hand in that he knows those woods better than we do."

"Keep in mind that Adelaide knows the woods better than he does. And Grady found his lean-to, but you're right, that could be one of who knows how many of his hiding places." Mike pulled into the parking lot of the grocery store to pick up some badly needed non-perishables and batteries before half the town descended and bought the place out.

"After this, we'll stop and top off the gas tank and fill up the gas containers I brought along for the generator, so we don't have to go out again for a while. That will give us plenty of time to get in some good hiking, or shall I say, some good hunting for Arnold's campsites, before nightfall," I said.

"Smart planning ahead. Let's get moving then, since we've got a few good hours of daylight ahead of us. I just know Grady wasn't thrilled about being out there with the White Lady."

"He really needs to get over his fears. She's not leaving the area, so it's time he learns to peacefully co-exist with her. He can't avoid her anyway, because you never know where she'll turn up. It's not like she leaves an itinerary around saying exactly where she's going to be and when. I've heard she travels on the highway as well as in the woods, stops on the roadside, just stands there. People have called 9-1-1 saying they've seen a woman standing alongside the road, dressed in her typical long white gown, and the Troopers have to go check it out, even though they know it's her. It probably drives the dispatchers crazy."

Mike grabbed a shopping cart, and said, "Do not tell Grady that she hangs out on the highway, he'll never drive again, which means he'll make me do all the driving from here on out. Come to think of it, he'll make a terrible passenger, too, whipping his head all over the place, looking for her. I really wish you hadn't told me that; now I'll be looking for her too." Mike shook his head, "Can we concentrate on shopping?"

"I'm on it, got my list from Adelaide with a few things thrown in of my own. Yours shouldn't be too difficult: Chips, salsa and anchovies. I've no idea how you've survived this long on the diet you're on."

"I'm fine, but thanks for looking out for me, pal."

"Let's try and be out of here in less than half an hour, okay?"

"No problem. Matter of fact, let's cut that in half and I'll be more than satisfied. I don't ever like shopping, but I especially don't like it when they've posted storm warnings and panic's about to set in. The gas station is going to be insane, so move it, Jensen."

"I'll take one side of the store, you take the other and we'll meet back here in a few."

"Nope, we'll stick together. My detective instincts are working overtime. I don't like the idea that Arnold disappeared the way he did, and he's out getting supplies the same as we are. Granted, he's most likely stocking up on more ammo, and I know they don't sell that here."

"Funny guy O'Malley."

"Who said I was joking?"

We went up and down the aisles systematically, following the list, tossing the items into the cart, in between grabbing others that seemed appropriate. Even though we'd tried to beat the rush, the place was jammed with what seemed like the entire town, stockpiling on all non-perishable items. The two hottest tickets were bottled water and toilet paper.

We debated, but then stopped at the DVD rental outlet and picked up a couple of action movies more to Mike's tastes, such as Iron Man, which he was convinced once Adelaide began watching, she'd love. I agreed with him, it couldn't hurt.

Both of us looked over our shoulders now and then, to be sure we weren't being followed. I knew Arnold wouldn't allow himself to be seen, if he was indeed trailing us. It would make sense to target us, and then there wouldn't be anyone to protect Adelaide, the remaining witness. Then it hit me. Adelaide wasn't the only witness, Alex could identify him too – and possibly Alex's mom as well. No one had mentioned whether or not the mom had seen him too.

"Mike, Alex never said if his mom saw Arnold, did he?"

"Interesting question. Not that I can recall. And you know, until I get the phone call from Grady, that won't be verified; that they're the same person, I mean." Mike reached into the cart, pulling out our things,

194

and began laying them on the conveyor belt at the register. He sighed, "I should have heard from Grady by now. Will you call him? If I do, he'll think I'm bugging him."

The cashier added up our items and I went behind Mike to start bagging our purchases. I was about to call Grady when my phone barked.

Can't leave things alone, can you?"

"Who is this?" I asked.

I slapped Mike's arm, covered the phone with my hand and spoke softly into his ear, "It's him. His voice is muffled, but it's him! Can Grady put a trace on my phone?"

Mike pulled out his phone and called Grady. Meanwhile, I held my phone to my ear, transfixed, vaguely noting as Mike paid, threw our bags in the cart, and wheeled it to the side.

"You know who this is Laura. What else do I have to do to get your attention? How many women have to die? This is all because of you, all these deaths, and they're all needless."

"What...?"

"Silence! I did not grant you permission to speak! You're identical to Gwen .She didn't know her place either. In the Bible, it is written that women are to be submissive to men, yet neither of you know that. That's what's wrong with the world today, that's why I wrote the note, "Never Forget." Even Adelaide has forgotten, and she's old school. I've tried to teach you, but you've failed to listen. You've made miserable students, all of you. It's useless, you're useless. So when the student fails, the teacher must punish. It is the teacher's duty."

"Sorry to interrupt, but you've got that last part backwards; when the student's ready, the teacher appears," I said.

"I did not give you permission to cut me off! You will be silent, You will listen to me! Some of what happened, Eliott asked for. He was after my wife and I can prove it. Aside from that, he's the one who killed Appleton. He was going against everything we were doing, and he was just as shameless as you and Gwen!"

At that, I turned to Mike silently and raised my eyebrows in intense surprise. Mike gestured to me to keep him talking as long as I possibly could.

I nodded.

"You're going to blame the murders on your dead partner, the one you just admitted to killing? Now, who's being shameless Arnold?" I asked.

Mike gave me a thumb's up.

"I didn't admit to any such thing!" Arnold screamed. "If this is being recorded, it won't matter, it's impossible to either catch me or find me." He went on, "I'm better than all of you combined, including your FBI friend Reggie. Just for the fun of it, I might make him my next target since I've only killed one male. Reggie would provide more of a challenge than Eliott, I'd imagine. I look forward to it; can you please pass the message on to him?"

I yawned as if I were on the verge of falling asleep from boredom, and said, "Sounded like an admission right there Arnold."

"Eliott and Gwen were having an affair, but that's not the only reason. It was all going along fine until he killed Appleton, and that was because she wanted her money back. If I'd been there when she showed up, I would have handled it. It was stupid of him to kill her. Gwen saw Eliott dump the body, so he killed my Gwen. She was out in the woods with her sketch book, and he killed her," Arnold yelled.

"So, you murdered your partner because he killed your wife?"

"Of course I did," Arnold responded with total calm. He added, "And, I would do it again. I've given you too much information, much more than I'd intended to at this juncture. I really must go, there's a storm coming and we have to complete our preparations. I hope you, Mike and Adelaide stay safe."

He hung up.

I tapped the phone to end the call, but not to delete the recording of what had been said. I knew Grady would want to play it back later on for documentation. I looked up at Mike, "I don't know what to say. I didn't anticipate even half of that." Oddly enough, I was feeling quite calm.

"Me either. That was the most oddball confession, but it's the evidence, or some of what we're looking for to bring to the prosecutor. It doesn't explain what happened to the other woman, Non Wrappe. I have to call Grady, but we do have to get out of here and get your phone down to headquarters so they can get that recording off of it. Good going Laura! You got so much information out of him." Mike rubbed his head, and added, "I'm impressed. If they had an Oscar for phone performances with murderers, I would nominate you. The yawn was perfect timing."

"Since you didn't get to listen to his end of things, I'll play it back for you. His justification is, well, mystifying best describes it. His view on and of women is so twisted, and that's not even an accurate word."

"Mike, there's something he did say that makes me wonder if he's got his sister with him. He does know the storm's on its way, but he said we need to make our preparations. Who else would be with him?"

"If that's the case Laura, we need to find him fast. She's not safe, especially if she's aware of the fact that he's killed either Eliott, Gwen or any of the other women. Damn, I wish we knew where he was," Mike said, shoving the cart through the door.

While packing the car, Mike looked over at me, smiled and said, "Thank God you had the common sense to record the conversation, otherwise I don't know where we'd be."

I grinned, tapped my phone and replied, "Good thing I remembered there's an app for that."

Chapter 26

Next stop was the gas station. While Mike topped off the car's tank, I went inside to get some coffee for us. On the way out, my phone barked once again. This time, it was Annie. I breathed a quick sigh of relief. Then I plugged in my earpiece, went around the back of the car and grabbed some gas cans. I might as well make myself useful while listening to her bitch about the kid who had ruined her interview and her life.

She surprised me. Instead, I listened to her apologize, while I filled one can after the other and sipped coffee in between. She said she felt silly being that upset with the kid, especially when, as I'd said, he'd been so brave to come forward. She now realized that he must've been so very frightened for both himself and his mom.

She went on to discuss the preparations for the Super Storm, as it was now referred to on the news, and asked if Adelaide and I were ready. I reassured her that we had all the necessities, and that Mike and I were filling up the gas containers for the generator, the final item on our list. Yes, then we were heading back, and yes, then we would begin our search for Arnold...oh, dang it, how did she do that? Pull information out of me when I wasn't supposed to release it? Damn, she was good, I thought. No way was I going to tell her about the call from Arnold and his confession to most of the killings. If I did that, Grady would hang me by my toes in the center of town, regardless of the incoming Super Storm.

I begged Annie to please not release the news that we intended to search for Arnold to the public. That tidbit of information would surely endanger Adelaide's life and the lives of anyone else Arnold might be going after. I reminded her that Mike and I were both staying with Adelaide, which would put our lives on the line, too. Annie gave me her word she'd keep quiet about it for as long as possible, and I reassured her that of course Grady would give her the exclusive. Didn't he always?

Mike was giving me the high sign. It was time to get rolling. I told Annie I didn't want to see her out reporting on the storm, hanging on to some pole for dear life in the midst of the high winds like a human weathervane, when in fact no one would be watching because they'd have lost power. She insisted that they'd be viewing on their iPad's. I reminded her that if they'd lost power, that meant they'd lost their internet connections too.

We both laughed at how silly we were being, realizing at the same time that we were both just concerned for the other's safety. I promised to keep in touch via cell phone, and to check in as often as possible, and Annie did the same. According to the latest "Storm Watch" news reports, the storm was still five and half days out. What if the trajectory changed and it wasn't as devastating for us as they were forecasting. I wondered about that possibility as I hung up with Annie.

Mike was fixated on the storm too. "Sandy's going to be one bitch of a storm, Laura. If that monster hits where they say it will, we're in for one hell of a time, and so are New York and New Jersey. We're in bullseye country, my friend.

He continued, "The fact that Adelaide's house has been standing there for as long as it has speaks volumes, but with all those trees around, well let's just say, it might be real tough to get any help out to us if we need it. The roads are going to be blocked due to fallen trees all over the place. Luckily, the house itself should be fine. Adelaide told me she and her husband had the property around the house clear cut so nothing can fall on it.

"Where Arnold plans on holing up during all of this is anyone's guess. Adelaide told me there are some caves deep into Trout Brook, so maybe that's his plan. Then, once the storm's over, he'll head back down her way. We need to be ready for anything and everything that he's going to throw at us, especially after the way you spoke to him, or didn't. And now that he's made a confession to you...well, half a confession anyhow, who knows what he's got planned."

"That was the idea even before his confession, to be ready for anything," I said.

"Oh." Mike interrupted, "Andy Griffith time...love that song!"

"Don't ever change Mike," I laughed.

Mike beamed, and answered his phone. His conversation with Grady was brief. It was a simple verification of what we already knew;

The DNA was a match, and Arnold and Brown were one and the same. Grady wanted us to be on our toes, and he was sending an extra team to us, regardless of the fact that the storm was on its way. He was treating Arnold as if he were a mini-storm. We were in that storm's path and needed protection too.

Grady promised that Alex and his mom were in safekeeping as well, and there they'd stay until Arnold was captured. He related that Alex was quite pleased with the Junior Detective badge Grady had bestowed upon him, and he had plenty to read and do to ride out the storm.

Grady listened quietly as I described Arnold's phone call, his admission to some of the murders, and his more-to-be-revealed attitude. It clearly unnerved Grady and it reinforced the need for him to send us a team. He directed Mike to stop at HQ ASAP so the computer forensics boys could get the recording off my phone. Mike assured him that we were already en route.

Grady said he'd personally check on us the following day, and to be extra cautious if we decided to go and search for Arnold. He told us that, aside from the lean-to with the cache of supplies he found when he'd first searched the reservoir area, he'd found no additional hiding places. Grady swore he'd spent a good hour up there. And he even agreed to join us in a brief search, along with whatever men he could spare, when he came out the following day. Mike said he'd have a merit badge made up for Grady for 'bravery in the face of seeing a ghost.'" No, Grady didn't feel a second merit badge was required; one was sufficient.

Grady gave Mike the location of the lean-to, to the best of his recollection, and sent him the photos he'd taken of the trail leading up to it. That way, Mike and I would be able to locate the lean-to when we went out. Mike said we'd begin our survey as soon as we could, in order to take advantage of the few hours of daylight remaining. It was worth it to see if there was anything we could turn up within a safe radius of that camp. We promised to check back once we'd surveyed the area.

"A tracking dog would be a good idea," I suggested.

"I know. That's why we're bringing Kola."

"Thought you'd never ask."

"Didn't think you'd want to risk it."

"It won't be a risk Mike. If Arnold comes anywhere near my pup, I'll shoot him."

Our stop at HQ was incredibly fast. The information was pulled off my phone and within several minutes, we were on our way. With any luck, there might be some background noise giving away Arnold's position at the time of the call. That would only be a starting point in tracking his location, as he would be long gone, but it was better than nothing.

When we reached Adelaide's, Officer Kindly greeted us at the barn and waved us through. We stopped and unloaded the feed for the barn animals and the gas cans for the generator in the garage. Then, we proceeded down to the house, where we unpacked the rest of our supplies.

"You two are as slow as molasses," Adelaide said. "I take that back, molasses is faster than you," she was sipping some tea while Kola and Chloe slept at her feet. "Day's not getting any younger, and that crazy man's out there plotting his next murder, while you two are out gallivanting about town."

Mike studiously ignored her comment, "We got some movies -- some good ones," Mike offered.

"Like what?"

"Iron Man. It's great, and you're going to love it," Mike said.

Adelaide raised one eyebrow, "Is that the one with Robert Downey Jr. in it?"

Mike elbowed me. "Yup, that's the one."

"How did you know I love him?" Adelaide said, and winked at me.

I rolled my eyes.

"Okay, you're off the hook Mike. Hope you got some fresh popcorn so we can watch it in style tonight?" Adelaide smiled at him.

"Sure did, with lots of butter. And we'll have a big fire. It will be loads of fun. First, Laura and I have to do a bit of exploring, or hunting, for you-know-who. Business before pleasure, as they say."

"We won't be gone too long, and we need to take Kola along on this trip," I said.

Adelaide looked down and patted Kola on the head. He sighed, stretched his front legs, rubbed his head on her foot and settled back in for a lengthier nap.

I walked over, bent down and patted him. I petted Chloe, too. They were becoming inseparable. Kola looked up at me, put his big paw on my hand, rolled over on his back as if bargaining with me; first a belly rub, and then, maybe he'd consider getting up. How could I possibly refuse such a simple request?

"Alright, my boy, a good old belly rub, then you'll be in the mood for a run?"

At the mention of the word 'run,' Kola leapt up and bounded to the door. He was more than ready to go.

"All right, crew of mine," Mike said, "we're going out for our excursion. Let's hope it's worth it."

"More to the point, let's hope all of you come back in one piece, dragging that you-know-what behind you," Adelaide said. She went on, "You could dangle him from two poles, tied up, and I'd be thrilled to high heaven to see that. Then I could thoroughly enjoy my popcorn and movie tonight, knowing he's where he belongs, behind bars."

She held up her cell phone, "I want you to call me when you're on your way back, so I don't worry about you. Chloe's going to be concerned about Kola, so skeddadle!" With that, Adelaide got up, and with her cane, per usual, dangling from her arm, walked into her bedroom with Chloe on her heels. Hearing Kola whine as the bedroom door closed almost made me cry.

Mike cleared his throat, rubbed his eyes, opened the door and followed Kola and I out. We started down the path behind Adelaide's house, moving down the embankment to the trailhead. Kola was in the lead, a pup on a mission, trotting along with his head held high.

Chapter 27

"What's that?" Mike asked, stepping on the back of my boot.

"Barred owl," I responded. "We're not going to get anywhere if you're going to stop every five seconds asking me to identify different animal sounds...wait a minute, that wasn't an owl, that was...quiet, we're being followed."

We ducked behind some bushes to see who was tracking us. I couldn't believe it, we were only steps over the Spencer property line. Why hadn't one of the officers spotted whoever it was and notified us?

"I see you," Crosby sung out. "Don't believe me? I'd toss a pebble at you, only it won't feel so good bouncing off your forehead, O'Malley."

"You two were supposed to wait for a responsible escort...okay, poor choice of words there. How's this? Under the Lieutenant's orders, you were told to wait for one of his men. Yeah, that's definitely better.

"Oh come on, don't look so disappointed, I'm a good shot, and I'm good company."

"That wasn't a look of disappointment, it was a look of fear! I'm happy to see you, but you scared the hell out of us," Mike said, while he smacked Crosby on his shoulder. "In case it slipped your mind, there's a killer on the loose. You could have called us."

"That's what the owl hoot was, that was, me calling," Crosby's eyes crinkled in the corners as he laughed. He bent down to pat Kola.

"The first hoot sounded like a real owl, so we didn't pay much attention, and the second one was so fake that it scared us. Next time can you figure out a better way of contacting us? After all, this is the modern age. We all have cell phones – and ours are on vibrate, by the way," I said as I smacked Crosby on the opposite shoulder.

"Damn, you hit hard."

"You deserved it."

"You ought to see her when she's angry," Mike laughed.

"No thanks, I'll take your word for it. Save the energy for when we capture Arnold."

"I'm all for that," I said. "So, let's quit chattering ladies, and let's spend our last few hours of daylight wisely. Crosby, we're headed to where Grady found the lean-to. We'll go from there and see what else we can discover. I'm determined to find his other encampments, along with the means he used to transport the bodies into these woods. Of course, there's always the possibility that he and Eliott lured the women into the woods together and then killed them here."

"Alright then, let's head out. You know where we're going Laura, so take point," Crosby said, while he slid his .308 sniper rifle off his shoulder, pointed it downward, and dropped back a few paces. Mike took the middle position and, in silence, we began our approach to the reservoir.

We maintained our quiet and stepped with care over loose stones and rocks. Each of us had dressed in muted tones, right down to our gloves. It was late October, and it was turning colder as the sun went down.

While we moved along, I wondered if Reggie had found the evidence he needed to put Arnold away. By now, Grady had most likely shared the recording of the phone call I'd had with Arnold. Once Arnold had been identified as the caller, it would add more ammunition to the case. I was dying to ask Crosby if he had heard anything, but I didn't dare break the stillness. I knew I had to be patient and wait until we arrived at the lean-to for our first opportunity to speak. I sighed; patience was not my strong suit.

As we approached the reservoir, Grady's landmarks became apparent. Suddenly, I stopped, bent down and pointed off to the side. Kola sat next to me. I turned and nodded silently to the guys. Both Mike and Crosby were tracking the direction of my finger. Mike shrugged. Crosby nodded, and tapped Mike's shoulder. He pointed and turned Mike's head. Mike stared for a few seconds and then a broad smile lit up his face.

Crosby gave a few owl hoots. Nothing. He tried a couple more. An owl responded. He made a circular approach to the lean-to, doubled back and came at it from the rear. He poked his rifle barrel in through the branches. Okay, then, no one is home.

He motioned for us to come forward. We did so with caution.

"Nice little spot away from it all," I said.

"Oh sure, right at the top of the list of spots I'd pick to go for my next vacation. I love how he's got the place decorated." Mike said. "I don't suppose you'd get any cable TV to watch football on Sundays?" he added.

"Not exactly my style, either, but as long as we're here, let's poke around a bit, shall we?" Crosby said.

"Grady said he went through the place," Mike said. "Said he didn't find anything interesting outside of survival stuff, but then he doesn't like it up here all that much, so he probably wanted to get out of here pretty quick. Hey, don't tell him I said that."

"I won't. We all know the White Lady stories and some guys get weird about them. If she's around, it's her turf. Doesn't bother me... well, what do we have here?" Crosby backed out of the lean-to, holding up a key on a lanyard in his gloved hand.

"Let me guess, it's not to his car?" Mike suggested.

"This is too easy," I said.

"Not really. Think about it, this place is off the beaten path, and so well hidden that the average hiker most likely wouldn't have found it. Looks like the raccoons have been here, though. I am surprised they haven't torn it up a bit more. They've scattered some of the cans, but that's about it.

"As for Grady, I know he surface searched this place, but to give him the benefit of the doubt, he was up here by himself when he got the call that Arnold took a shot at you two, which interrupted him before he could complete his task. I know the Lieutenant to be a thorough guy, and there's no way he would miss this gem of a find. Wow! Let's go find the boat this key starts, shall we?"

Crosby pocketed the key after first putting it into an evidence bag. I took the lead and we resumed our hike in silence. This time, we were not following the trail. We were snaking alongside the edges of the reservoir, seeking a well concealed, small boat that our key would fit.

Chapter 28

By my estimation, we had two hours of daylight remaining. Normally, it wouldn't bother me if we made our way back in the dark -- we had flashlights for that -- but it left us exposed if Arnold was out and about. It was clear to me that we didn't have much time to search for the boat and get back before dark, a topic we needed to discuss prior to putting too much more distance between ourselves and home base.

"Why are you stopping?" Crosby whispered.

"We're getting short on time, and who knows where the boat is. We want to be smart about this, right?"

"Laura, you're right, time is our enemy, along with Arnold and this storm. I don't think we have a choice. We have to keep going. We need to find this evidence if we're going to nail this guy. Put it this way, what if he's out here and decides to sink the boat, especially when he realizes the key's missing?" Crosby raised his eyebrows.

Kola growled.

"Even he agrees with me," Crosby said.

I leashed Kola, and said, "I don't think that's it."

"Coyote?" Mike asked.

"Could be," Crosby responded. "Probably a good idea to keep him leashed for a bit," he petted Kola, contemplating his next words. "We need to stay ahead of this guy, if at all possible, and mostly, we need to catch him alive. Reggie's gotten ahold of some solid stuff that will put him away for the short term, but we need to rope him in for the murders in order to keep him behind bars."

"I wanted to ask you about what Reggie found, but Mike and I have got some interesting things to tell you too."

Mike said, "Laura, Crosby has a scanner, he most likely heard about all the commotion."

Crosby glanced back and forth between us for several seconds before speaking. When he did, it was in a hushed tone, "I know we only met a few days ago, but when I heard the call go out over the radio for Tactical, and I knew you two were in the area, my heart was in my throat. The pounding didn't quit until the all clear was given."

Mike and I nodded. He and Crosby shook hands. Then Crosby surprised me by reaching out and giving my arm a reassuring squeeze. I barely felt it through my thick jacket, but the sentiment was clear.

I realized that Crosby must not have heard about Arnold's call. I glanced at Mike and he mouthed, "Tell him." I waited until Crosby sat back, and then I revealed that Arnold had called me. Crosby was just as shocked as Mike and I had been at what Arnold had said. It literally reshaped all that we thought about the case and our approach to it.

Crosby held his hand up for a minute and said, "Much as I'd love to believe Arnold's phone confession Laura, he could be purposely trying to throw you off the scent. Don't forget we're dealing with a guy who's not all there, and who's also a planner and a schemer. He's above average in intelligence too." Crosby glanced around and continued, "He's had us going in circles and has enjoyed watching us do so at every turn."

"Man's got a point. We're not going to know for certain until we have him and all the evidence, and we can question him," Mike said.

"That's not to say that I'd discount what he said to you Laura, but we have to continue gathering all the evidence before we come to a conclusion," Crosby said.

I nodded. I had a lot to learn and I was being educated by the best in the field.

"So, I guess some of what I've got to tell you is old news, from before Arnold's call," Crosby said. "I'm guessing that old Reggie's up to date on everything -- the phone call as well as the fact that Gwen had a copy of the client list hidden in her safety deposit box. And of course the new evidence that Reggie, himself, turned up."

Mike and I nodded.

"But anyway, I'll fill you in on what I know. This just gets more bizarre by the minute. Reggie did locate the flash drive that Eliott had hidden away, with all the names of the people they'd stolen from and the exact dollar amounts. I'd guessed that Eliott figured that, someday, he'd be able to repay them and wanted to have an accurate record of all of them. We assumed Arnold discovered the flash drive, blew his stack, and that in his mind the flash drive was reason enough to kill Eliott. In other words, I was surmising that Arnold killed Eliott because of the flash drive, until you both told me otherwise. I believed that Arnold was a total crook and Eliott was a real honest guy, but I may be wrong. At any rate, Eliott hid the drive in the metal frame that holds the box spring for his bed. He slid it underneath. Pretty ingenious, huh? I don't like it when crooks and killers get the better of me. "

"Cheer up Crosby, we all got suckered on this one. How do you think Mike and I feel?" I asked. "We let a diabolical killer hire us to look for his missing dead wife. In spite of our obvious mistake, we're keeping the money since it's already in the bank. We can do that, can't we?

"We can discuss the legalities of that later. In the meantime," Mike said as he started down the path to the lake, "we have just one hour to find a boat, but we do have three sets of eyes."

"That's the spirit! Crosby nodded. "Getting all caught up on current events seems to have inspired you. And think of all the fun we're going to have when this is all over, swapping tales while we're out fishing. We don't have to wait until next spring, either, if that's what you're thinking. I keep my boat in the water all year round. If that's additional inspiration, then so be it."

I followed Mike down the path and Crosby came close behind. We once again kept our heads low and our speech to necessity only.

Within five minutes of reaching the reservoir, the sun glinted off an object at the water's edge. My first thought was, this has to be a trap.

"Hey guys, I see something. I mean, I think I do -- in the water. The sun's hitting something shiny. See it?"

"What do you know; our boy didn't completely hide what our key goes to. Good eye Laura," Crosby said.

"It was the reflection I caught."

Mike cautioned us, "Let's move in slowly, just in case this is a special invitation from you-know-who."

"You're right, Mike," Crosby agreed. "Matter of fact, let me scope around a bit before we get any closer, just to be on the safe side. We're this close; I don't want anything stopping us from making this haul. Let's not slip up or get tripped up."

We patiently waited while Crosby scoped out the perimeter. To me, it felt like hours. I wanted to run in and swab the boat from one end to the other myself, checking for all kinds of evidence that I knew had to be there. I wanted the entire forensics team out here, and I wanted them immediately. But I had to stop and realize that neither of those things was going to happen, at least not for now. There was a system in place for this kind of thing and that's why Crosby was here.

"Okay, coast is clear. Let's check her out. I'll call Grady and let him know what we've found. I'll see how fast he can get another boat out here to tow this one across to the parking lot. They'll have to swab her first, take some samples, get any and all prints that can be gotten, and then trailer her back to headquarters for further analysis."

"Putting her in a giant Ziploc would be a great way to go," I said.

Crosby laughed, "If only that were possible, boy that would make things simpler."

Crosby had no sooner put the call in to Grady, when we saw the detective crew in a boat similar to the one tied up, making their way across the reservoir. They tied off onto a nearby tree, hopped ashore, and wasted no time beginning the collection of evidence. I recognized most of the crew from the first crime scene, when Kola and Casey had discovered Non Wrappe's body. That seemed like ages ago. It wasn't.

"This crew is fast. They'll have this boat processed, back and trailered before you know it," Crosby said. "Hey, should I ask them for a ride for the three of us, or do you want to hike back? There's really nothing for us to do. It's in their hands now."

"To be on the safe side, why don't we hitch a ride?" Mike asked.

"Better safe than sorry," I agreed. "Arnold could be out there, watching the proceedings, seeing as that's what he likes to do. Can we stick around for a minute to see if they find any blood evidence?"

"That we can do, but then I think we should get out. I scanned the area pretty thoroughly, so it's very unlikely Arnold's close by, but you never know. Anyway, let me check on what they've discovered so far. You two stay with me, and keep Kola close by," Crosby said.

We walked over and remained about twenty feet away, watching the team hard at work, measuring what to us were unseen things, but to them was crucial evidence. They placed rulers next to what had to be photographed prior to photographing, bagging some items. All of it was done systematically and with a great deal of patience. I knew why it had to be done this way. It was a defense lawyer's job to rip all of this apart with equal patience and just as systematically as it was a prosecutor's job to knit it together. A prosecutor's job relied entirely on how meticulously the officers and detectives did their job.

Joanna Hitchens leapt up and shouted, "I found blood!" She covered her mouth, and whispered, "Sorry, I get so excited when I find what we're looking for."

I wanted to run over and hug her. Instead, I grabbed Mike and Crosby and began jumping up and down. Kola put his front paws on me, and knocked me to the ground.

Crosby gave me a hand up, while Joanna snapped photo after photo of the blood spatter she'd located.

My heart soared as we climbed aboard the police boat that was taking us to the opposite shore. From there, we'd be given transportation back to Adelaide's, where we could enjoy a lovely dinner, a fire and a movie. We were moving in on our man. I had a good feeling we'd catch him before the storm hit us. For the first time, it felt as if the tide had turned in our direction.

JEAN MARIE WIESEN

Chapter 29

Crosby sat in the stern of the boat, rifle resting on his knees, while we crossed the reservoir. He kept a pair of binoculars glued to his eyes, and scanned the terrain surrounding the team as they scooped up any evidence that might have been left behind.

"You've got your guard up" I noted.

"Yup. Got a bad feeling about this, and it has nothing to do with not trusting my buddies. I do. I train with them all the time, but this guy is devious, and he has no conscience. Look what he did to you and O'Malley. Look what he did to his own partner? Nothing's off limits to him."

Mike turned around, "Crosby, they'll be okay. You've scouted the area once already, and like you said, you all train together. So you'd better believe they're also keeping a close eye on their surroundings. Now you have another job to do, and that's to move on and protect Adelaide. They have to stay behind and finish up with processing the scene. As soon as they get us ashore, this boat will make the return trip and tow that one back. You'll see, and all your worrying will be for nothing."

I pulled my hat down and wrapped my arms around Kola for warmth. In hindsight, I'm still not sure if he jerked and then laid flat on the boat bottom first, or if the gun shot came first. All I remember is everyone yelling and screaming, the boat speeding up, and Mike shoving me down. I do recall a few shell casings hitting me on the cheek, and the bow of the boat hitting land. Sergeant Richard Kirkland, who had been driving the boat, hauled me and Kola out. He led us behind a building and told us not to move. That was not going to be a problem.

Shit, my phone was barking. It was Annie. I had to answer it to at least let her know I was okay.

"Yep, I'm fine. Your timing is ridiculous, though. One of these days, we seriously need to discuss it."

"Not funny. I'm just glad to hear your voice," Annie cried. "You do know that law enforcement is losing their ever loving minds, between the storm and knowing there's a killer on the loose?"

"Kind of in the middle of it, if you know what I mean?"

"Do you know who, if anyone, got shot?"

"No idea at all. I'm stuck behind a building on the reservoir dam, while they're getting a handle on it." I realized I was shaking.

"You're by yourself? No one's with you? What if he comes and gets you?"

"Gee, thanks. I hadn't thought of that. Guess, I'll take a peek over the dam and see if he's there right now. Hold on. Nope, don't see him. Guess he's still on the other side."

"That's not what I meant, silly. I can't believe they left you alone with a shooter out there."

"I've got Kola and a gun. What more do I need?"

"Not implying or even saying that you can't take care of yourself, but until they catch this guy, I'm going to worry. That's how it is." Annie released a heavy sigh.

"I know. Me too, sister friend." I sighed also. "Uh-oh, Mike's coming over and he doesn't look good. Hold on a second, okay?"

"Right here Laura, I'm not going anywhere."

Mike knelt down, put his head on my shoulder and began crying. Crosby came up behind him and mouthed to me that Joanna was gone. Crosby took his sunglasses off and wiped his eyes and then put a hand on Mike's shoulder. In all my years of knowing Mike, I had never once seen him cry. I put my arms around him, held him and felt my own tears begin to flow. I put the phone to my mouth and whispered Joanna's name to Annie. I could hear her crying too. We both hung up.

More officers from neighboring towns and cities, as well as State Troopers, pulled their crews off of storm preparations and linked up for the search. Reggie had joined the hunt too, expressing his intense dislike of the woods, but Arnold had to be found; it was mandatory. It was going to be an incredible crunch time, Sandy preparations be damned. Arnold had to be captured prior to the storm's landing. That meant, no days off for anyone, and overtime for everyone.

"Let's get you two back to Adelaide's before she hears about this on the news," Crosby said. "Actually, I'm surprised she hasn't already called to find out what's going on. Let me give her a call right now.

"Hey Adelaide, this is your friendly cop Crosby, checking in. I've got your two wanderers with me, just wanted to let you know all is well…Okay, okay, you're right. All is not well…Yeah, they said you're too smart for that and I shouldn't try to pull one over on you. Yes, I took it upon myself to call you to let you know that we're on our way back. Mike's not in very good shape. As one would expect, you're correct. Yes, they were good friends and it's a terrible loss for everyone. You'll make a nice dinner for both him and Laura, and me, too? That's very kind of you, and I will take you up on it. Yes, I will pass your condolences on to everyone. To Grady also. What? If anyone wants to stop in for some food, they're welcome to? That's very generous of you Adelaide. And, while the search is ongoing, you want me to put a large coffee pot in the barn for the team? Muffins, too? I know they'll appreciate it. Okay, we'll see you in a bit."

Crosby walked over to Mike and me, stood in between us, put one arm around each of us, and walked us to the nearest police vehicle. He opened the back door for Kola and Mike and then the front door for me. He slid into the drivers' seat and off we went to Adelaide's.

Chapter 30

Those aren't bran muffins, they smell great," I said, "not that your bran muffins don't smell good too."

"I'm not baking bran muffins for the search team, silly. They'd be running behind every tree and bush and messing up my woods instead of hunting down their prey. I'm making my specialty, apple spice muffins with a bit of icing on top. They're healthy and they've got just enough sugar to keep the team going for hours. When they come back, I'll have whipped up a batch of blueberry pancakes for them. Can't have enough carbs; have to keep those fires stoked. They can take cat naps in the barn if they need to, plenty of hay stacks to lie down on, and I've got loads of blankets for them. Don't want any of them to catch cold. There's a bathroom in there, so they don't have to use the outdoor facilities."

Crosby stood by, looking at Adelaide with obvious admiration. "You're very kind to do all of this. It's a pleasure to finally meet you," He said, extending his hand to greet her.

Her brown eyes lit up, "You're dive boy. Pleasure's all mine." She gripped his hand and looked up at him, "Get that rotten bastard out of my backyard, son! Forgive me my manners, I forgot to say, 'please.'"

She walked over to Mike, who remained in the doorway, and hugged him.

"Laura, will you please toss a couple of logs on the fire while Crosby and Mike take the coffee pots and containers of pasta and meatballs to the barn. I'm sure everyone will be interested in dinner by now. Don't forget the bags of plates, cups, utensils, milk and sugar. Right, and the muffins too. That ought to cover it. If anyone needs anything else, let me know. Hurry up and get back so we can sit down and eat; I know you boys want to go out again. Laura's staying put, I'm guessing," Adelaide pinned her eyes straight on me.

"Not moving an inch. Except to help with cleaning up and feeding Kola," I said.

Adelaide smiled.

I exhaled.

"I heard that," Adelaide said, as she brought a plate of pasta to the table.

"I'm meditating. It's part of the process."

"Nice try."

I dropped into the chair and put my head in my hands, thankful the guys were gone. I didn't want them to see me cry.

Adelaide came around the table, and hung her cane over the arm of the chair. She leaned against the table, put her hand on mine and in the softest tone, said, "If you ever tell Mike I've got a sweet side, I'll deny it." Her eyes had a twinkle I'd never seen before, and when she spoke, her voice was not only gentle but had a slight lilt. "My Henry was everything to me Laura, he was my world. We didn't need anything or anyone else. We had this place and each other, and of course all the animals, both the domestic ones and the ones in the woods. Oh, my, when we first built this place, it was the most tranquil, idyllic wonderland you could possibly imagine. Yes, it was fifty years ago and we had horses then, so we would ride along the stream down into the valley. We'd bring picnic lunches with us in the spring and summer and late into the fall. Sometimes, we'd brave it in the winter months too. Henry would build fires and we'd make ourselves some coffee. We'd stay there until the sun went down over the hillside.

Do that nowadays, and someone will call the police and fire department on you. Yes, things have changed mightily over the years since it was just our valley. There are rules now, but it's like that everywhere you go. We used to have so much wildlife come right up to the porch, and we'd throw extra feed out to them if the winter was harsh. They didn't always survive, but they're not meant to, which is why it's survival of the fittest. Now, they allow the animals to be hunted, of course not close to the house, even though the hunters try to now and again. But, we sure as shootin' didn't have humans hunting each other and dumping remains out here.

"I'll tell you something else Laura, when I lost my Henry, my heart broke into a million pieces and I was convinced I would never heal. I was so afraid to be close to anyone again, because what would happen when I lost them too? Then, along came Mike and he was in a dangerous job, so I kept him at arm's length until he retired. I've slowly let him become my friend. I know, it's hard to tell, but I do care about him."

She wiped a tear from her eye, patted both Chloe and Kola, put her hand back on mine and continued, "Then, he brought you into my life, and I softened up a bit, because you were the daughter that Henry and I never had. That's why I couldn't stand it if you went out with Mike, Crosby and the rest of the group to search for this psycho. Besides, he already attacked you once.

"Eat your pasta before it gets cold," she patted my hand, stood up and walked back into the kitchen.

"We never had this conversation," she yelled from the kitchen.

"That's what I thought, and I'm guessing I don't get to respond?"

"Nope."

"You going to join me?" I asked.

"Have to feed the pups, first."

"I was going to feed them. Pasta's great, by the way"

"Glad you're enjoying it."

"So you come and eat, and I'll feed them"

"Can anyone join this argument, and this meal?" Crosby asked, poking his head through the doorway.

"The more, the merrier," Adelaide answered.

"Great, because Mike and I are starving and we've got some info you might be interested in."

"Please sit down, and spill the beans," I said.

I brought over a couple of plates and table settings for them, and retrieved the re-filled pasta bowl for them. Adelaide brought over fresh bread and salad.

"Is this dinner conversation?" she asked.

"We'll leave out the gory details, I promise," Mike said.

"No worries, it's info that you need and besides, you two already ate, right?" Crosby looked back and forth between us.

"Crosby, what have you found?" I demanded.

"Okay, here's the deal, a couple of officers did find a .308, same rifle as what I've got, up high, about fifty yards out from where Joanna was hit. The problem is the serial number has been sandpapered off to the point that it's completely untraceable, even with forensics. As in, there's nothing there. In other words, Arnold bought the gun off the street. Not only that, he had to have been wearing gloves when he fired it, not one lousy fingerprint on it. So, when we find him, there won't be any gun residue on his hands. Doesn't mean there won't be any on his clothing, unless he ditches what he was wearing.

"The only good bit of news is, we got a bootprint that's a match to a print Adelaide showed you two a while back, and that proves he's been in this area, not only on foot but most definitely on horseback too. So, all's not lost, we're piecing this thing together. We've got blood evidence in the boat we found and we've matched up some prints. In other words, we've identified his two modes of transporting bodies here. I don't believe he brought them from too far a distance, that's my personal feeling, and I happen to think they were alive until he got them here."

"What are you saying Crosby? The ME already said the women were killed by an injection of potassium chloride?" I asked.

"Yes, he did…"

"You're disagreeing with the ME?" Mike shook his head.

Adelaide took a bite of bread and said, "I warned you about discussing this at the dinner table."

"Please listen for a minute. Hear me out on this," Crosby continued. "It's a plausible theory and that's where we're at."

"I know where I'm at, and that's starvation station," Grady said as he stepped into the room, rubbing his hands together. When Adelaide's cooking, I'm ready,"

"Hi Lieutenant. Pull up a chair, grab a plate and tell me what you think. I'm theorizing."

"Crosby, I need to have at least a few bites before I think about this, okay?" Grady took a few fast forkfuls, and then signaled for Crosby to go ahead. He sipped some tea that Adelaide had brought to the table for everyone.

"Thanks Loo. As I was saying, under protest from these two, my working theory is that Arnold might not have killed these women right away. He might have injected them with a partial dose to incapacitate them long enough for transportation purposes only. When he reached his destination, and they awakened enough to resist, he finished them off. Follow it and give it some real consideration. It speaks to his psycho sociopathic personality in that human suffering means nothing to him. It's water over a dam, if you will, and look where he picked for his dumping ground, that exact metaphor."

Grady pointed his fork at Crosby and said, "That last bit, the metaphor thing, you just came up with that, didn't you?"

Crosby smiled and responded, "Yeah, I did. It was pretty good, though, huh?"

"I'm inspired. Do you have your own personalized cop trading cards?" Mike asked.

"I'll admit, I'm impressed too," I said. "I'll trade for one of those cards."

"Let me get this straight," Grady took another mouthful of pasta, swallowed some tea, and wiped his mouth before proceeding. "Crosby, you're saying that Arnold quasi-incapacitated his victims long enough to move them, either by horseback, or boat, and then finished them off?"

"That's what I'm surmising Loo, on the evidence we've currently gathered," Crosby answered.

"I have had some reports of horses being taken, but then returned within several hours," Grady said.

"Which substantiates my horseback theory," Crosby said.

"That sounds pretty methodical to me, and pretty damned calculating," Mike said.

"As in pre-meditated and toss insanity out the door," I added.

"We're not the jury, nor are we the defense attorney. We simply collect the evidence and keep it intact as it makes its way through the chain of custody to the prosecutor's desk. If we're called to testify, we do, and in the interim, we keep meticulous notes," Grady said. He slapped the table for emphasis as he got up to leave. "No more break time. I guarantee you, Arnold's plotting his next move with the precision of a chess player. I say it's time we checkmate his ass."

Crosby and Mike grabbed their coats and followed Grady out the door. Crosby picked up his .308 at the coat rack, next to Adelaide's Winchester. He stroked her Winchester affectionately, turned and nodded his approval before closing the door.

When they had gone, I briefly checked in with Annie. She wanted more information than I had to give her, of course. Adelaide and I cleaned up the dishes. Then we sat in silence in front of the dying fire with the remnants of our tea, each lost in our own thoughts of the day's events. I hoped Adelaide was reminiscing about Henry and the good old days. Meanwhile, I could still feel the heat of the spent shells on my cheek.

"I'm going to bed, Laura, to discuss with my Maker why he took

Joanna this day. There are some things I will never understand. When someone's doing good in this world, like trying to catch a killer, for example, and suddenly they're gone, well I just don't know. I don't expect an answer, but I do expect the talk to knock me out. Sleep well."

"Thanks Adelaide. You too."

Chapter 31

I awakened with a hand over my mouth. It was Adelaide's. It was still dark out, and Kola was standing next to the window. He had pushed the curtains aside with his nose.

Adelaide was dressed the same way she had been the last time I was yanked from dreamland by her in the middle of the night, right down to the shotgun cradled in her arm. If this became a regular thing, Arnold wasn't going to kill me; I was going to die from a heart attack.

I gripped her wrist in a futile attempt to remove her hand from my mouth. I put my other hand on my neck in the universal signal of, "I'm choking!"

She nodded and said, "You have to whisper, there's someone out there."

"Right, the two officers assigned to protect us. They're on the porch, and a barn full of cops, detectives and state cops are all over the place. Adelaide, there are cops crawling all over these woods. You're hearing all kinds of noises you're not used to, including me choking!"

I leaned over to get a sip of water from the night table, then sat on the edge of the bed and froze. Out of the corner of my eye I caught a glimpse of a shadow passing by the bedroom window. The hair on my arms stood up, and now I understood the meaning of your blood running cold. I reached for my flannel sweats, which were on the chair back, my socks, shoes and my coat. I grabbed my Glock from underneath my pillow and picked up my cell phone from the night table.

"Isn't under your pillow the most obvious place for your gun?" Adelaide whispered.

"Not any more so than the coat rack is for your shot gun."

"Touché."

"We're staying right in this bedroom until we establish where everyone is, got it?"

"Clear to me. I've got Chloe with me."

"I see that. Good thinking. Let me give Mike a call. In the meantime, we need to be quiet and stay away from the windows – the pups too." I crouched and went to Kola's position, leashed him and took him over to Adelaide and Chloe, who were on the floor next to the bed, which provided a barrier between them and the windows. I too, sat down on the floor. I phoned Mike.

"Yeah, it's me." Mike sounded groggy. "It's really late, what's going on?"

"I know it's late, but something's not right. Neither officer is on the porch like they're supposed to be. Kola won't quit with his growling. It's too quiet out there Mike, and…

"What was that?" I asked.

"Sounds like the kitchen window breaking," Adelaide answered.

"What? The window broke?" Mike asked. "That's impossible. How the hell could he get through the perimeter we set up? Don't hang up. Stay on the line, I'll use my other phone and call one of the guys in the barn. There has to be someone there."

I grabbed Adelaide by the collar of her coat and forced her down to the floor. "You are not going out there." I knelt down on the floor next to Adelaide and felt something sharp in my knee. It was silver with an arrow on it. What a time for this find.

"Look what I found sticking in my knee, Adelaide?" I held up her long lost Sherwood Archery pin.

She arched one eyebrow and then grinned, in spite of our dire situation. "You are one mighty good detective. Now, let go of me young lady, so this bastard doesn't attack us."

"Stay put, Adelaide. You'll get us both killed. Let him come to us, then we'll shoot him."

"Promise?"

"Cross my heart and all that stuff. You can even take the first shot if you'd like."

She smiled, rested the Winchester on the bed and aimed it straight at the door.

"Hey Mike, did you get ahold of anyone? Adelaide's ready to blow away whoever walks through the door, so we'd better make sure it's not someone we like."

"Uh Laura, the guys on the porch were hit over the head, they're out cold. Whoever's in the house is not a friendly. I repeat, whoever is in the house is not a friendly. Acknowledge."

"Received Mike."

"Crosby is outside with Grady and a few others. They made the determination on the officers and are figuring out the best means of entry at the moment. They've got the house surrounded. There's no way for this person to escape. We assume it's Arnold, but we don't… wait, yeah, we do know now. We have confirmation; it's Arnold. He's moving from the kitchen, down the hallway, slowly. Laura, if you can, put the earpiece to your phone in, I don't want him picking up any sort of noise, okay?"

I kept the earpiece in my coat pocket. It was a bit tough to keep my hands from shaking, but I managed. One of these days, I would go high tech and use Bluetooth.

"Got it Mike. I can't hear any footsteps. Rotten SOB! I gripped my Glock with both hands and rested them alongside Adelaide's. We glanced at each other and resumed our gaze on the bedroom door.

"Okay Laura, he stopped, for no reason that can be ascertained, their words, I'm relaying what I'm hearing. Seems to be taking in his surroundings, why? Don't know. Now, he's flipping through some papers on the table, the dining room table. Did we leave anything important out that you recall?"

"No."

"I didn't think so either. Crosby was tossing out theories, right? Yeah, he wasn't scribbling. I know he doodles, sometimes when he's working his theories. Was he doodling when he was going through that whole potassium chloride thing? Think Laura, this is important. And you have that photo memory recall thing."

I closed my eyes and relived the conversation, down to the minutiae. I could visualize Crosby doodling but didn't see him drawing any chemical compounds, so I felt comfortable enough responding in the negative. I whispered, "Not even a syringe."

"Good enough for me. The guys are discussing not wanting to mess up Adelaide's house and the fact that you two are in there. My guess is, flash bangs are out due to her age. Even though you and Adelaide are in the bedroom, they'd hurt her ears and could do permanent damage. And tear gas is out too. It could burn the place down. We all want this jackass to go to jail, not the morgue. Plus it would be tough to get you out safely. I don't think Adelaide would mind a couple more broken windows and maybe a broken door, right?"

"No."

"We'll have it fixed right away, as in by first light.

"They'd better hurry up! Where's Arnold now?"

"He's still rummaging through the papers on the desk. Okay, here's what they're going to do; they'll shoot through the windows to hit him below the knees, don't want to cripple the guy...Oh, and they'll go for the arm holding the rifle too. At the same time, they'll be breaking through the front door. It will be over within less than fifteen seconds."

"Good, I have to pee," I muttered.

"This is news? Thanks for the much needed laugh. God, I wish I was there, but this is sort of like being the behind the scenes director. Damn concussion and doctor's orders to stay out of action, but as soon as they get him, I'll hop in my car. I can't miss seeing his arrogant self in cuffs. I'll bet you can't wait to call Annie? Well, after you go. Speaking of 'go,' you ready? Three seconds from go time. It's been a pleasure being your emcee this morning."

I looked at Adelaide and blinked three times. I mouthed that it would be over in three seconds.

She nodded and steadied the shotgun.

I readjusted my grip and double checked that Kola's leash was well wrapped on my ankle. I heard Mike's countdown in my ear, then all hell broke loose on the other side of the door. More breaking glass, numerous shots fired, Arnold swearing, the splitting of wood -- had to have been the front door -- followed by a thump and more expletives both from the cops and Arnold.

We heard cheers, and rounds of, "job well done," coupled with, "get the stretcher in here and make sure you cuff the prisoner to it." We could barely make out Grady reading Arnold his rights.

Mike phoned Annie for me on his other phone, so she could get the exclusive footage of Arnold being wheeled to the ambulance with an escort of police officers. I could hear her laugh and say she was already on her way. "It's all clear ladies, safe to come out," Crosby announced. He opened the door to both of us still hunkered down on the opposite side of the bed, shotgun and Glock aimed right at him.

"I come in peace, please lower your weapons," he smiled. "Oh, and until we get the glass swept up, keep the pooches in here, okay? We've got a crew coming in to clean it all up and replace your windows and the front door, well just the frame. We didn't kill the door itself. We were careful." Crosby was beaming.

"What was the thump?" Adelaide asked.

"That was the beautiful sound of a criminal hitting the floor, Adelaide. Music to my ears. The only thing better than that is landing a tuna in my boat. Doesn't make quite the same thump, but it does give me similar satisfaction.

"I don't think I'll quit smiling over this one for a long time. The only thing better than this will be the day he gets sentenced by a judge. Yeah, we'll have to listen to him blabber for a minute or two, but the judge gets the last word, and it will be over. What a great day that will be," Crosby sighed, then said, "soon as Mike gets here and sees this fool in cuffs, let's go get the biggest breakfast we can find. That will give the clean-up guys time to do their thing, and I don't know about you, but I'm starving.

"Speak of the devil, here comes Mike now. Gang's all here."

As we made our way carefully through the debris and onto the porch, we could see the news cameras focused on Annie and Grady. He graciously gave her a few moments of his time, going through some of the information regarding the capture, focusing mostly on the fact that Arnold had been taken alive, and so, yes he would indeed face a jury of his peers for all his crimes.

After they'd wrapped up the interview, Grady walked over, and he and Adelaide and I stood there, looking at each other, not quite knowing what to say.

Despite the racket of brooms and shop vacuums that had already been brought in to begin cleaning up the mess, our moment of silence was deafening. I was the first to break the silence.

"Is this how it's supposed to be Grady?" I asked.

"A little anticlimactic, huh?" Grady said.

"That's an understatement," I said.

"That's why we all have outlets," Grady mused. "Crosby has his fishing, and, well, I dabble in it too. Mike rides his Harley, you hike a lot, and I'm guessing you'll probably do a lot more of it." He put his arm around me. "Come on, you two, get dressed, we'll go eat a good breakfast, then this place has to get put back together before Sandy hits. Remember the storm? We'll go through the debriefing after breakfast, and last but not least, we still have all the evidence to sift through, and the files to make nice and neat and pretty for the prosecutor. Don't forget, Arnold has to be questioned by both Reggie, myself and the Captain, so the fun's not completely over." Grady winked, "And of course don't forget about the arraignment and the trial."

I grinned, and went off to get dressed. So much, indeed, to look forward to. We had captured Arnold after a long, arduous hunt. He'd believed he was impervious to capture, but we had proved him wrong. Now, we would sew up our case. It would be airtight, perfectly packaged for the prosecution to present to the jury, and I would be there each and every day until sentencing day, alongside at least one detective and/ or officer of the Soundview Police Department, who would be present to honor Detective Joanna Hitchens. On sentencing day, it would be standing room only. Arnold would never breathe free air again, not after all the lives he'd taken.

Chapter 32

Annie promised to leave her iPad and all recording devices in her car while she joined us for breakfast at our favorite local spot, the Olde Bluebird Inn. I checked her pockets, just in case. Crosby wanted to frisk her. Annie both dared him and glared at him. Adelaide insisted they sit at opposite ends of the table to avoid her getting gastric upset. Mike wanted to leave them both outside while we enjoyed a quiet, well deserved meal.

"We're all adults, I think." I pointed to a seat next to me, "Crosby, sit, stay and don't speak unless you've something nice to say. Understood?"

"I like women who take charge. If I'm good, may I please have a biscuit?" He leaned his head over as he took his seat.

I patted him on the head, "Good boy, good stay.

"As for you, dear friend, if you don't cool it, you're going to be banished to your car and your food will be sent out to you. Is that clear?"

Annie answered, "Yes, and I'm sorry. This is the biggest story to hit, probably ever, and I got carried away. I really mean that everyone, especially in light of the loss of Joanna."

"Apology accepted," Grady said. "Now, let's get on with the business of ordering our food, so we can get back to the task at hand; getting all our ducks in a row. That's what Joanna would want us to do."

The waitress arrived with six steaming cups of coffee, and we each took a moment to peruse the menu. My stomach growled. It seemed like years since the pasta dinner we'd had at Adelaide's. I chose my usual order of scrambled eggs with Swiss cheese, wheat toast and fresh fruit on the side, while Mike chose the house special, a tall stack of pancakes with bacon and two eggs over easy. I told him that if he'd ordered anchovies on his pancakes, he too would be banished to his car.

After we'd all ordered, Crosby began, "Hey Loo, so who's interviewing Arnold before he goes into surgery? I thought you'd be doing it? Unless of course he's got a lawyer and has nothing to say,"

"Nope, the Captain and Reggie are taking it. They want first crack at him, especially Reggie. I'll get the follow-ups with Reggie after surgery. That's fine by me. Captain's an ace interviewer, and the initial one will be short and sweet. There will be plenty of time to watch the Captain in action later on.

"As to the lawyer issue, Arnold says there are a few things he's willing to discuss with us prior to his lawyer's arrival. Could be a trap he's laying for us, but I'm not concerned, the Captain's not going to fall for his antics."

"They'll be operating on him for a while, I'm guessing," Mike said.

"The leg wound was a through and through, so that's a clean-up. The arm might take a bit longer if the broken bones have to be pinned back together. Could be a long one. Our tax dollars hard at work," Crosby said.

"Look at the bright side, his golfing days are over," Mike grinned.

"Last I heard, they even took away miniature golf in prison," Adelaide smirked.

"I suppose the Masterson Club will have to find someone else to run their charity event next spring." I mused.

Crosby laughed, "Wow, can you imagine their surprise when they discover who we've arrested? I'd love to be a fly on that boardroom wall.""

Annie sipped some coffee, and said, "I do believe I'll hop on over to get some members' reactions while it's still early." She put some money on the table, winked and added, "Parts of this job can be a bit entertaining at times. Stay tuned."

"She's entertaining," Grady said.

"Sorry you two got into it, earlier," I said to Crosby.

"Not a big deal. We're all tired and we all want the same thing; we want Arnold to go down for this. It's been a long drawn out saga, and she's your best friend, I get that. Come on, this guy comes into your office, all innocent, pretending to hire you and Mike, and look what happens. You could have been killed. Like Annie said, this turned into one hell of a story for her, but don't think for one second she wasn't scared to death for you. Arnold was after you too, in a convoluted way. I mean, you even resembled the women he killed, and I think it creeped out all of us. Oh, geez, I just used one of Mike's words, or is it Grady's?" Crosby covered his face in mock embarrassment.

Mike slapped him.

It felt so good to laugh, to release the pent up energy without the fear of looking over our shoulders, or ducking for cover from the sound of something dropping or a branch breaking.

Grady surveyed what little remained of our breakfast. "Let's get out of here, and get back to headquarters to start all this lovely paperwork," he announced, to collective groans. "I don't like it any more than you do, but it's a necessary evil, and we've gotta get it out of the way before Arnold gets out of surgery and there's more of it. There are two things we've gotta get going on besides the paperwork; we need a detail to oversee his transfer to the jail as soon as he is able to be moved, and I want it done before the storm. I do not want him in the hospital when that thing hits. Also, I want him arraigned, pronto. Find me a judge who's willing to go down and do this, bedside, as soon as he's awake from his surgery. Find me a defense lawyer, too even if he's in the lobby of the hospital, because I do not want this tossed back at a later date, Arnold saying he didn't get his due process. We all know he's got enough tricks up his sleeve to pull out who-knows-what at the last minute. I don't want him saying his lawyer isn't a defense lawyer, only knows about taxes or real estate, or some other excuse, so he can hold us up and then point to us for not having gotten a fair trial down the road, and I definitely don't want him alleging that we didn't adhere to procedure."

"Yes Sir," was said in unison by all seated at the table.

"Excellent. I'm picking up the tab," Grady said.

I raised my hand.

"What do you have Laura?" Grady asked.

"Much as it bothers me, I know everyone's entitled to a defense. Well, a friend I went to John Jay with went on to law school and works in the Public Defender's Office. I know they're assigned cases, but he's been there for a while, high up in the pecking order as it were. Would you like me to give him a call?"

"Definitely. Since it's such a high profile case, I'm sure they're already wondering who's going to get it, if anyone. They most likely figure he's got his own attorney. Little do they know, the guy's broke and there's no way he's going to make bail -- and you know he's going to ask for it. Well, that and any lawyer worth their salt will, regardless," Grady answered.

"All right, I'll give him a call. His name's Jack Highgate." I got up to make the call.

It wasn't necessary to let Grady and everyone else know that Jack was intended to be an integral part of the firm that Matt and I had planned to open all those years ago. But when the need for an attorney arose, Jack's name was the first to come to mind, and I knew he would appreciate the call along, with the notoriety. It might be just the thing, the incentive he needed to get him out on his own, or to get a partner as I'd done.

I was back at the table in two minutes flat. "What do you know, not only is Jack interested -- who wouldn't be, right? It's a case maker, as they say in his business -- but he thinks he can find a judge who will go to the hospital, along with the bail commissioner, as soon as Arnold's been awake for at least twenty four hours. He said Arnold's got to be coherent enough to comprehend the severity of the charges against him. That brings us to tomorrow, Friday, and that still gives you until Sunday to move him to the jail, a sufficient amount of time before the storm hits," I said.

"When will he know for sure about the judge?" Grady asked.

"He said he'd get back to me in about an hour," I replied.

"But it's a go on the commissioner?" Grady asked.

"Yes," I answered.

"Excellent networking," Grady said.

"I have a stupid question Loo," Crosby said.

"No such thing, but go," Grady said, standing.

"Suppose for a minute he's got the money for bail. You figure he's going to put his house up, right and it's worth what, around eight hundred thousand or so?"

"It's not enough," Grady responded. "Add in whatever assets you think he's got and it doesn't matter. Those monies aren't his. He stole money from that list of people that Reggie's got on the flash drive. Remember? Besides, the commissioner has to ask for the maximum amount of bail allowed by the state in a case as serious as this, and that's a million, so he's short."

We walked outside. Crosby stretched, took a deep breath and said, "I believe Joanna will help us out with this one."

"Yep," Mike said. "We've sure had some supernatural help before; maybe now it's Joanna's turn."

Chapter 33

❝Get out!❞ Arnold screamed, as Reggie, Grady, Mike, Crosby and I walked into the hospital room. "I'd throw something at you, but you've got me cuffed to the bed -- for no reason, I might add, and my other arm's in a sling. You're holding me against my will, and I didn't do a damned thing. When the hospital releases me, I'm suing each of you for everything you're worth. You've ruined my reputation in the community and you're collectively responsible for my wife's death. Not only that, my sister left town after reading the headlines, claiming she'll never speak to me for the rest of my life."

Reggie held his hand up and said, "Hold on fella, you killed Gwen and we've got ample proof." He waved the flash drive in Arnold's line of sight at the foot of the bed, and watched Arnold writhe against his cuffs. "You know what this is, huh?" Reggie smiled. "We found this in Eliott's secret hiding spot, and no I'm not revealing to you what's on it.

"We've got enough evidence to keep you in prison for years, if not forever. We've got you for everything from embezzlement to murder and all sorts of stuff in between. We're only here to take your pretty little mug shot, get some fingerprints and inquire as to whether or not you'd like a public defender present while we question you or a lawyer of your own choosing. Or, whether you'd like to free yourself of the burden you're carrying and tell us what you know. The Captain will be here in a minute. Your call, as they say?"

"I already said I didn't do it … and you stole from me," Arnold said.

"Wait, can you repeat that, please. That last part," Grady asked. "Exactly how is it we stole from you? And assuming for one second that we did, what is it that we stole?" Grady crossed his arms.

"My flash drive."

Grady raised his eyebrows and turned to Reggie, "I thought you found that in Eliott's house Reg?"

Reggie turned the drive over in his palm and showed it to Grady who nodded. "What initials do you see engraved there Grady?"

"What a fascinating question Reggie. Why, I see 'EP.'"

"That's amazing, since Eliott's last name is Potts," Reggie said.

"You don't say," Mike chimed in.

"But, Arnold is claiming it's his property. This indeed is confusing," I said. "Good thing all of you are detectives," I added.

Reggie said, "You went to a top of the line school Laura, so don't sell yourself short. I'd like to toss in that you're cutting your teeth on a tough case, a headliner, as they call it in the business. I'd like to say, you're growing up P.I. and rather quickly," he smiled and tossed the drive to Grady.

Grady snatched the drive mid-air, rubbed his fingers over the initials and stared down at Arnold, "You want to continue to maintain that this is your property, even though we found it hidden away at Eliott's? Or, would you like to take this opportunity to tell the truth?"

Arnold shut his eyes and pulled hard at his cuffed wrist.

"Keep that up, and you'll break it," Mike said. "Your wrist, not the cuffs," he added.

"Then, it will be real tough to sign your statement," Reggie reminded him.

Arnold suddenly stopped straining at his cuffs and went completely still. "If I tell you the truth, will you make a deal with me?" he asked.

"It all depends on what you tell us," Reggie answered.

"Hi, sorry I'm so late. Hope I haven't missed too much?" Captain Winston said, as he strode into the already crowded hospital room. He closed the door behind him.

"No, not really," Grady said, "we're discussing the flash drive and the importance of Arnold's cooperation. You know, the impact that will have on the judge's sentencing."

"Oh, absolutely, Arnold. The Lieutenant is right on the money in that regard," the Captain said calmly. "The judge looks very highly on someone's assistance in an investigation, and that's where we are at this stage. The more you play ball with us, the better it is for all concerned; and that's what we're all after, the best outcome for all involved, you included. We're interested in your welfare at the end of the day, Arnold."

"You seriously expect me to believe that?" Arnold said.

"Yes, I do," the Captain said. He walked over and pulled a chair next to Arnold's bed, sat down and looked him straight in the eye, "Arnold, look at the top notch care you're receiving; state of the art hospital, state of the art surgery, no expenses are being spared here to get you good as new. Whatever you need, you're going to be given, be it rehabilitation for your arm, your legs, all at no cost to you. You're not being charged for any of this, not one dime. All we're asking is that you tell us what happened, and after that, Arnold, we can all move forward."

"With one exception," Arnold said.

"What's that?" the Captain asked.

"I'll go to prison," Arnold responded.

"We don't have any idea what a jury of your peers will say, do we?"

"I suppose not."

"No, we don't. I'll grant you that first we do have to have a conversation about what happened, and that's why we're here, to listen to your side of things. I'm not going to lie to you Arnold, there are some things we're going to charge you with, some things that we've got strong evidence on, which is why you were read your rights at the house when you were arrested. I know it was a long list of things, but we had to do it. Now we have to take all of that a step further, all of which is a legal process, a process that protects your rights, okay?"

"I understand."

"Great Arnold. Because we've got a judge coming in, along with a bail commissioner, a court reporter, and a prosecuting attorney; and all the charges are going to be read off. We also have a public defender coming, unless of course you have an attorney that you'd like to call?"

"No, I don't. I've never been in trouble before, so I don't have that kind of lawyer. This is embarrassing. What are you going to do?"

"It's called an arraignment, Arnold. Like I said, this is when all the charges against you are read aloud into the official record, and the bail will be set by the commissioner. Also, you will be officially identified as the defendant in this case.

"Okay, I might have done one thing, but that's it... Okay, more than one thing."

The Captain put his hands on his knees and asked, "I appreciate your willingness to work with us, Arnold, I really do. Confession's good for the soul. What is it that you did?"

"I did embezzle the money. Eliott wanted to give it back, which was impossible because I'd lost most of it in the stock market and bad investments. He didn't know this until I told him. He thought that if we sold our homes and came clean, we could repay some of the monies and turn ourselves in. I had a lot of money in off-shore accounts that he didn't know about, but I figured if I agreed to sell the house, it would get him off my back long enough for me to leave the country. Why bother being straightforward with a guy who's going behind my back and sleeping with my wife, right?"

The Captain nodded and motioned for Arnold to continue.

"I thought you might understand," Arnold said, as the corner of his mouth curled up. "What happened next was quite unexpected, to say the least. Eliott tells me that one of the clients, a Wendy Appleton, came to his home and confronted him regarding her and her husband's losses in their investments with our firm. By the way, I know some of this was recorded in my phone call with sweet Laura, but I'm willing to go over old ground in the spirit of cooperation."

I stared at the linoleum floor to avoid what I knew was Arnold's stare.

His monotone voice continued, "Eliott said the confrontation became ugly, as in a push turned into a shove, and she fell, hitting her head. He said his attempts at reviving her failed. He panicked and dumped the body. He claimed that while doing so, he was spotted by Gwen, who was out sketching, so naturally he had to kill her. I'm supposed to believe this insane story? My beautiful wife just happens to be out in the woods at the exact time that he's dumping a body? Then, I'm at home when Gwen's sister shows up, a sister I never knew she had, a twin no less. We're outside on the walkway when Eliott comes back from his body dumping, he sees Gwen's twin and flips out. I can understand, I would have, too. He screams, thinking that it's Gwen haunting him, and that's when I discover that he's murdered my wife. Sorry if I'm telling this story out of order, I'm still in a state of disbelief. So, he pleads and begs for his life, insisting that he and Gwen never had an affair, when Gwen's twin starts yelling and runs in the house. Fortunately, I live in a relatively quiet neighborhood, and everyone was at work, otherwise all hell would have broken loose. Can you believe it? The audacity of Eliott is mind boggling."

The Captain looked at the camera to be sure it was still running. He nodded to Arnold to resume.

"No comment, Captain?" Arnold asked.

"This is your story Arnold. If I need to ask any questions, I will. At the moment, you're doing just fine," the Captain replied. "I take that back, what's Gwen's sister's name?"

"Toska," Arnold answered.

"Thank you. Please go on," the Captain said.

"Okay, I was waiting for you to ask that, now I can proceed." Arnold stopped, mumbled for a bit, looked away before beginning again, "I lost my place for a minute. I believe I was speaking about that little snipe begging and pleading for his life, and insisting that he hadn't had an affair with Gwen. He must have thought I was stupid, when I was the brains behind the operation. Yes, that's right, it was all my idea. All he did was sit on some silly board and obtain inside information. Anyone can do that, for heaven's sake! It's not rocket science. Once you have the information, you use it and you make money, lots and lots of money. Granted, we were stealing, I'll give you that, but the murder thing, well I've no idea how that all started. It's a bit like when a ball begins to roll downhill; it simply won't stop.

"So, Eliott kept up with his sniveling, begging and all that, as he was backing down to the lake, and things took on a life of their own after that, what can I say? I know, a surreal quality...yes, that's it, as if it was all meant to be. The rope was on the dock, right next to the cinder block. He fell right into the boat and passed out. I wrapped him up in a blanket, put the cement block around his leg and dropped his body in the middle of the lake."

"Arnold, what happened to Toska?" Captain Winston asked.

Arnold narrowed his eyes, and stared at the ceiling before replying. "I need some water."

Mike stepped over with a glass and held the straw up to Arnold's mouth.

Arnold sighed and said, "She was so annoying. She showed up on my doorstep unannounced, looking for Gwen. Like I said before, I'd never met her, never knew she even existed, and was completely floored to discover that Gwen had a twin. She lives in some state in the southwest, and wanted to mooch off Gwen and I to advance her own art career. Somehow, she'd gotten the idea that she could live with us. Anyway, I brought the boat back in to the dock, went into the house, and couldn't find her. I took a walk down the street, and ended up in the woods, and that's when I discovered Gwen's body with all that silly stuff on it, the bear and the rest of it. Toska was following me; crying her eyes out, so putting her out of her misery seemed to be the right thing to do. Besides, I couldn't have any witnesses around reporting me to the authorities for, well, I didn't exactly kill Eliott... he fell into the boat, the clumsy fool. Collecting all that stuff, the bear, the flag, the note and the KA-BAR knife was a tremendous effort. I only did that to protect Eliott's reputation. I didn't want anyone to think he was a killer, or me, for that matter. The plan was for you to believe that there really was a serial killer running around town, so I had to make it look that way"

Reggie rubbed his chin, stared at the floor for a minute, then looked at Arnold and said, "Arnold, let me see if I understand you correctly. This is some story you've told us. I want to be sure I've got it straight, so bear with me. You're an admitted thief and an accidental killer, is that the size of it?"

Arnold became wide-eyed, and said, "I'd love to shake your hand, but circumstances prevent me from doing so. You got it, Mr. FBI Agent!"

"Is there anything else you'd like to tell us?" the Captain inquired.

"Like what?" Arnold said.

Mike walked over and whispered into the Captain's ear. The Captain nodded, got up and stepped over to Reggie. The two of them walked out of the room.

Mike sat down, crossed his arms, yawned and said, "Just the two of us pal. What do you say we tie up a couple of loose ends, so to speak?"

"Why? You're not a cop. I don't owe you a thing. I already paid you," Arnold laughed.

"He might not still be a cop, but I am," Grady said, stepping up behind Mike. "If he's got questions, answer them."

Arnold adjusted himself, and looked back and forth between Grady and Mike. He tried to look at me, but couldn't due to Grady's frame blocking his view.

"You're looking a bit pale Arnold. Do you have to eat on a regular basis?" Mike asked.

"Yes, why?"

"Are you insulin dependent, Arnold?" Mike asked.

"So what if I am. It's not a crime to be." Arnold's lips tightened. "One of my investors owns a medical supply business."

"Lucky guy," Grady quipped.

"I've one more question for you Arnold, how do you make string when you're in the woods?" Mike asked.

"It's easy, if you're a woodsman. You take the inside part of bark, the stringy looking part, wet it a bit, roll it in your palm, hold one end in your teeth and the other in your hands, and it twists up very nicely on its own. You're asking me very strange questions," Arnold said, averting his gaze.

"Not if you think about it, we're not," Mike said as he got up. "You're our guy. I'm not completely convinced Eliott had anything to do with the killings, but it's going to be next to impossible to prove it, since you killed him too."

"One thing you're definitely going down for is killing a cop," Grady said, standing tall over Arnold's bed. "You forgot to dispose of the clothing you were wearing when you shot and killed one of my detectives. That includes the gloves you wore at the time. Yup, we found all of that hidden in your lovely boat house. Shame you weren't a tad bit more careful about getting rid of the evidence. You've an ample supply of KA-BAR knives, Marine teddy bears, and US flags at your house, too. We know the Marines turned you down. You most likely failed the psych exam, so not following in your uncle's footsteps put undue hardship on you. Face it Arnold, you failed across the board. We also have a photo of you leaving the pizza place after you fired off a shot. You were dressed in your nifty Brown outfit, and you might have forgotten admitting to Laura that you were indeed Brown when you had her pinned down outside of Adelaide's barn.

"I believe it's time for his arraignment," Grady said. "Let's leave them to it."

Arnold slammed his head against the pillow as we exited the room.

Captain Winston, who had been listening from just outside the door, shook Grady's and Mike's hands, "Stroke of genius there men, getting the information out of him regarding one of his investors owning a medical supply company, along with him being a diabetic. He never saw it coming. He's diabolical, alright, and that's where he got his needles and potassium chloride from. I guarantee it was stolen, but now we know. We'll have them check for missing supplies. Good work gentlemen."

"And getting him to tell you how he made the rope," added Grady," that ties it up nicely, so to speak."

I looked up and down the hallway, then back at the Captain.

"If you're looking for Reggie, he's gone. Something about

rearranging his tackle box," Captain Winston said.

The Captain signaled to the Judge to enter the room. Behind the judge, a bail commissioner walked in, followed by a court reporter, then the prosecuting attorney with an assistant, and then my friend Jack Highgate, the public defender. Reggie and Grady had already done the necessary fingerprinting and mug shot with the portable equipment. The judge verified that the official identification had been taken care of, since the arraignment couldn't begin unless it had. He waited until Grady answered in the affirmative and the proceedings were under way. The prosecutor read all of the charges, including the five murder charges and the embezzlement charge, the only one that Arnold would readily admit to.

As expected, the commissioner set the bail at one million dollars, the highest the state would allow. The judge asked Arnold if he understood the charges. Initially he nodded. The judge informed him that a verbal response was required. Arnold glared at the judge and gave him a, "Yes."

The judge remanded Arnold to custody as soon as the hospital deemed him fit for release. He clearly did not have the funds for bail. The treating physician's notes indicated that Arnold could be discharged the next day, which was Saturday. The judge marked his calendar accordingly, for a pre-trial conference the following month. He wished everyone a safe passage during the coming storm and exited the room, with the court reporter right behind him.

We cleared out, per Jack's request to spend time with his new client.

I pretended not to know Jack as I passed him on the way out of the room.

We walked down the hallway, out of earshot, before anyone spoke. Grady was the first to utter a word, "Shame they took the death penalty off the table."

"I don't think so," I said. "He's the perfect candidate to spend the rest of his life rotting in prison."

Chapter 34

I kept my promise to each of the victims and attended every day of the trial, beginning with the pre-trial conference. That first day, Arnold arrived in his orange jump suit with DOC stenciled in large black letters across his back. As I waited for the conference to start, I wondered vaguely if other prisoners in the Department of Corrections had the job of stenciling letters onto jumpsuits. Naturally, Arnold pled not guilty after which he lost his temper, picked up a pitcher of water and lobbed it straight at the judge. Four Judicial Marshals tackled Arnold and brought him to the ground. It took several minutes to subdue him, cuff and shackle him, and get him seated once again.

At his next court appearance, he was brought to the defense table to meet his lawyer, shackled at his hands, waist and feet, with a Judicial Marshal at either side holding each elbow. The shackles and chains clanged with every step he took, and banged against the chair and table as the Marshals helped him take his seat. When the Judge addressed him, the Marshals had to assist him with standing and again with sitting, due to the chains. Because of this, Jack requested that during the trial, his client be unshackled and dressed in a suit, so the jury would not be biased against him. The Judge agreed to allow Arnold to wear a suit, but he would not back down on him remaining handcuffed when entering the courtroom, both ankles and hands. He said if Arnold had not thrown the pitcher of water at him during the pre-trial conference, things would be different. He did, however, say that once Arnold was seated, the leg shackles could be removed. Jack was less than satisfied, but it was the best he was going to get under the circumstances.

Within a week, a jury was seated and in two weeks the trial had ended. Jack had put on a great show, but the prosecution had an open and shut case, and Jack knew it. There was a literal arsenal of evidence. Arnold wanted to depend on the kindness of his peers, well so be it. When it came to witnesses, none had shown for Arnold, because there weren't any. Not even his sister showed up as a character witness. The prosecution had a few witnesses that were strong and viable, coupled with the forensic evidence that made their case solid. As to the embezzlement charges, those would be tried separately in a federal court. In other words, this was only the beginning for Arnold. He would face a slew of new charges, a new set of witnesses, and yet another jury.

Sentencing day arrived, and as predicted, it was standing room only. We'd been smart and shown up an hour early, to be sure to get a seat on the one side of the courtroom that was supposed to be reserved for the family of the defendant. In this situation, that was Arnold. So far, I hadn't spotted anyone, but we still had to leave that row open, just in case.

The other side was filled with several rows of families of the victims whose lives Arnold had taken.

"Do you know anyone over there?" I pointed.

"Don't recognize anyone," Mike said. "I don't think Joanna's family lives in the area, what there is of it. I think her parents are deceased, and she had one sister and that's it."

"Someone's got a big family, don't know who it is, unless it's several families," Grady said.

"I'm sure glad we got here early, this place is filling up," Mike said.

"Good thing you listened to me," Adelaide said.

"You're not kidding. Look," I pointed to the door.

The Captain walked in with the Chief, the Deputy Chief and the entire squad behind them. Neighboring towns would be covering while they were here for the sentencing, in case any criminals had some otherwise brilliant plans. Grady and Mike got up to join the police entourage, while I remained in my seat with Adelaide next to me. A reporter nearly dove into the empty spot, all smiles. Every major paper and not so major paper in the state was here to cover the story, along with large news outlets, since the case had garnered nationwide attention.

The bailiff walked out, slowly scanned the crowd, and then announced, "All rise, the Superior Court of the great State of Connecticut is now in session, the Honorable Judge Anthony Richard is presiding."

"That was a fast hour, feels like we just got here," I whispered.

"Quiet, you'll get us thrown out," the reporter said in a loud stage whisper.

"You, sonny boy, keep quiet with your notepad. I've waited a long time for this day. I don't want to miss a word that the Judge has to say. Got it?" Adelaide held her cane up.

The reporter looked at her and gulped.

I bit my lip.

Judge Richard peered over the rim of his glasses, took his seat, adjusted his microphone and motioned for the gallery to take theirs. He glanced around the courtroom and waited for everyone to settle in, as did the Marshals. There appeared to be extra Marshals on duty in light of the overflow crowd. I didn't expect them to ask anyone to leave.

"There doesn't seem to be enough seats for everyone who showed up for today's business. This is an unusually high attendance, but then it is a high profile case, therefore I will allow for standing in the aisles if you can possibly keep them clear, otherwise the Fire Marshal will clear them for you," the Judge said.

He took a sip of water before continuing, and surveyed the room while he spoke, without looking directly at Arnold. Whenever his eyes traveled in that direction, they stopped and met with Jack's eyes instead of Arnold's.

I noticed that Arnold didn't seem to be paying attention anyway. He was either adjusting his handcuffs or tracing the grain of the table wood with his fingernail.

The Judge reiterated the charges against Arnold, discussing the severity of the crimes, the heinous nature of them, essentially justifying why he was about to impose the sentence, or in this case, string of sentences, since each charge carried its own individual one. I felt Adelaide's hand rest on mine as the litany went on. It was becoming too much to bear. Cut to the chase, already.

"Will the defendant rise?" Judge Richard said.

Adelaide and I looked at each other and grinned. We gripped our hands.

The Marshals stood behind Arnold, one on either side of him and one directly behind him.

"You have been found guilty by a jury of your peers. Therefore, I sentence you to five consecutive life terms without the possibility of parole."

Cheering and clapping broke out in the courtroom.

"Order, there will be order in this courtroom." He banged his gavel. "I will not tolerate any more outbursts. If there are any, those persons responsible will be asked to leave the courtroom. We're not finished. We still have the statements from any of the family members of the deceased who wish to make them.

"The defense may be seated so we might begin with those statements."

One by one, relatives came up and spoke about how the death of their loved one had impacted them, what the loss had done to them. They choked back tears while they talked. Some tried to look at Arnold, but when they saw him picking at the table, they became angry or disgusted, stopped speaking and walked away.

Listening to this was positively brutal, and it got worse, if possible, when Joanna's sister spoke. She told of how all Joanna wanted to be when she grew up was a cop, to help people. Then she burst into tears and took her seat.

The Judge gazed down at Arnold and asked if he had anything he wanted to say.

Arnold shut his eyes, bent his head down for a minute, then stood and without turning around to face anyone, said, "I'm sorry for your loss."

Jack buttoned his coat while standing next to Arnold and leaned over to say something to him, but Arnold backed away.

Judge Richard nodded to the Marshals who grouped around Arnold and immediately removed him from the room. It took five of them to get him out, and back down to lockup. Afterwards, he would be taken back to the local jail to await his federal trial, and later on he would be assigned to a federal prison to serve out his term.

I made a mental note to ask Grady or Mike about how the consecutive life terms worked. I'd always wondered about the theory behind that... I never understood why they didn't just call it life in prison. It wasn't like you were going to come back in your next life, get dragged out of the nursery and taken to prison. Or were you?

Chapter 35

Our fishing expedition day had arrived, and Crosby was anticipating great things from me, or so I'd heard through the grapevine. I'd been instructed to pick up Adelaide and to be at the dock no later than eight AM, which was fine by me. I'd also been told that we could bring Kola and Chloe along for the trip. I was informed that there was ample room below decks for them to stay while we fished.

Annie was to meet us at the dock on her own and was just as excited about this trip as I was. She'd spent the night before going through her attic, pulling out all of her dad's old fishing equipment. Knowing her, she was most likely already at the tackle shop getting the reel restrung with fresh line.

I arrived at Adelaide's with what I believed to be plenty of time to spare, a full hour ahead of when we were scheduled to be at Crosby's boat. I was in no hurry, but Chloe was already out front, whining. Then I noticed that the front door had been flung wide open.

"Adelaide, are you okay?" I yelled, running inside, fully expecting to discover her sprawled on the kitchen floor.

"No, I can't find Chloe's life jacket and if she falls overboard, she'll drown." Adelaide was inside the hall closet on her knees, tossing all manner of objects out into the hallway. "It was in here the last time I used it, at least this is where Henry put it."

"Your front door is wide open and Chloe's outside crying, I thought something had happened." I bent down to pick up the life jacket she was searching for and handed it to her. "Let's go and have some fun, shall we?"

"Chloe must have dragged it out when I wasn't looking. She plays tricks on me. I'm not a silly old woman; I've just been up for hours. It's been a while since we've had a good time here. We went for a lovely walk and had a great breakfast Laura. My woods are back in order for the first time in I can't tell you how long," Adelaide smiled. "I guess

I've forgotten how to relax."

"That's the whole point of today. Let's get going."

I picked up her bag while she pulled on her hat and coat and grabbed her cane. The pups jumped into the car and we were off. We reached the docks in no time. Crosby had a pot of coffee on and mugs out for everyone down below. We were the first to arrive, but within moments, Mike, Grady and Reggie pulled in with their gear, ready to get going. Annie jumped onboard, laughing like a little kid, with her tackle box in hand and clutching her dad's fishing pole. She too was ready for action.

Crosby untied the lines with the help of Grady and Reggie, and we were under way, heading out of the harbor. He'd thought ahead and stocked up on plenty of New England clam chowder, stuffed clams and some bay scallops at Sono Seafood, his favorite haunt. He figured we could cook up some of whatever we caught, but just in case, he didn't want to be left short-handed for lunch. With an oven onboard, everything could be kept warm. A hibachi was on hand so we could barbecue our catch.

"She's gorgeous Crosby, what kind of boat is she?" I asked.

"My pride and joy, that's what she is. She's a Grady White Express, all thirty three feet of her."

"Now, ask what he named her," Grady smiled.

"I'll bite…"

"She's quick, that's very close. You must have peeked at the stern," Reggie said.

Crosby laughed, "Her name is Please Bite."

"You get it?" Mike asked.

"I don't," Adelaide said. "Never mind, I got it. Clever boy."

We took in the early morning air as we cruised out of the harbor, sipping coffee and watching the gulls playing at their aerobatics and calling to each other. Adelaide had brought along some slices of bread. She broke them into pieces and giggled with delight as the gulls dove after them. Kola and Chloe viewed the game with fascination, sniffing the fresh air while it blew their ears back. With Arnold behind bars, everyone was relaxed.

Soon enough, Crosby informed us we were at the first of his fishing grounds.

He grinned at me, "Ready for class?"

"I thought I was going to watch?"

"Not a chance. This is a working boat, and this is a fishing pole. Hold onto it no matter what. Got that?"

"Aye, aye Cap!"

"Again with the quick learning," Reggie commented as he baited his hook and cast his line out what seemed like a mile away. He noticed me watching and said, "Someday."

"I don't think I'll ever be able to do that."

"Me either," Adelaide said.

"Hey, a little support, here," I said.

"Did you see how far that went Laura? Be realistic," she said.

Crosby baited my hook and said, "For now, why don't we stick with the simple stuff and you can drop it over the side. Once you've caught something, and you will, I'll teach you how to cast. I promise." He crossed himself.

"Sure you will. Okay, fine, I'll hold you to it," I said, as I dropped the line over the side. I watched as the bait swirled through the water and made its way down until I could no longer see it. I returned to watching the gulls, the blessed silence, punctuated only by their calls and the sound of the water lapping against the sides of the boat.

I was lulled into a sense of peace, until the calm was broken by a jerk of my rod. "I caught something! Look, my pole is bent nearly in half. It's got to be the biggest fish, ever! Crosby, get over here. I need help; I can't hold onto it and it's my first fish, I don't want to lose it."

Everyone turned to look at what the commotion was, caused by the first timer.

"Beginner's luck, that's always the way." Reggie shook his head. "It's not right."

"Well Crosby, get over there and help her out before she drops the darned thing," Mike chimed in.

"I'm coming already, hang on will you. I have to put my pole down, and...wow, you weren't kidding were you? Your pole really is just about bent in half there, Laura. Hang on, I'm right here; let me get it." Crosby took the pole out of my hands and tried to reel it in with no luck. "Maybe, you're stuck on the bottom." Crosby turned to look at his navigation equipment to check his water depth and realized that was not possible. He'd watched me and knew there was only about twenty feet of line out, and according to his depth finder, we were in sixty feet of water. "Something is definitely wrong here. I just don't know what it is. Guys, I need some help here. Seriously, guys, I think I see something and it's not a fish."

"What, oh what, did Laura catch?" Mike asked as he leaned over the side.

"I'm going with, who did she catch?" Reggie said. He and Mike both grabbed nets.

"Oh dear," Annie said, putting her pole in a holder.

"I think we need a harpoon, the big tuna harpoon," Crosby said. "You ought to be able to get that hooked onto his belt and hold him long enough to drag him back to the swim platform."

"You're taking him swimming?" Adelaide asked.

"No, he's had plenty of that," Crosby said.

"Never mind, I figured it out," she said. "This has turned into an interesting trip."

"Not what I had in mind," I said.

"Me either. I'd like my clam chowder, now," Adelaide said, heading down below decks.

"Okay guys, drag him back here. Good, keep going. Okay, got him. Nice one Laura. Your first fishing trip, and you catch a dead body. I'll leave the high five for the next time."

"Not funny, Crosby."

Crosby, Mike and Reggie managed to pull the waterlogged body up and onto the swim platform, and secured it with a rope.

Crosby dug into the guy's back pocket and pulled out a soggy wallet. It held an ID, along with a laminated map. He handed the map to Grady and Reggie.

"Our dearly departed has a name, and it's Charles Draco Wastrel," Crosby said.

"He's up to some interesting stuff," Mike said.

"None of it good," Reggie added, handing the map back to Crosby.

"Is this what I think it is?" Crosby asked.

"What is it?" I asked.

"Our next case," Crosby replied.

"It's going to take all of us to solve it," Reggie replied. "It maps out where nuclear warheads have been planted along the Eastern seaboard."

"I don't suppose the White Lady travels outside of her woods," Mike said to no one in particular.

Crosby laughed and replied, "If you're subcontracting her, you're going to have to alter the name of your firm so it reads, 'Occasional usage of the supernatural.'"

Adelaide came up from below with a cup of steaming clam chowder and asked, "Did I miss something?"

"Not much, Adelaide," I said. "Only that it looks like we've got a new case we'll be evaluating, one warhead at a time."

www.ingramcontent.com/pod-product-compliance
Lightning Source LLC
Chambersburg PA
CBHW070915180626
46817CB00003B/1065